Later, I found the bed firm, the sheets crisp, the pillows ample, yet I tossed and turned long into the night with visions of Mimi Trinler dancing through my half-dreams. In my waking moments, I wondered if there might be any way at all to make them come true. I realized there was not, and felt absolutely no better. I thought of her comment about my needing a longer rope and appreciated what she meant. I decided I was sort of like a para-phrased St. Augustine: Tie me to someone, Lord, but not too close.

Finally, I slept. So, of course, the next morning I resented get-ting up. But I turned off my alarm and grumpily arose. Unsurprisingly, I got shampoo in my eyes and managed to put my finger through my hose as I dressed. I must say I have never given much thought to witches in my young life, but I never thought unkindly of them. Why was all this happening to me?

Turning The Tables

AN ALEX PERES MYSTERY

JESSICA THOMAS

Bella
BOOKS

2005

Bella Books, Inc.
P.O. Box 10543
Tallahassee, FL 32302

Printed in the United States of America on acid-free paper
First Edition

Editor: Karin Kallmaker
Cover designer: Sandy Knowles

ISBN 1-59493-009-0

For the Jimenez/Dravida Group.
You are right, Jacques—it's a heart thing.

For Ronnie, with thanks for making so many things
easier and more fun.

And for my editor, Karin Kallmaker,
whose iron fist always wears a lovely velvet glove.

Chapter 1

"From ghosties and ghoulies,
And long leggity beasties,
And things that go boomp
In the night . . .
Mae the guid Lord protect us."

I recited the medieval prayer with great feeling and gestures, watching my partner out of the corner of my eye. "You'd better pay attention to that prayer, partner. Halloween is only two days away. Times are getting parlous."

He stirred slightly and blinked one expressive brown eye, just to let me know he was awake and listening but unimpressed by my warning of supernatural activities.

"There could be witches and black cats riding on broomsticks," I added. He grinned to show strong white teeth and closed his eyes again. Nothing much frightened my partner.

I continued my dressing routine as he lay on the bed. Getting dressed involved more than the usual thought today. I had an appointment with the senior vice-president of the bank and thought it might be wise to look the part of a solid citizen, especially since I didn't know what the meeting was about.

Yesterday the vice-president's secretary had called and asked if I could make a two o'clock appointment with her boss, Mr. Ellis. I said Sure, why? She said she didn't know, she had merely been asked to make the date. I was curious. I didn't think I had an overdraft and doubted Ellis would know or really care if I did.

I had, however, applied for a home improvement loan the week prior. My roof had molted a bunch of shingles in the last storm and I knew the time was nigh for repairs. I figured while they had the roof off, it might be time to add that "master suite" the contractor had been suggesting. While no work would be done till spring, I had approached the bank to find out what I could spend and had not yet heard from them.

Still, I saw no reason why someone of Ellis's exalted rank should be involved in that either. But I would visit those august halls and find out.

Even as a child I had been fascinated by the big old bank, and my mother had sometimes entertained me with stories of its history. It had been established in Provincetown, Massachusetts, in the early 1800s and called itself the jaw-breaking Fishermen's, Widows' and Orphans' Savings and Loan Association Bank and Trust. An enterprising Boston businessman had secured a banking charter, and sent his younger son across the bay to set up the bank and run it.

Jericho Ellis had proven perfect for his assigned mission. A plump, friendly young man, he loved to stroll Provincetown's streets and waterfront and engage in pleasant conversation. He never forgot a name or a face, he was honest and he was shrewd. He soon discovered that the Portuguese baker's daughter was as sweet and warm as the rolls she sold, and he got her into bed the only way he could—he married her, although I don't believe my mom had phrased it quite that way. Thus cementing Provincetown's English and Portuguese populations, he could but prosper.

2

The young Ellises' mutual pleasures produced enough heirs and spares to guarantee a succession of officers at the bank, and a series of sons and sons-in-law and nephews appeared on schedule over the years to run it. It remained a private family business up to the present, with no attempt to open a lot of branches and snappy refusals for offers to merge. Even in these days of 800 numbers and fax numbers and electronic requests to *Press 1 now*—the Bank still knew its customers well enough for loans and mortgages to be issued more on personal information than collateral and credit ratings.

As time passed, the name reduced itself to a more easily handled Fishermen's Bank. Now that the fishermen themselves, thanks to various quotas and shortages, were an endangered species, I wondered if the name would be reduced to a minimalist's delight: Bank. I hoped not.

The current building for Fishermen's Bank had been erected in the late 19th century and was probably the most impressive edifice Provincetown could boast, if you didn't count the rococo phallic symbol of the Pilgrim's Monument. The bank was located in the East End, in what had been suburbs when it was erected. In addition to the imposing building itself, there had been world enough and time in those days to include a pocket park with a couple of now-large oaks and a small fountain with pond, with nearby benches for those who wished to rejoice over or recover from their recent banking activities. Much of the park had later been paved to accommodate those newfangled motor cars, but the fountain and trees and a patch of grass remained to give the illusion of space and serenity, although the benches were now usually occupied by footsore tourists.

I loved the bank with its massive granite exterior and heavy doors, its polished marble floors and interior supports, the gleaming real brass tellers' grilles, the thick vault door that stood open all day—reassuring you that the bank was well and truly solvent.

Somewhere in there, I was sure, lay bags of old English shillings and Portuguese *escudos*.

I liked the way that voices seemed hushed in the high expanse,

3

as if only important business was to be discussed, and soberly so, in those noble environs. After all, the business of a bank, whether yours or theirs, was *money*. I liked the fact that it took itself seriously and required that you do, also—unlike most of today's banks, where you feel you could be in the waiting room of an upscale car wash.

Finally, I was ready to keep my appointment. I added a raincoat to my nifty ensemble—the morning mist had lifted, but it was still cloudy. While the forecast had not called for rain, I decided to drive, just in case. I didn't want to arrive looking like a misplaced muskrat.

When I picked up the car keys, my partner jumped off the bed and went into his act. My partner is Fargo, my best friend and the absolute love of my life: a large black Labrador retriever with a heart the size of New Jersey, a beautiful deep bell of a bark and a talent for acting that would put him up there with Olivier and Branagh in any match.

He began by nudging my hand that held the keys and wagging his tail in a frantic sweep, then he moved to stand between me and the door. Finally, he lay down in front of it, head between paws, eyes rolled sadly back, whimpering. My "Oh, come on," as I opened the door brought him scrambling to his feet and running for the car.

Traffic was light as I circled to go down Bradford Street, partly due to the weather, but also the month. October was transitional in Provincetown. Most stores were still open, but merchandise was thin. Restaurants were cutting back on hours and help. The larger motels were closing off rooms or wings. Some cottage units would stay open, hoping for winter rentals, and B&Bs were open for as long as it paid to heat the guest rooms. Tourists, our collective *raison d'être*, were thinning out.

They weren't yet gone. Weekends still saw considerable influx. Two weeks ago had been Women's Week, when what appeared to be the entire lesbian populace of the East Coast had arrived on Ptown's welcoming doorstep. There were daytime seminars on subjects ranging from how to handle male advances to adoption procedures to portfolio diversification. There were special night-club acts, and various parties, culminating in the Saturday night prom, when all the locals came out to cheer the lesbians as they entered the Town Hall in their fancy dress or tuxedos or ubiqui-tous jeans. We've come a long way, baby.

Usually I prefer groups of six or less, and I don't tend to be a parade marcher or sign carrier, but I must admit, I loved this week-end. There was a feeling of sisterhood, a focus on the positive side of lesbianism and a united activism that moved me more than I cared to admit. Of course, there were some women who drank too much, some who became publicly obnoxious, a few who got into fights and doubtless many who found their way into beds where they didn't belong. But all in all it was a very satisfying time.

The last big weekend of the season would be Halloween, which conveniently occurred this Saturday. The costumes for the parade rivaled Greenwich Village in originality, if not in quantity, and both the private parties and the bar scenes had the raucous inten-sity of "live tonight for tomorrow we leave the trenches." But it was a great season finale.

After Halloween, Provincetown pretty much cleared itself out and cleaned itself up and shut itself down. People either went away or settled into a winter siege mentality—which was actually kind of cozy. There were more year-round people than there used to be, but after the seasonal throngs one still felt a very welcome sense of space and quiet.

Like other businesses, mine slowed in the off-season months. My business? I'm a private investigator. My name is Alexandra Peres, but if you have any instinct for survival, you'll call me Alex. Like most PI's, I deal with life's less blissful side. Most of my busi-ness involves insurance fraud. An amazing number of tourists decide to finance their vacations by falsely claiming to have gotten food poisoning or been injured in some motel or store, or clipped by a "speeding" car in Commercial Street's endless stream of turtle-paced traffic.

Several insurance companies keep me on retainer to sort out these claims, separating the possible from the merely frivolous. I also track down heirs named in wills, people who have used creative pseudonyms on checks and teenagers who have run away from home. These last assignments are usually sad. Most times the kids are never located. Once in a while there is the joyful, tearful reunion, where all involved promise to do better—a promise unlikely to last past next Tuesday. And finally—occasionally—as my least favorite part of my occupation, I snoop around some spouse whose affections would seem to have wandered afield.

Anyway, private investigation, that's my main occupation. My secondary one, which gives me great satisfaction, pleasure and surprising income, is nature photography. Nothing spectacular, just things that happen to catch my eye . . . like a dog curled up, safe from the wind inside a coil of rope on a trawler's deck. Or a rain-wet starling on a fence, scowling mad at the world. Maybe a cat looking pleased under a sign saying, "Bait for Sale." I shoot them in black and white mostly, blow them up, mat them and put a simple frame around them and *voila*! Several local art galleries take them on consignment and sell them for absurdly high prices. But I don't complain.

I reached the bank and left Fargo sitting importantly in the driver's seat, while I headed for the side entrance. Inside, I made my way to a secretary perched behind a desk on the main floor. "Hi, Florence, I've got an appointment with Mr. Ellis. Is he in?" The question was unnecessary. I could see him through the glass door of his office, going over papers with the head teller.

"Sure, Alex. He's expecting you. Let me just tell him you're here."

She returned a moment later, followed by a teller, who sloped off to his cage with a preoccupied nod, and Ellis himself, who greeted me with a paternal pat on the shoulder and led me to his office. "Alexandra! How good to see you! Come in, come in. You don't mind if I call you Alexandra, not Ms. Peres, do you, dear?"

Actually, I minded Alexandra a lot less than I did *dear*, but I merely smiled. I still didn't know why I was here.

I sat down, then realized he was still standing, looking down at his desk, and I started to get up again. *He* sat down, looked up to see me standing, and started to rise. By then I had sat down again. It reminded me of those films where Americans meet Japanese and nobody can quit bowing. Finally, we both managed to stay in a chair.

"Well now, Alexandra, how are you? I can't remember the last time we were together, though of course I've known you since you were a baby. Your brother, too. How is Sonny?"

What the hell was this trip down memory lane? "I'm fine, sir, and so is Sonny. Mom, too," I threw in for good measure. The only family members left were my Aunt Mae and Fargo.

"Good, good. Of course I see your mother frequently at church and other functions. A lovely lady, dear to my heart, a truly lovely lady. I cannot tell you how I admire her."

What was he babbling about? I remembered Ellis was a widower and for one insane moment wondered if he were going to ask me for my mother's hand in marriage. Fortunately, before I could make a total ass of myself, I realized I was about two hundred years out of date (this bank did that to you) and the wrong gender for him to be asking my permission anyway. I managed to mutter some sort of thank-you and finally he got down to business.

"I understand you're planning some additions to your house and have asked us for a little help."

So it was about the loan. All that blabber about my mother. Had he just been leading up to wanting her to put her house up for collateral? I had a good bit of equity in my own and didn't like the idea of involving her. What was going on here? "Uh, yes, I did. I brought in the application last week with all the details."

He nodded and gestured toward a stack of papers. "I have it right here—somewhere. Anyway, there's no problem with the loan. We can handle that for you. You'll hear from the loan department at some point. You're not in a rush, are you? You know how they are." He gave me a rather wicked grin. "Now, another reason I asked you to stop by. We are going to be doing some redecorating ourselves here. I believe the last time we did that was in 1948." He flashed that grin again. Who said bankers have no humor? "In the big conference room we're going to purchase and display paintings by several local artists. In the small one, we figure to use some of your more sizable photographs, probably five or six of them."

I took a deep swallow. What luck! Not only a nice chunk of money, but the exposure—you should pardon the expression. I had visions of writeups in the local papers, other decorators using my photos, visitors asking, "Who did the photos?" and "Are others available?"

"Thank you!" I breathed. "That's extremely kind . . . thrilled to be selected . . ." I murmured on.

"Just telling you now, my dear, so when our decorator calls to look at what you have available, you'll know what it's about. And now—heh, heh—we always like to make sure we get at least a *few* payments back on our home loans, so I have a little assignment for you."

He shuffled some papers meaninglessly around his desk. "We bill ourselves as a full service bank, and nowadays that can mean anything, including a self-serve gas pump out by the ATM. But the one place I have always thought us to be remiss was in financial planning, and I have finally convinced the board to change that. We are going to have a Financial Planning Service, wherein we can offer expert advice on retirement needs, estate planning, savings for college expenses, etc. We'll be able to suggest securities, mutual funds, annuities, et al. And the customer will be able to purchase them right here through the bank."

"That sounds great," I said, and meant it. "My financial planning right now is a couple of CDs, some low-interest savings and a mutual fund recommended by one of the local bartenders."

"Exactly. And I'm sure many of our customers haven't even had the benefit of Joe's financial acumen." How the hell did he know I was talking about Joe at the Wharf Rat? Talk about knowing your customers!

He looked at me with a small, astute smile and continued. "To begin with, our new department will have a couple of clerks, a secretary and a young man with a broker's license to handle actual purchases. We've got them lined up already. What we don't have yet, to head up the department, is a Financial Planner. We've narrowed the applicants down to one man and two women. We'd like you to check them out for us. One's in Boston, one in Providence and one in Norwalk, Connecticut, so you'll be running around a bit, I guess. And, of course, now that we're finally going to do this, everyone is in a hurry. What's your schedule?"

I thought for a moment. "Well, tomorrow's Friday. I can't get very far in one day, and I doubt if I'd find people I need to see over the weekend. If I leave Monday I can probably have a report to you by the next Friday. Would that be all right?"

He nodded and handed me a folder. "I can't see how you could do it any faster. That's about what I had figured. Here's the pertinent information on the three of them. Take a look at it and call me at home this weekend if you foresee a problem. Otherwise, we'll hear from you in about a week." He stood and I followed suit. "Oh," he added, "don't bother getting deep into their personal finances. I do believe we may be slightly better equipped for that than you, heh-heh."

Obviously he expected a return laugh, so I lobbed one over his desk and said good-bye. "Thank you again, Mr. Ellis, for everything. I'll be in touch."

Fargo woke up and yawned as I approached the car. I let him out to stretch his legs, and he stood a moment, undecided. Then he trotted to a nearby tree and took care of fluid output. Next he walked over to the fountain's pool for a gulp of fluid input. I called him back to the car and put him in.

I tousled his marvelous big wide head. "Fargo, my angel dog, we may not be among the rich and famous, but we are definitely among the solvent and may even become locally renown! If you will let me have a beer at that classy spa, the Wharf Rat Bar, I promise you your very own hamburger for dinner!"

He sealed the pact with a great slurp of my face and we drove away. If there were clouds in the sky you couldn't prove it by me. I couldn't stop grinning. And I had totally forgotten any medieval Halloween warnings.

As it would turn out, neither Fargo nor I would encounter a single ghostie or ghoulie over Halloween weekend. As for long leggity beasties, my good friend Cassie was definitely long-legged, and God knows she was in a beastly mood by Saturday night's end, if that counts. Not a single thing, however, would go *boomp* in the night within my hearing.

On the other hand, we would have a few unusual occurrences. Peter Pan would fly into a rosebush. A good-looking blonde would have me using the guid Lord's name in resounding tones. Judy Garland would sing again. I would receive a witch's curse. And the entire town, especially the gay community, would wince over a particularly brutal murder that looked as if it had been committed by one of our own.

Chapter 2

I leaned on the bar and waited for Joe to see me. He straightened and spun a beer down the gleaming mahogany with a "Hi, Alex. This Bud's for you!"

I caught it with a grin, replying, "You're three m.p.h. under your usual speed, my man." Great barroom wit taken care of by both parties, I had put money on the bar and begun to climb onto a stool when I noticed my brother sitting at a back table with a pile of colorful brochures spread out in front of him like a giant game of solitaire. I walked back for a closer look.

Sonny, a.k.a. Lieutenant Edward J. Peres, pride of the Provincetown Police Department, glanced up from his travel flyers and smiled. "It's the decisions that kill you."

"Every time," I agreed. "La Costa del Sol? Montmartre? The Lido? Buckingham Palace? Whither goest?"

"Gatlinburg, Tennessee."

"Oh, of course. Where else? Are you serious?"

"I didn't collect all these for my scrapbook. Of course I'm serious. Paula and I are going down in a couple of weeks. I'm just picking out where to stay, and I've about settled on this one. What do you think?" He passed me a folder.

The picture was of a large attractive building called the Riverside Crest. As I opened the folder and glanced at the photos and text, I thought about my brother. Sonny was bright, ambitious, well trained in his profession, an excellent cop, generally a nice guy and—in a small town—regarded as quite successful. That is, until it came to women. There, he was an unmitigated idiot. In his still-young life, he had managed to become involved with an older woman, a married woman and numerous young single women—from which pool he had acquired two ex-wives, each now rearing one of his children at his expense and with as much time as he could give them.

At the moment, he lived at home with Mom, that being about what he could afford under the circumstances. The arrangement also included great meals, laundry, housekeeping and no questions asked about his weird hours—which were usually, but not always—a part of his job. Now, it seemed, he was involved with Boston-based Paula Wagner. She was—according to Sonny—beautiful, gracious, charming, great fun, uh-sexy, smart, friendly and good humored. And probably, I thought, had *praying mantis* tattooed on her forehead for all but Sonny to see. Sonny was looking at me expectantly.

"Well," I enthused, "this looks just great! Private decks overlooking the Little Pigeon River—sounds like a fresh, bubbly mountain stream! And rooms with real fireplaces. You'll love that, I'll bet. Dining and dancing, how elegant! Unless of course, it's square dancing. Uh, but tell me, Sonny, why Gatlinburg?"

"It's the heart of the Great Smoky Mountains," he poeticized. "Everywhere you look it has beautiful mountain peaks and crags, with all the leaves turning this time of year. They have all sorts of great old mountaineer and Cherokee Indian craft places, and horses to ride and hiking trails and trout fishing out of this world and helicopter rides and a golf course and—"

"You don't play golf," I pointed out.

"Paula does. I imagine we can rent some clubs. Hey, I can bat a ball around, it can't be that hard."

"No, I imagine Tiger Woods picked it up in no time."

"Oh, you know what I . . . Anyway, we're not going all the way down there just to play golf."

"I'm sure you're not," I smirked over my glass of beer. Sonny blushed, much to my sisterly satisfaction.

"Dammit, Alex, you know full well—"

"Sonny!" A breathless, raspy, beer-and-garlic-tainted voice floated between us. It was Harmon, uncontested winner for the title of Town Character. He drove a battered red-turning-pink pickup truck, somehow supported himself doing odd jobs, occasionally helped out on a fishing boat and had cast himself as a grizzled, overall-clad Hercule Poirot in an ongoing crusade against drug dealers.

"Sonny, I'm glad I found you! There's a boat down to the docks you'd better go see. It's one of them cigarette boats, looks like she could go a hundred miles an hour! All painted black with lotsa brass all over. Now don't that tell you something?"

Sonny deliberately misunderstood, hoping to turn off the fountain. "Sure sounds like a beauty! Thanks, Harmon, I'll try to get a look at her."

"No, Sonny, that ain't it. These two fellas got off her, along with two women—all dressed fancy. They're gonna freeze later. And the men was wearin' them blazers with gold buttons and shirts with them ashcats tucked in the collar . . ."

I managed not to laugh but didn't dare look at Sonny, who erupted with a sort of gargle. "You're getting to be a regular fashion expert, Harmon. Are you going somewhere with this style show?"

"Yeah. See, I knew right off they was suspicious characters, so I walked straight up and asked real casual-like where was they from and why was they here. The one guy points at the boat's transom and says, 'Taking a ride in the *Black Duck* out of Boston.' 'She's a beaut,' I say, to take him off guard. And he says, 'Yep. She's a repallecate of my great-grandfather's boat by the same name, which was a famous rum-runner back in the twenties.' There it is, Sonny."

"There is what?"

"Why, there ain't any *need* of *rum*-running these days, but there's other kinds of running. The boat's even named after a runner, and it's a family business! So then I asked them if they was leaving soon. The older man, he says, no, they aim to walk around some and then have dinner—I reckon just killing time till they rendezvous with the mother ship and pick up the drugs—and was there anything else I wanted to know. One of the women, she giggles and says maybe I'd like her mother's maiden name. But I figured you could find that out easy enough, so I just said I hoped they had a nice evening in our lovely town . . . so as not to make 'em suspicious, you know, and I came looking for you."

"Okay, Harmon, thanks. I'll look into it." Sonny had his head bowed over the brochures. "You run along and don't worry about it." Harmon left to join his cohorts at the front table, and Sonny shook his head. "Not make them suspicious! 'In our lovely town!' God, if they've even got an unpaid parking ticket, they're headed full-throttle to Bermuda by now! But you know, truth to tell, I'd kind of miss Harmon if I left."

His statement startled me. "I hope you're not planning on leaving," I said. "I might even miss *you.*"

"Well, you know, my paycheck is pretty well gone before I even see it, between taxes and child support. And college—the thought of college for two kids is a nightmare. With the way things are now, anybody with fairly good police experience can do pretty well in the security business."

"Sonny, I can't see you guarding a parking lot or pacing hotel halls." I made a circle of my thumb and finger and pretended to peer through a keyhole.

"Me neither," he laughed. "No, Paula and I have talked about it. Her father and his partners own some big condo complexes and office buildings around Boston. There could be a job coordinating all the security departments. A good job . . . three or four times what I'd ever make here. And you know, I'm pretty well equipped to do it. I've gone to every police seminar the state gives. I've taken courses in criminal law and psychology, disaster response, etc. I'm not entirely the dumb village cop."

"Far from it." I smiled. "That's what worries me. Well, just make sure you'll be happy wearing a double-breasted suit every day." Sonny's job did not require that he wear a uniform all the time, nor suits and ties. Today, he had on tan slacks, a forest turtle-neck and a tweed blazer, looking more like a young professor than a cop. Only the spit-shined low boots gave a clue to the cowboy who lurked inside. The colors looked good on him. He took after our Portuguese father in coloring, with a complexion that always looked just slightly tanned plus dark, wavy hair and big brown eyes to kill for.

"By the way, how old is Paula?" I asked innocently.

"Around your age, give or take."

That put her in her early thirties. Very definitely time to be getting married, if that was her game plan. Paula began to sound like a wealthy young woman who wanted/needed a husband but couldn't possibly marry a small-town cop and move to the boonies. She could, however, move the husband to the big city, get him a cushy job with Daddy and ease him gently into the country club set—where he might or might not be happy. Of course, I had never met this paragon. Maybe she was all Sonny thought her to be. But I doubted it.

Sonny and I had an agreement between us that was etched in steel, although we never discussed it: *Thou shalt not comment upon any of my romantic partners.* It was the only way we could remain friends, as well as relatives. Neither of us had a track record to brag about. I had about the same luck with women as Sonny, and the last thing either of us wanted was advice to the lovelorn from the other.

Of course, Sonny had bent that rule rather sharply last year when he rescued me from being shot when my lover turned homicidal, but I forgave him that trespass, since it had saved my life. I remained neutral and said merely, "You'd miss the kids if you moved."

"Yes," he admitted, "That's a definite. But, remember, my time would be pretty much my own, barring emergencies. I could come over any time, and they could come to visit me . . . us. Paula says she knows she'll love them."

I didn't even try to field that one. I just said, truthfully, "I'd love to meet her."

"You will. She's coming down tomorrow. We'll have lunch or something. I'll call you." He stuck a pencil in his mouth and wiggled his eyebrows like Groucho Marx. "You look kind of dressed up. Something I don't know about?"

"Not that kind of something, unfortunately. But, yes." I told him of my visit with Mr. Ellis and he was genuinely pleased for me, especially about the photographs.

Sonny had always supported my efforts in that field and treasured one particular photo I had given him of Fargo, front legs stretched to full height against a scrub pine and laughing at a squirrel, who was poised head down, two inches above Fargo's nose and laughing back.

"I have to go," he added and began scooping brochures into a large envelope. "Got to see about reservations and plane tickets. But if you like, we can run your three job applicants through the computer for you. Probably clean as a whistle, but you never can tell. Call Nacho tomorrow. I'll tell her it's okay."

"Thanks, I was going to ask you about that." Sonny nodded, gave a half-wave and walked out. I heard Fargo give a joyous bark of greeting and knew they'd be communing for a while. One more beer, I thought, would make the afternoon perfect.

I drank the beer and idly listened to the fishermen at the front table, conjecturing over who the people from the cigarette boat might be. Opinion was about equally divided between bored over-rich or drug dealers who felt fancy clothes cloaked them in respectability. I tuned out and thought about photos for the bank's walls.

The increased noise level broke into my daydreaming. Four

tourists had taken a table nearby. A cell phone rang and all four of them immediately reached for pocket or purse. Actually, the call was for a man sitting at the bar. I looked more closely at the tourists—two couples about my age—and wondered why on earth they bothered with cell phones on vacation.

I hated the tyranny a cell phone tried to impose. It attempted to invade my privacy anytime, anyplace, and completely forgot that *its* place was to be used for *my* convenience. In fact, mine spent most of its life safely locked in my glove compartment where it could ring its little head off—instead of my wringing its little head off. Sonny swore someday I'd be trapped in a cabin with a bear coming through a window, and I'd wish to hell I had my cell phone. I told him when the bear came in one window, I'd just go out the other.

I became aware of three young men at the bar, giggling and punching each other as young men will. One of them seemed to have a small photo which was the cause of the merriment. He was a tall, nice-looking redhead, and I thought he was a houseboy at the Old Boat Dock, a motel on the bayside catering mainly to gay men. In all probability his services there went far beyond that of sheet-shaker, and for which services he would receive sizable tips. I doubted the snapshot was of his mother. I didn't know the other two but assumed they held similar jobs.

At the other end of the bar was retired police chief Jared Mather. He was rumored to be a descendant of Cotton Mather and I saw no reason to doubt it. He was a spare, upright man with gray hair and eyebrows and deep-set unreadable eyes above a firm and humorless mouth. It was not hard to imagine him delivering a three-hour sermon of eternal hellfire and placing someone in stocks for mild blasphemy. He came in every late afternoon and had two scotch and sodas—never more, never less—and left. That told me he watched his drinking *very* carefully. Most people would occasionally go for three or be happy with one. He rarely conversed with anyone except to order his drinks. Smiles were even more rare, and I wondered why he came.

I'd known Jared Mather forever. He'd been a good friend of my

17

Aunt Mae and Uncle Frank, and I think she may even have dated Mather a few times after Uncle Frank died. He'd also been a good friend to Sonny. After graduating high school, Sonny had seemed at loose ends, drifting from one no-go job to another. With both our father and Uncle Frank dead, he'd had no male figure in his life, until Mather stepped in to fill the vacuum.

He got Sonny into the army and, when his enlistment ended, into the Provincetown Police. There, Mather had proved a good mentor, making sure Sonny took advantage of all special training available, providing guidance on how to handle the people he encountered on his job, turning him into more than just a good cop . . . into a professional who took pride in his work and in himself. I think the two were very good for each other.

Yet my feelings about the chief were ambivalent. I greatly appreciated what he had done for my brother. I did not appreciate his feelings toward gays. The chief was deeply involved with some hard-nosed religious sect down in Eastham, and the word *gay* to him was the proverbial red flag to the bull. He felt that homosexuality was an egregious sin against God, that being gay was a first-class ticket to literal hellfire and damnation, and that homosexuals should at the least wear a brand to warn off innocent potential victims from their seduction.

That said, he never took his prejudices to work with him. I never heard even a rumor that he ever mistreated a homosexual in any way. I never heard any gays complaining that Mather had roughed them up, "framed" them, abused them vocally or even been impolite. If you found yourself in his custody you were treated by the book, whether you were a boxer from Buffalo or a hairdresser from Harlem. I didn't like him, but I respected him.

After his retirement, when various gays had by then been elected to the Town Council, the Zoning Board and even the School Board, Mather ran for selectmen on a "Take Back Our Town" ticket, against a young gay lawyer. Even the town's most conservative citizens preferred the lawyer to the ex-chief and Mather had received a humiliating paucity of votes. Now he lived quietly in his small house out near my Aunt Mae. He made wonderfully crafted wood furniture and occasional truly striking carvings that found their way to some of our better galleries. It was amazing to me that such a bitter man could produce such beauty.

Before long my stomach told me it was about time to live up to my promise to Fargo. I collected him and we headed for the drive-in where I ordered a double bacon cheeseburger for him and a lobster roll, fries and coleslaw for me. We took them home where I changed clothes while Fargo guarded the kitchen counter. I cut his burger into bites and put it into his dish, whence it disappeared with amazing speed, and took my own dinner into the living room to watch the news.

After I ate, I realized that I must have been more keyed up about my interview than I had thought. I felt that almost overwhelming fatigue that comes with the letdown from stress. I clicked over to the History channel and propped my feet up on the coffee table. I would have sworn I was watching a program about the development of modern battleships, but suddenly I was looking at the pyramids instead. I had just settled into learning whether or not they had been built by aliens, when I woke to find myself in the midst of men marching toward the battle of Trenton.

The phone caused me to levitate about three feet and wonder briefly how I had got from Egypt to Trenton so seamlessly.

Sonny laughed in my ear, then said, "Well, Harmon was at least partly right, for a change."

"Why? How? What happened?" I was coming awake.

"It seems that as our boat people walked around town, they got a small following. By the time they got to the Sea Bounty Restaurant, it was a bit larger. When they finally came out, there was quite a crowd."

"Why? What had they done?"

"Nothing. It developed that the owner of the boat is some rich Boston lawyer who was with his wife. The other man and woman were his guests—Mel Gibson and Jodie Foster, no less. They're shooting a film in Boston and took the day off for some R and R.

19

Instead, they damn near got mobbed. It took three of our people to clear the crowd and walk the foursome back to their boat."

"Oh, God, that will be all Harmon needs to hear!"

"Alex, Harmon gets enough crazy ideas on his own. Don't help him, or there'll be his picture in the *Enquirer*, pointing at an empty boat slip, and an article stating that Ptown has been invaded by people dressed as movie stars who are really secret aliens selling drugs."

"I'm going to bed now. My heart isn't up to all this excitement."
And so I did.

Chapter 3

The next morning felt chilly, although sunlight peeked disarmingly through the blinds. Fargo was a warm, welcome ball in the middle of my back. When he sensed I was awake, he sat up, yawned, stretched and thumped his tail on the bed. Nice thing about dogs, they always awoke in a good humor. If he'd had a problem yesterday, he'd forgotten it; something might go wrong today, but he wasn't projecting about it. A great way to live. I was envious.

I let him out in the backyard, turned on the coffee, took a fast shower and dressed in my usual uniform of sweatshirt, jeans, crew socks and sneakers. I let the dog in and he addressed himself to the dry food he'd ignored the night before. I addressed myself to a cup of steaming Costa Rican coffee and the first of five cigarettes I allow myself each day. I sometimes exceed that number, but lecture myself sternly whenever I do.

I was halfway through the second cuppa when Fargo began his

"To Beach or Not to Beach" soliloquy. He sat looking longingly at his leash as it hung by the back door. He rested his chin on my thigh and rolled his eyes. Finally, he pawed my leg and let out a frustrated yip. Before he could call the SPCA and report my cruelty, I stood up, grabbed my jacket and his leash and we headed for the car and Race Point.

On arriving, I parked and let him out of the car to run and fished my camera out of the compartment in the ever-present hope of a good shot. I never knew what it might be: a surf fisherman reeling in a catch, gulls fighting over a dead clam, a little fiddler crab standing beside his hole, waving his single claw and daring the tide to cover him.

It was a top-ten morning, so fresh and crisp and sweet you couldn't help thinking of apples. It was windless and the ocean was calm. As I walked down the dune and along the waterline, tiny wavelets whispered that the ocean was still there, however. It might be serene today, but tomorrow it could be raging. It was always well to be reminded of that.

Fargo ran—a satiny, powerful, burnished black bundle of energy. He sported in and out of the chill water, sounding that deep bell from sheer exuberance, biting playfully at the water as it splashed him. The tide had uncovered what looked like part of an old railroad tie, and on its upper end sat a seagull, gazing keenly about for the unwary crab. I angled slowly around him, looking for the best shot, and took one I knew I'd like. I was about to take a second when Fargo could resist no more, and charged him.

The gull flew, complaining loudly, gaining height slowly in the still air, and Fargo jumped hopefully upward. I got a shot of Fargo at the full extension of his leap, straining every muscle, as the gull flapped and struggled for altitude. Fargo missed, but I didn't. I should have a photo that was a winner! Maybe I'd offer it as one to be used at the bank, give Fargo his place in the history of the town. It seemed like a great idea. It also reminded me that I had work to do, and I turned for the car.

At home I settled dutifully at my desk with the folders of the three finalists for Mr. Ellis's job as head of his Financial Planning Department. Two women and a man—well, ladies first.

We had Nancy Whitfield Baker. Hmmm, I thought, good power-name. It would sound impressive over a phone. Yeah, well, Nancy, what else about you? Brought up in Weston, Mass. An only child, thirty-three years old. BS in business from Boston U. and advanced courses for a Certified Financial Planner at Rolles. Heavy-duty stuff. Mother a housewife but "very active in charitable works." How nice. Father a VP at Independence Bank in Waltham. Now, that wouldn't hurt a kid going into finance for a career.

There were no surprises thus far in Nancy's dossier. She'd worked over a year at Dad's bank in Waltham, but then probably wanting a wider horizon, or less of Mom and Dad, she went with Fleet Boston Financial, stayed nearly five years and moved to Merrill Lynch. Now, after two years there she had worked her way up and was handling some smaller corporate 401-k-accounts on her own. It all sounded very good. Ambition, ability. Question, Nancy: Why do you want to move to a rather small family bank in a tourist/fishing town?

The next folder belonged to Cynthia Alice Hart, born thirty-one years ago and raised in Oak Hill, Connecticut. Two older brothers . . . she'd probably learned to defend her rights. She was also probably Daddy's little girl. Mom and Dad owned a bookstore in Oak Hill, a bedroom town for Hartford. Cynthia took her business degree at UConn and her advanced courses at Brown University in Providence. She, too, had worked in a local bank before returning to Providence to work as an assistant broker for Morgan Stanley. Two years later she went with a small firm named Kudlow Investments (here someone—I assumed Ellis—had penciled in "small old-family firm; excellent reputation"). She'd been with them over four years now and handled most of their IRA and SEI accounts.

Cynthia had noted in her application that it was okay to contact Kudlow as a reference. That was unusual—ordinarily you don't want your current employer to know you're shopping around for a new one. That bothered me a little. Had Kudlow suggested she find a new home?

I moved on to George Hampton Mills, a Harvard man, who said he was forty-two. I mentally added five, since he had not mentioned his graduation year. That didn't bother me—people were afraid to be over forty nowadays, sadly. They all lied. On the surface his career was impressive. He'd been with several prestigious brokerage houses, but his next-to-last job had been with Thalgrun Investors in Norwalk, Connecticut. He lived in Norwalk, and now worked for a firm I didn't recognize in Darien. He was not a Certified Financial Planner like his two female counterparts, but "felt that his long experience in, and personal studies of the market and its investors, rendered him more than competent in that arena." Thank you for sharing, George.

George hadn't put any dates on his recitation of jobs, either. That usually meant you hadn't stayed long and/or there were some other jobs in between that you weren't mentioning. Not pertinent in a guy his age. Most people had a skeleton or two.

His wife was a part-time real estate salesperson—just the addition Provincetown needed. We already had about one real estate broker for every three buildings in town, including phone booths. I didn't need to wonder why *he* thought of asking for this job; he gave his reasons forthrightly in his application. "My wife and I wish to leave the hurly-burly of the New York City/Fairfield County society and return to a more value-oriented life, where we can appreciate nature and enjoy the company of those for whom we truly care."

Sounded great, grammatically, if nothing else. Of course, since they had no children, I wondered whom they were bringing along that they truly cared about and whose values concerned them. The family cat? Oh, well.

Adhering to Sonny's offer, I called Nacho at the police station. I had gone to school with her when she was called Mary Patricia Malley. Even then, she always had a snack in hand: nachos, chips,

24

peanuts, popcorn, cookies. The nickname of Nacho appeared when she joined the police force. By now, most people who ate like Nacho would be a 400-pound toothless wreck. Not her—she still slid easily into a size eight dress and had lovely straight, white teeth. She was, in a word, *disgusting*.

She was also a computer whiz and a nice person. She agreed readily to "run your critters through and see what floats up. I'll fax you whatever I get." I knew if there was anything to float, it would do so for Mary Pat. I just had to give her a little time.

While waiting, I began to draft a rough itinerary. It seemed that the quickest, easiest and probably cheapest way to go would be to take the first flight Monday morning to Boston, rent a car and check out Ms. Baker first, visiting BU and Rolles and Fleet Boston. I wouldn't phone ahead for appointments. I'd learned that people found it too easy to avoid seeing you, and you ended up getting a minimum of information over the phone, from a file often in the hands of a person who didn't even know the subject of your investigation. Anyway, I liked to see faces when I asked questions. So even though it sometimes meant waiting awhile, I preferred to arrive unannounced. Those three calls should about finish Monday, and Ms. Baker.

I pulled out a road atlas to plan my remaining trip. It looked as if any way I went would be a great circle route. So I figured I'd visit the University of Connecticut Tuesday morning to check on Ms. Hart. Then I'd go down to Norwalk to see what Mr. Mills' stint at Thalgrun had to offer. Finally, on Wednesday I could swing back through Providence and polish off Ms. Hart. Unless I got tied up somewhere by something complicated, I might make it home by Wednesday night! Great! Being on the road had long since lost its charm for me, even when someone else was paying.

I saw Fargo trot purposefully across the front yard and looked to see what he was after. He went up to the gate, where the postman gave him his daily biscuit payola and then began to stuff things into my mailbox. I was not at all interested in the bills and junk he was delivering, but his very presence told me that it was lunchtime, and that I had little in the house to eat. It would be impractical, I told myself, to bother shopping today, when I was leaving Monday. And there was nothing I could do for my trip until I heard from Nacho. As I tended to pack while chasing down the runway after my flight, I wouldn't do that today. So-oo, why not just whip down to the Rat for one of Joe's delicious pastrami sandwiches? Why not, indeed?

As Fargo and I walked toward the Rat, two men approached us. Fargo moved closer to me and eyed them appraisingly. One man steered the other into the street to give us more than ample right-of-way, and both nodded politely as we passed. Most people didn't tend to argue with a ninety-pound Labrador, and I always felt safe with Fargo in attendance. He and I did, however, have one little secret we had never shared with a soul.

In moments of great stress or alarm—like the time a duck hunter fired both barrels of his shotgun as we stood nearby, or the time a little cocker spaniel bitch found Fargo's sniffs a bit too friendly and nipped his ear—in times like that, Fargo tended to leap into my arms for safety. Or at least try. On two occasions I had found myself flat on my back with the dog sprawled across my chest, which had been humiliating for both of us. I had now learned to do a quick sidestep and grab his collar in moments of crisis.

We never discussed this one tiny fault. He was always there. He loved me. He looked impressive. It was enough. And never—*never*—had he asked me why on earth I was wearing that blouse with that pair of slacks.

Turning down the alley to the Rat, we were confronted by a witch, wearing the traditional black hat and some sort of black cape over what looked to be a nightgown. At first I thought she was wearing a mask, but then realized she really was an old woman. A gray pigtail hung partway down her back. She had large, almost bony-looking ears, and her beaked nose and up-tilted chin almost formed a C clamp across her toothless mouth. Her liver-spotted hands and wattled arms were outraised as she quavered, *"Beware!*

Stay away! Visit not the den of Satan. Of demon rum do not partake. Your world will reel and objects break, and you will rue the day! Stay away!"

I looked down at Fargo, pressed close against my leg, eyes rolling to show the whites. "Easy, my love." I chuckled at his strange behavior. "We have just been cursed by a real live witch, that's all. Tomorrow is Halloween, you know." I stroked his head and knelt to hug him, as he was truly frightened. After a few comforting murmurs he stopped quivering and I stood up to confront the witch. "Well, you sure impressed my dog." Where the hell was she? Where could she have got to? She must have gone around me, up the street—funny I hadn't heard her.

I walked on down the alley, tied Fargo to the anchor and went inside the Rat, half expecting to see the witch at the bar. As I paused to adjust to the dim light, I heard my name called and spotted my friend Cassie, waving me to her table. I walked through the determinedly nautical décor of the room. Fishing nets were draped along the walls, sprinkled lavishly with starfish, plus scallop and clam shells. Lobster pots and markers dangled from open rafters, and a couple of kedge anchors lurked in dark corners to bark the shins of the unwary. The engine telegraph from a long-forgotten ferry stood stiffly under the back window, its indicator frozen on "Dead Slow Astern." Which just about said it all as far as the Rat was concerned.

I sat down and asked, "What's new?"

"I ran away from home," she answered. "Lainey's on a cleaning binge."

"I hear things like that and it makes me glad I'm single," I answered.

"There are those times, even with the best, which of course Lainey is."

Joe appeared to take my order. I looked at Cassie's platter of stuffed clams, sliced tomatoes and fries and immediately forgot pastrami. "Just ditto Cassie's order, Joe, only bring me a Bud instead of a Coke."

Cassie sighed, looking sadly at her glass of soda. "Want a beer?" Joe asked her.

She shook her head. "Can't. I'm flying." He nodded and walked away.

We both knew what she meant. Cassie owned Outer Cape Charter Service, of which she was president, pilot, receptionist and mechanic. Her plane was a lovely little twin-engine Beechcraft which would carry six passengers, seven if she let someone ride in the cockpit with her. She cared for the plane like a mother with a newborn babe, and I would have flown round the world with her in an instant.

"Got a busy weekend?" I asked.

"Yeah. Halloween's always a buster. I'm picking up four guys at three o'clock, another four at five o'clock and five gals at seven. Hope I'm not late for that one. Then, I bring over six guys in the morning. And I get to take them all back on Sunday, except for the six guys who're leaving Monday midmorning."

Joe set a platter in front of me and I began to eat. His wife, Billie, made great stuffed clams—lots of clam, little stuffing. I was happy for Cassie's busy weekend. I knew her business, too, would drop off during the winter. "I'm going over to Boston myself Monday morning," I said. "I just got the last seat on the Cape Air eight-thirty. I wanted to catch the early bird, but they were sold out."

"If you've got a problem, I'll run you over early," Cassie offered.

I shook my head. I knew she meant it, but all she would charge me would be regular commercial rate, and I sometimes wondered if she charged me full price for that. "It's not a problem." I explained my trip and she nodded.

"Okay. But, anytime. You know that. Well"—she wiped her mouth—"into the wild blue yonder. Oh, say, you *are* coming to our party tomorrow night, aren't you?"

"Hell, Cassie, I don't know. You know, nobody I really want to bring, yet I don't much want to come alone, either. I'm kind of a drone lately."

"Oh, come on, you'll enjoy it. There might even be somebody interesting. And Lainey will be disappointed if you don't come. Oh, remember, you gotta be in costume!"

"Well, yeah, I guess."

As Joe placed Cassie's check on the table, I asked him, "Say, Joe, who's the witch spouting curses outside?"

"I dunno, what's the punch line?"

"I'm serious, some old lady was waving her arms around warning about demon rum and things spinning and breaking. I thought maybe you'd hired your mother-in-law to provide a Halloween scare or something."

"My mother-in-law would make the Marines run for cover, but fortunately she's parking her broom in Orlando these days. I'll go see who it is. Maybe scoot her down to Fisherman's Cove . . . she'd be right at home."

As Joe turned to leave I raised a big bite of stuffed clam, covered in sauce, toward my mouth . . . and dumped it in my lap. Joe gave his familiar sour grin and handed me his bar towel. "Hex working already, I see."

We all laughed, and he and Cassie walked away, Cassie calling over her shoulder, "Stay away from my airplane, lady, you're jinxed!"

I concentrated on lunch and tried to get my good humor back, difficult with a splotch shaped something like Idaho on my pant leg. I heard Fargo give a couple of sharp barks outside. That was extremely unusual here, and I looked up quickly. What I saw sent my good mood receding further into the background.

Ben Fratos walked in with his usual swagger. Ben was my only "competitor" in town. He'd retired from the police force with an injured leg and supplemented his pension by becoming a private investigator. He was almost the perfect caricature of a slimy PI, with sparse oily hair, a beer gut, an abrasive personality and an intense interest in anything scatological. Until a few months ago

Ben had made some inroads into cases that might have been mine, simply because he was a man and an ex-cop.

That is, until a fairly famous lesbian artist had rented a condo in town—complete with skylight, of course—to do some painting and, rumor had it, recover from a broken romance. One step toward recovery is always a new hairdo, and while at the hairdresser's she met and became friendly with the town manager's wife. As time progressed, the manager began to wonder if his wife were not participating too intimately in the artist's emotional—and possibly sexual—recovery and decided to find out.

Now me, I would have set a lesbian to catch a lesbian, but the town manager picked Fratos. Ben trailed them hither and yon, subtle as an elephant behind a teacart, had they been alert, but apparently he turned up no romantic activity. Then, the wife began visiting the artist's condo. Aha! The husband was said to be leaning all over Fratos. But poor Ben had a problem: there was no easy way to see into the second-story unit—no nearby buildings with facing windows, no nearby trees with sturdy branches. One evening the women went out to dinner and then to the condo. Ben was desperate.

He climbed the fire escape and onto the roof to peer through the skylight. He saw, doubtless to his disappointment, the wife seated demurely on a straight chair and the artist standing several feet away at her easel, brush in hand. What the two women saw was a skylight falling around them, and a yelling fat man flailing the air and thudding to the floor in front of them. Sensibly, they exited the building at warp speed, screaming bloody murder.

His fall had cost Ben some painful cuts and a nasty back sprain, so he lay there among the shards until several of his ex-comrades rushed in to investigate. The entire situation was ludicrous. The women were simply friends. The wife was having her portrait done as a surprise for her husband's birthday. The story took about two minutes to go all over town, providing considerable amusement to all who heard it.

Of course, it would have died down shortly, but some wit came up with the cry of, *It's a bird, it's a plane, it's Super Ben!* The kids in town picked up on it, and the call still follows him from time to time. The ridicule cost him more business than his ineptitude ever had. And most individuals, plus the insurance companies, had decided that my less dramatic approach was preferable to their needs. I, for once in my life, maintained a discreet silence throughout.

Somehow, though, Ben got it into his head that I originated the *Super Ben* sobriquet. I had not, and I deliberately never used it. But to no avail—in his mind I was guilty. I could feel his hateful little porcine eyes follow my progress through the platter of food I was trying to enjoy, and decided to hell with him. He was not going to ruin my day. I was a better investigator than he was, any way you looked at it.

And if I ever decided to leap through a skylight to land at the feet of two beautiful women, I'd try like hell to handle it more like Errol Flynn than Jerry Lewis.

Chapter 4

Fortunately, I'm a simple soul. A full tummy, a coffee and cigarette number three restored my good spirits. I leaned back in my chair and idly listened to the Rat's fishermen harmonize on their familiar screed: quotas, shortages and price controls. Their outlandish threats to take up more profitable sidelines included running drugs, running guns and running people who wanted either to leave or to enter the country illegally. They would do none of it, of course, but it sounded macho. Harmon sounded the only note of caution.

"You want to be careful who you deal with nowadays. Seems to me, ain't hardly nobody who acts like you think they really oughta be, no more." He was more right than any of us knew, but at the time I simply found his syntax amusing.

People not being who they seemed turned my mind to the problem of a Halloween costume, which thrilled me right up there along with root canals. A lot of people in town went to great trouble and considerable expense, renting costumes in Boston or even New York. Some actually had them tailor-made. Of course it was entirely too late for that, even had I been so inclined. And the only thing I owned that even vaguely resembled a costume was one of those little black raccoon masks, tossed somewhere in a drawer. What a pain in the royal bootay!

Then I had a bright idea. I'd borrow Sonny's camouflage fatigues left over from his army days. They'd be comfortable. I couldn't stand the thought of tripping around in a sheet as a ghost or something. With the uniform cap and the mask, they'd have to do. Problem solved.

I unhitched Fargo and we started for my mom's house. I'd pick up the uniform and ask if she could keep the dog while I was on my trip for the bank. She always loved to do that. She was sort of like a grandmother with Fargo, spoiling him rotten while she had him and then returning him to me with a comment that I really should take him to obedience school.

Coming from the Rat, the easiest way to reach Mom's house was to walk up the Francis's driveway and climb over the low wood fence that separated the properties. Or, if you were Fargo, to leap the fence gracefully and pause for a brief roll in the still-green grass. The house was typical for the Cape: pretty much square, two stories and an attic, with a small ground-floor room added on long ago to accommodate things like the furnace and hot water heater, washer/dryer and a few shelves. The house was in good repair, painted a light yellow, with a green roof and dark green shutters . . . the color scheme it had shown throughout my memory.

Mom had seen us coming and held open the kitchen door. Everyone said I was the spitting image of her when she had been in her thirties. I hoped that comparison still held when I was in my middle fifties!

As she leaned out the screen door to laugh at Fargo's antics, I saw a woman of some five feet eight inches, with a straight build and square shoulders and long, good legs. She had an almost-pug nose, a mouth that liked to laugh and hazel eyes that gave away her thoughts and feelings. Her hair had been light brown with red highlights, but now held enough white hairs to give it a blondish-red cast. She looked great, my mom.

Inside, Fargo got water and biscuits. I got coffee and pie. Then I turned to the business at hand. "Mom, I'm going to a party at Cassie's tomorrow night, and the price of admission is wearing a costume. I thought I'd wear Sonny's fatigues. Do you know where he keeps them?"

"In the upstairs hall closet. Is it okay with him if you borrow them?" Always the mother.

"Sure." I lied easily. Well, I'd call him later. I knew he wouldn't mind. Always the younger sister.

A few minutes later I came downstairs in my costume. The pants drooped over my shoes onto the floor, my hands were half hidden by the shirtsleeves and only my ears kept the cap from covering my eyes.

My mother looked at me critically. "Well, at least you'll never have to shoot anybody. The enemy will take one look at you and die laughing. I suppose you want me to hem them."

I did. While she sewed, I explained my trip for Mr. Ellis, which pleased her greatly. She was always happy when my business didn't involve someone having done something illegal. And she was thrilled with the bank's choosing to display my photographs. As expected, Fargo was more than welcome to visit while I traveled. She showed me how to fold some paper towels and put them in the lining of the cap to make it fit and then I asked casually, "Have you met Sonny's new girlfriend?"

"Yes, I have been presented to that young lady of countless virtues. Did you know they're going down to Gatlinburg on a vacation?"

"So I hear," I answered.

"She's here for the weekend, you know. She flew over this morning and Sonny brought her by for coffee." Mom pushed her teaspoon around on the butcher-waxed white oak table. Something was bothering her.

34

"Is she staying here? At the house, I mean." Had she plopped her suitcase down in Sonny's room? No, he'd never let that happen.

"Why, heavens no, she didn't want to impose upon my gracious hospitality, and she felt the Tip of the Cape Motel would probably do for a weekend."

"Do?" I asked. "It's the best place in town."

"I'm sure it beats heck out of your old room," she laughed. "I actually served them coffee and homemade crumpets in the dining room. Even so, she kept looking as if she'd like to turn the cup over and see if it had a 'Made in Korea Exclusively for Kmart' imprint."

I laughed. "That bad, huh? Do you think he's serious?"

"I think *she's* serious, and that's worse. He won't stand a chance if she really means it."

"You'd miss having him around." I raised my cup and looked at her over the rim.

"Yes, I would," she answered. "But I'm terribly afraid he'd miss having *himself* around. I don't think Sonny is meant for that kind of big city corporate life and country club society. And the last thing he needs is another failed marriage." Her voice trembled and then steadied. "She calls him Edward," she added drily.

I didn't mention that I thought Sonny might feel he was hostage to two college educations and that a job with Paula's father might be the ransom. "Oh, God. Say, Mom, how did *Edward* get to be Sonny in the first place?"

"Just one of those stupid things. Your Uncle Frank's father used to love to hold him in his lap when he was a baby and sing some old song to him—something about climbing on my knee, Sonny Boy. Somehow everyone started calling him that. I know it's—what do the kids say?—hokey, but it stuck. By the time we realized it wasn't cute anymore it was too late."

She snipped a final thread and began to fold the jacket. "Well, here's your costume, m'dear. You will remember to wash, starch and iron it before you bring it back, won't you?"

"Wouldn't have it any other way! I'll drop it and Fargo off—washed starched and ironed—Monday morning." She gave me a yeah-sure look and I went out the back door. I managed to catch my elbow and drop the uniform onto the grass. Picking it up and refolding it, I muttered, "Damn that witch, she's following me!"

"What did you say, dear? A witch is following you? I don't see one."

I explained my encounter and Mother laughed. "Probably a disgruntled tourist. Buy some garlic and drive a stake through a head of lettuce or something. Bye, darling."

I grinned and felt silly. An old woman enjoying moments of a second childhood was hardly threatening.

As Fargo and I walked home, I decided for the thousandth time I was lucky in my family. The three of us loved each other and we liked each other. We were there when it counted without being all over each other. We tried to help, if needed, without sitting in solemn judgment. Aunt Mae completed our little family with much the same attitude.

It hadn't always been that way. When I was a kid, tension had been constant. I realized now it had emanated from our father. He was a rather bitter man who tried to cover that with strangers by being spuriously jolly. He was assistant manager at the local A&P, and I always thought he felt he could have done better, that Mother and Sonny and I held him back in some way. He frequently drank more than he should, and while he was never physically abusive, he was often depressed or sarcastic and unpleasant.

When I was twelve and Sonny fourteen, the edge of a powerful hurricane hit Provincetown. My father struggled home from the store to find that we were already without electricity, the house cold, dark and dank. I was terrified, and so was Sonny, though he tried to cover it by being loud and unconcerned. Mother tried to get some sort of cold dinner on the table. And Dad drank. It was a frightening, nervous evening. And we were all restless and uneasy through the night.

Next morning a gale still blew and rain still came relentlessly

36

down. Power remained off. In the night a tree had come down, taking power lines with it, leaving some of them draped across our driveway and blocking my father's exit. He was hung over, tired, hungry and as miserable as the rest of us. He paced and snarled as the battery radio repeatedly warned listeners to avoid downed lines and stay inside until things improved.

Finally, exasperated, he donned his coat, saying, "I have to get to work. Those lines haven't sparked once since I got up. I know they're dead."

In less than a minute, it was not the lines that were dead but our father. Dr. Marsten tried to comfort us by saying, "He didn't suffer. He just touched the line and that was that."

That was far from that. In seconds we had gone from a family with a father, who may have been far from perfect but was present and reliable, to one without. We had changed from a family with a breadwinner to one without. It was not easy, and I've never been entirely sure how Mom held it together, although Sonny and I tried to help as best we could.

Of course Sonny did not go to school to become an airline pilot. He spent a couple of years in the army and returned to become a police officer, now being groomed for a someday chief. And he would be a good one.

I didn't become a lawyer, but I did manage to go to community college and get my PI license. A devoted, if not particularly devout Episcopalian, Mom had gone to work for—and still worked part time for—the local Catholic Church. Both the priest and her rector regularly teased her about being a spy in the other camp and she loved it.

Over time we discovered a great pleasure in each other, in the lives we led, separately and connected. And we lived—although not in the lap of luxury—at least on the knees of comfort. I looked at Fargo and realized you couldn't really ask for a helluva lot more. Well, maybe one or two things more.

As I draped the fatigues over a kitchen chair I heard the fax machine growling and walked into my office as the last of several pages came through. Nacho had not let me down. I took them into the kitchen, poured a Sprite and sat down to be informed.

Nancy Baker seemed a young woman of true virtue. Nacho had checked police records in Boston and in her hometown. Her only "oops" was going forty-five in a thirty-mile zone, which ticket she had paid with a check which did not bounce. No civil suits, past or pending. She might be dull, our Nancy, but she might be just what Mr. Ellis ordered. Boring, bright and hardworking. A woman you would trust with your money, even if you didn't want to sit next to her on a long flight.

George Mills surfaced on the next page with considerably more entries, and disturbing ones at that. He'd been pulled over for a couple of DWI's, which had been reduced to reckless driving charges. He must have had a good lawyer and a friendly judge to get that done. Another DWI, a couple of years later, had cost him six months loss of license.

Norwalk police had twice been called by neighbors to his home on domestic incidents, no charges filed. Then they'd been called to his home by neighbors again, this time for disturbing the peace during a Halloween party almost a year ago now. This sounded interesting. I hoped Nacho had been able to get the police report. Well, she'd gotten at least some details and included this note:

Cops went to Mills' condo and finally got someone to answer the door. The place was a mess—table filled with food overturned on rug. Mills (in a toga) had accused a guest of hitting on his wife. The guest told Mills to cool it and stuck his head in the bobbing-for-apples tub. Mills retaliated by beating the man with a violin—you suppose he was Nero? Other guests—and Mrs. Mills—cheering on the fight. Everybody busted for disturbing the peace. Assault charges dropped. Some party! Nacho

I was laughing aloud by the time I finished. It certainly had been a lively little evening. It did seem, however, as if Mills had a problem with his temper, his wife and his booze. I wondered if his ex-employer knew Mills had a drinking problem or perhaps if this incident had inspired him to correct it.

Just one more to go—and here it was. Ms. Cynthia Hart

seemed quite law abiding. Nacho's fax told me that Cynthia, too, had gotten a speeding ticket at one time and, in addition, had forgotten to renew some safety sticker demanded by the State of Connecticut. She had paid both fines. End of story. No, not quite.

A separate page reported that Ms. Hart had been arrested for running a yellow light, speeding, reckless driving, endangering the life of an officer, leaving the scene of an accident and resisting arrest. Good God, these Connecticut people were a spirited group!

According to Nacho, the charges had been dropped, but somehow Cynthia had ended up cited for contempt of court. She added that the officer's notes mentioned, of all things, a stray cat. Now here was a story I wanted to hear in detail! I hoped I might be able to pry it out of her employer when we met.

I made copies of the faxes and put them in my briefcase to take along on Monday just in case I wanted another look, placed the originals in a folder marked *Ellis* and filed it. Then I decided I really had to go to the supermarket. I needed things like dog food to take to Mom's, beer, maybe some chips and at least enough food to last me till Monday. I was tired of eating out and I'd be doing more of it, so off we went.

Later that night I forewent watching a Celtics game for an educational docu-drama about Ernest Shackleton and his second trip to Antarctica. After two stark, horror-filled hours I was shocked to learn he returned to London to a hero's welcome although he had lost his ship, failed in his mission, shot his sled dogs and fed them to the crew and caused at least two of his men to lose part of their feet to frostbite while he left them marooned.

So much for explorers. As I thought of it, they all seemed rather drearily alike, with a kind of heartless tunnel vision I would never understand. Maybe that's what it takes. If they waited for people like me to explore them, places like the polar regions, darkest Africa, the Himalayas and the Gobi Desert would all have map notations of *Here Be Dragons*.

Disgusted, I turned to the weather channel, where I learned

that it would rain tomorrow morning, clear up for the afternoon and early evening, and rain again tomorrow night. That put the rain exactly at times I did not want it.

For tomorrow morning, when everybody else would be sleeping late or partying early, I had let myself be trapped by Mary Sloan into helping get her boat out of the water and into her garage. Twice a year Mary stalked the unwary to assist in getting her boat in/out of the bay, always approaching those she would not have to pay. She felt free to criticize every move, and somehow remained dry while you got wet. I did not look forward to it.

Tomorrow night, of course, was the big Halloween parade, which I really did enjoy watching, followed by Cassie and Lainey's party, which might—or might not—be fun. In either event, it all looked to be wet.

Sighing, I let the dog out.

Chapter 5

I made three bad mistakes Saturday morning. First, I should have called Mary Sloan and told her I couldn't help her with her damned boat, that something terribly important had come up—maybe flying down to Washington to advise the President on gay issues, advice he sorely needed. Second I should have driven, not walked, down to the East End where she moored her boat. Third, I should have left Fargo home.

As it was, I put on a jacket and my old fisherman's cap, picked up the dog's leash and set off on a cloudy, chilly, but blessedly dry walk. We got to the public access way just as Mary pulled up in her tan Hyundai Santa Fe. It was always so pristine that I wondered if she drove home from work every night and put it in the shower. She frowned on seeing Fargo, but then, he didn't seem overjoyed to see her, either. She tapped her foot impatiently while I took off my jacket and laid it on a nearby retaining wall.

As I straightened up, something thumped lightly against my

41

chest and I looked down. Automatically I felt for the locket and gold chain I always wore. It had been my grandmother's, and the locket was engraved with her initials, which were also mine. It was unique and opened to form three small picture holders. In the largest was a cropped photo of my grandparents as a young couple. In the two even smaller areas were tiny headshots of my mother and Aunt Mae as little girls. I treasured it. Thank God I had noticed it. In the activities to come I might well have broken the chain and let it fall into the water without noticing. I carefully removed it and placed it atop my jacket while Mary cleared and re-cleared her throat.

We started to work, and the first problem was Fargo. He raced in and out of the shallows, thinking this was a fine new game with me in the water, too! He also tried to help by jumping against the side of the boat and then jumping on me with sopping wet legs and paws. Certain he would either cause an accident or find himself in one, I leashed him to a nearby fence. There he alternately whimpered and barked and whined, while I gritted my teeth and Mary sporadically called out, "Silence! I say be silent, sir!" as if she were an English lord correcting a recalcitrant royal hound. I assumed she had heard it somewhere on TV.

The rest of the job went about as efficiently and pleasantly as those things usually do, but we finally got the boat winched onto the trailer without serious incident. Mary still looked clean and dry and terribly competent. I had knocked my cap into the water, so it was cold and soggy on my head. I had somehow scraped my shin and it hurt. Half the bay had come in over the tops of my Wellingtons. As I dumped the water out of them onto the side-walk, I realized disconsolately that—from the point of view of comfort—it didn't much matter. I felt chilled and unusually clumsy as Fargo and I grumpily walked the couple of hundred yards to Mary's house.

It was easier to walk than try somehow to get Fargo dry enough and clean enough to ride in the SUV.

I helped her disconnect the trailer. As we pushed it into the garage, the rain started—immediately heavy. Mary looked uncomfortable. The normal thing would be either to invite us in or take us home. This was not to be. "I have a dentist's appointment in a few minutes," she said, truthfully or not. "If you want to wait while I run in and change, I'll give you a lift downtown." She did not invite us to come in while she changed. I was too discouraged to do other than nod.

Fargo and I stood in the garage doorway, watching the deluge with mutually disgusted expressions. I was swearing never, *ever* to let this woman talk me into anything again. Fargo, I think, was mentally composing his newspaper ad for a new owner. As we rode downtown (with Fargo in the back on newspapers and Mary ostentatiously sniffing), the rain obligingly stopped. We exchanged curt farewells and Fargo and I began the squishy walk home.

When we were still blocks from my house, it started to sprinkle. By the time we reached the Green Mansions Inn, a gay men's guesthouse, it was a steady drizzle. Green Mansions was a marvelous old Victorian house on the bay with green shingles and white trim and a wonderful wraparound veranda. Usually studded with large Edwardian wicker fan chairs and small tables, it was bare now except for a rather badly warped wooden table, with what looked to be a broom handle serving as one of its legs. For years the inn had been owned by two gay men named Peter and the Wolf. Their real names were Peter Mellon and Frank Wolfman, but some long-ago wit had coined the sobriquet and so they had remained. Now in their early sixties, they catered to an older crowd, and it was said their invariably pretty houseboys would do considerably more than bring you fresh towels if you asked nicely and tipped hugely.

Wolf was on the porch collecting the mail, and looked up as we passed. "Alex! You're getting soaked! Get in here and dry off till this passes. Are you crazy? It's cold out here! Let me give you a warm drink."

We had already ascertained that I was crazy and God knew I was cold. My feet felt like those of Shackleton's feckless crewmembers. Someone sounding motherly and holding out promise of hot drinks was welcome indeed. I climbed the steps and shed my jacket and boots in the hallway. Wolf hung up the jacket and wisely left the boots alone. As Fargo and I padded damply into the living room, Wolf called up the stairs, "Peter, Alex Peres is here. Bring down a pair of your heavy crew socks, they're smaller than mine. And a towel for Fargo."

Peter came downstairs with towel and socks in hand and a quizzical expression on his round face, took one look at me, said "Oh, you poor thing," tossed me the socks and called over his shoulder, "Lewis! Dear boy, do make a pot of tea quicker than quick! Bring it in the living room, please. Tea for three, dear boy."

Following Peter was an enormous gray-and-white cat named Pewter, after the cat in the Rita Mae Brown books. Fargo tensed and I muttered, "Far-go!" warningly. He seemed to sense this was not the time to rearrange this Victoriana-filled room, and Pewter strolled casually toward the kitchen as if it had been her original plan. I began to towel the dog. One crisis avoided.

The socks felt almost sinfully soft and warm, and the tea tray made me feel better by its very appearance. Lewis set it on the coffee table and began to pour. It struck me as somewhat incongruous, as the tea set was obviously sterling, that there were three nondescript mugs on the tray instead of cups and saucers of the Royal Doulton I was sure they possessed. Maybe Lewis figured I wasn't worth the wash-up.

He asked me if I wanted milk, and as I looked at him I realized he was one of the three young men I had seen in the Wharf Rat the other day. I asked merely for one sugar. He complied and as he handed me the mug I observed a recent bad scar on his hand and wondered idly what had happened. It looked as though it should have been stitched.

Reaching for the mug, I noticed his bright little eyes drop with interest to the heavy signet ring I wore and then rise to stare at my breasts. Clever detective that I am, it took me almost no time to determine that he probably was not admiring my sexy sweat-shirted figure, but my locket. I looked at him sharply and he covered himself with a simpering smile on his full, pouty mouth. "I was just admiring your beautiful gold jewelry, Ms. Peres. I'll bet they're both your favorite family heirlooms, aren't they?"

I murmured noncommittally and wondered why anyone would call him *dear boy*. And I thought that if he were *my* houseboy I'd keep my jewelry in the safe, along with any cash. I realized Peter was standing over me with a bottle of rum and extended my mug gratefully. I explained why I was wandering the streets in my soaked condition and they both laughed.

"Mary got you, too, did she? She's gone through about everybody in town by now. She got Wolf a couple of years ago. He stepped in a hole and hurt his ankle and she never even drove him home! The poor baby had to hobble to a pay phone and call me to come and get him." Wolf looked more like a fading Ashley Wilkes to me than a poor baby, and Peter was surely a chubby leprechaun with male pattern baldness. No matter—they were both white knights for my money today.

"Yes," Wolf sighed dramatically. "It was extremely painful. Now, when we see her coming, we cross the street and make the sign of the cross." He held his crossed index fingers in front of him in the universal keep-the-vampires-away sign. We all laughed and began to chat, of course, about the weather. Peter was afraid it would ruin the parade.

"Are you two going to be in it?" I asked.

"No," Peter answered. "Those *darling* people at the Crown and Anchor have asked me to do my little Judy Garland piece and I just couldn't refuse. I'll be busy getting all made up while the parade's on. I'm getting too old, of course, but one hates simply to *give in*, doesn't one?"

"One does," I concurred. "What about you, Wolf?"

He shrugged and placed his mug on the coffee table. "I'm not much on costumes or parades. Oh, I love to see them. I just don't care about being in them. And you, Alex?"

"I'm with you. I'd rather watch than march. I am wearing a cos-

45

tume only because Lainey and Cassie's party demands it. And the costume itself is hardly inspired—it's my brother's old army uniform."

"You should wear a tux," Peter stated. "Have you ever noticed how great women look in tuxes? Really feminine women look terribly *soigné* and sexy, and masculine women look terribly *suave* and sexy. You'd look good in one—a little mixture of both, I think." He eyed me appraisingly.

I felt myself blush and hated it. "Well, it's too late now," I replied. "And I am taking up your day. Is the inn filled this weekend?"

"Oh, yes, every room and then next week we drop dead." Wolf waved vaguely toward the two upper floors. "A few rooms booked in November, but I think we may cancel those and leave early for Florida. We have a marvelous condo on South Beach that looks better all the time. We are getting tired of all the guesthouse turmoil and may just put Green Mansions up for auction to whoever wants to work more hours than a fireman. I may take Rima, here, with me—and Pewter of course," he added with a grin.

"Oh, don't leave, Ptown wouldn't be the same." As I heard myself mouth the platitude, I realized I meant it.

"Well, we may do one more season."

"You've been saying that for two years," Peter pouted.

I laughed. "Well, listen, thank you both for resuscitating me. It was truly a noble deed. I think the rain has stopped again, so I'll run while I can." Somehow I set the mug down on the edge of the coaster, and it tipped over. Tea immediately formed a growing circle on the antique coffee table and began to drizzle onto the Persian rug.

"Oh, God, I'm so sorry!" I tried to wipe up the mess with a hopelessly tiny napkin.

Wolf called Lewis to bring paper towels, and the young man began the mop-up with an amused glance at me. Even as he mopped, I noticed that either the heat of the tea or the alcohol was making the top of the table turn white. That didn't help my embarrassment.

"Wolf, Peter. What an oaf I am! Look, if you need to refinish the table . . . have the rug cleaned, please, please don't hesitate . . . bill me . . . be more than happy . . ."

Peter rescued me from my rambling monologue. "Dear Alex, stop fretting. A little furniture polish will get rid of the spot, and you wouldn't believe some of the things that have spilled on that rug with no harm done. Now just shush!"

"I think I really am bewitched!' I blurted.

"What?" They chorused.

"This crazy old woman in a witch outfit stopped me outside the Rat the other day and screamed something about devils' dens and demon rum, and then that things would reel and break. Scared poor Fargo half to death. And, idiotic as it is, ever since, I've been dropping things and walking into doors. I don't believe in witch-craft but it's maddening!"

"Oh, my dear," Peter chortled delightedly. "Maybe she really was a witch. Dogs *know!* Now"—he turned to Wolf—"right after Halloween we'll have a small party and do an exorcism. Won't that be fun?"

Wolf smiled and nodded and I took the opportunity to get out before we all sat down to make up the guest list. I went to the entryway, followed by the two men. "I really must go before I do further damage. Peter, I'll get your socks back to you soon."

"No rush, sweet girl, no rush. Forgive *me* for rushing, Alex." He consulted a spot on his wrist where a watch should have been. He looked blank for a moment and then said, "Oh, I must have left it in the kitchen. Anyway, I've got a rehearsal shortly." He called after me as Fargo and I reached the sidewalk. "Stop by the Crown tonight . . . around nine!"

"I will," I called back, deciding that I really would. I had never seen his "little Judy Garland piece." I wondered if he would do it straight or, as he would say, camp it up.

Fargo and I made about fifty feet before the drizzle started yet again. I was quickly beyond feeling, and didn't much care when it stopped once more. I took off my sodden cap, shook it out and held it in front of me to drip as I ran my other hand through my equally sodden hair.

"Paula, you will notice this poor woman is one of Provincetown's sadder cases, a combination of drunkenness and paranoia."

I recognized my brother's voice, and looked around just as his hand reached out and dumped a bunch of coins into my extended cap. "You've been sleeping under the docks again, Alexandra. Now why don't you go home to your poor mama and behave like the young lady you were raised to be?"

I pocketed the coins and turned toward him. "Thankee, kind sir, for the money which I will spend on cheap whiskey, and for the good advice—for which—I—will—kill—you!" I put my hands around his throat and began to shake him.

He was laughing too hard to fend me off successfully, but he did manage to gasp out, "The pastries! Don't make me drop the pastries!"

I let go of him and turned to Paula, who was working on a small, tight smile. I could hardly blame her. "I've heard so many nice things about you, Paula. It's good to meet you at last." I had to admit, she was super good looking! Blonde hair in a carefully careless cut, blue eyes and a figure that belonged on a fashion show runway. But her mouth, I thought, was the just teeniest bit hard and her eyes just a smidge close.

I put out my cold wet hand, which she took for a nanosecond and murmured something inaudible.

Sonny then took over. "Here, the car's right here. Get in, Alex. And you, Fargo, poor boy. You both look like tornado victims." He shooed us to his car and put us in the back seat. He and Paula got in front, and she turned partway around, graciously hobnobbing with the serfs.

"We were on our way to your place anyway," she said. "How very fortunate we found you when we did." She sniffed and rolled her window down an inch. I had the uncomfortable feeling that my nose was running and reached into my coat for a packet of tissues. Instead, I pulled out a grubby sock, which I hastily shoved back, in the hope that no one had seen it. Unhappily, I noticed Paula's eyebrows were just about up to her hairline. I thought of trying to explain and gave it up as impossible. Then I sniffed too, and it was inescapable . . . the unique and all-pervading aroma of *parfum du wet dog*.

The three-block drive lasted about an hour, and then Sonny was hustling us all into my house. "Come on, come on. I'll rub Fargo down. Alex, go get a hot shower—now! You're so cold you're twitching and that's not really good. Go!"

I went. By the time I returned, miracles had taken place. Sonny—somehow I knew Paula had had no part in the activity—had made the dirty dishes disappear from the kitchen sink, made fresh coffee, and put a cloth on the dining room table, along with my good luncheon plates, cups and saucers. The platter of the pastries he had brought included my favorite French crullers and cranberry-walnut scones. Even Fargo was dry and shiny and already snoring lightly in his bed. I was impressed. I was also starved but made a desperate effort to mind my manners. I figured Sonny deserved it.

"Well, you look better," Sonny said. "You really were not in great shape. What on earth happened to you?"

I told them. Sonny laughed and Paula tried to look interested. "Mary got you, too, did she?" Sonny asked.

"That seems to be the standard reply whenever Mary Sloan is mentioned. A couple of years ago she trapped Frank Wolfman and sprained his ankle for him and left him to walk home. That also seems standard." I pulled up the leg of my slacks to show my wounded shin.

"Ouch," Sonny winced.

Paula grimaced. "Ooh, grisly! Should you have someone look at that?" Did people really go to doctors for scraped shins?

"Oh, I imagine she'll make it," Sonny replied for me. "Yeah, Mary got Mitch last spring. She got the boat in the water by herself but then got her SUV stuck in the sand. Mitch happened to be driving by and stopped to help—in uniform, on duty. Instead of putting him in the cab and her pushing, she drove the SUV and

Mitch was in back. They got her going and she took off like a jet— and just kept going. Left Mitch standing up to his ankles in water and looking like he'd been sprayed with stucco."

"God," I sighed. "Mary Sloan is a real threat. Does she have a list of victims or just throw a dart at the phone book?"

"I think it has something to do with chicken bones and the full of the moon." Sonny tipped back in his chair. I hated it when he did that.

"Look, Alex, we really were coming over here. I wanted to tell you that we moved our vacation up. I managed to rearrange the tickets and hotel reservations." He sounded slightly harried. "We're going to fly to Boston late this afternoon with Cassie. Otherwise she'd be deadheading over to pick up a fare, so she gave us a good price. And we'll fly down to Knoxville in the morning and rent a car to drive over to Gatlinburg."

"Why the sudden change?"

Paula looked at me earnestly across the table. "I really feel that Edward is so stressed out, it's just imperative he get some relax- ation right away. And I'm done in myself." She gave a brave little smile. "I had to decorate a five-room model apartment in one of Daddy's condos and it's about finished me." She sighed, and her head drooped piteously.

I was curious. "What's got you so worn out, Son . . . ah, Edward?"

Paula answered for him. "Well, first, there's been that terrible arson case."

I was startled. Fire was always a danger in Provincetown. Lots of old wooden buildings built close together, a hot blaze and a high wind could spell disaster. But arson? I looked at Sonny.

He looked back neutrally. "Liz Mason," he said succinctly.

Oh, I knew about that. Liz's boyfriend kept a bunch of tools and fishing gear in her garage. It burned down, and she swore her ex- husband had set it.

"Ah, the Mason case," I nodded sagely. "It'll be a long time before Provincetown forgets *that* conflagration!"

Sonny glared.

"And that giant car-theft ring," Paula added.

Goodness, we were beginning to sound like Chicago in 1930. But I figured that one out myself. A few weeks back, a bunch of teenagers got beered up and made some sort of bet about who could hot-wire and joyride the most cars out to Race Point in a single night. They were perking right along, emptying out the town, when a cop noticed what seemed an awful lot of traffic for an October night.

I shook my head. "Yes, that was a mind-boggling challenge. Well, Edward, I can see why you need to get away. I take it you got the time off okay?"

"Yes. Chief Franks will be available if needed. His wife is doing much better. They seem to have stabilized whatever was causing her irregular heartbeat. And Captain Anders is around. At least he *looks* like a cop, until you see the only paper on his desk is *Barron's*. So yeah. It's okay. Mitch will be able to handle things. He's a lot smarter than he thinks he is, kind of a nice reversal nowadays. He just needs a little confidence."

Sonny leaned across the table and handed me a three-by-five card. "This is where we'll be—phone and room numbers are there, too. You are the only soul who has this, so don't lose it. And do *not* give it to anyone unless you think something is really wrong. Mitch or Anders will want to call if somebody runs a red light. Mother will want to check on us if she hears a plane crashed in Argentina. Mary Sloan will call if her Santa Fe gets splashed. Don't ruin the first real vacation I've had in years."

"Don't forget, Sonny, I won't be here either." I gave in and hooked a second cruller. "Not Monday through Wednesday, anyway. You sure you don't want to leave it with Mom? You can trust her."

"Nah, not for just three lousy days."

"Well, I'm sure you'll have a really grand time," I said.

Paula placed her hand tenderly on Edward's arm. "He just *insisted* that's where we go. It sounds just a tiny bit touristy, but I'm sure the scenery is lovely."

I took the last bite of my cruller and managed not to lick my fingers. "Well, I'm sure it is, too, and Edward tells me the crafts are quite beautiful. They fashion lovely pottery and hand-woven cloth. Not to mention old-time instruments like dulcimers, hand-carved just like they were nearly four hundred years ago." Why did my conversation with Paula sound as stilted and Victorian as the Green Mansions décor?

"Yeah." Sonny had no such problem. "That fascinates me. I read up on the area a little bit. Did you know there are some back-woods areas down there where the people still speak a sort of Elizabethan English dialect?"

Paula slapped his hand playfully. "Oh, Edward, *of course* they speak English. I know it's terribly—ah, rural—but even so, it's still America down there."

I did not look at Sonny. "I'd better let Fargo out." I excused myself. By the time I got back, they had their coats on. Sonny wished me luck on my trip. I wished them fun on theirs. Sonny and I hugged. Paula favored me with another brief handshake and they left.

Fargo and I both made it to the couch before we fell asleep.

We awoke two hours later, and I at least was much refreshed. I let him out, filled his water dish, filled his dry food dish and started frying some bacon. He had two slices, plain. I had two BLTs with extra mayo, thanks, and it was time to begin my evening.

The fatigues now fit reasonably well, and after some moments of panic I found the little raccoon mask in a file drawer. I began to explain to Fargo why he had to stay at home tonight. He explained fervently to me why that should not be so. This time I won.

The players were now all in their places in our little microcosm of the world's stage, ready for their entrances and exits, and some in their time to play many parts.

I put on my cap and went out.

Chapter 6

Just in case I was fighting any residual chill, I decided a drink was in order. Also, that would give me a chance to give my costume its first tryout on Joe, the bartender. I turned down the alley toward the Wharf Rat, pulling on my little mask as I walked. In reality, I wasn't chilled at all. Not wishing to wear a coat, I had put on a long-sleeved T-shirt under the uniform and was quite comfortable. I just wanted a drink and some conviviality which might put me in a holiday mood, okay?

The place was fairly busy despite the early hour. As I walked up to the bar I noticed Chief Mather in his usual spot, staying late on this spectral eve. He glanced up briefly, but I wasn't sure whether he recognized me or not. In any event, he didn't speak.

Joe, on the other hand, ambled over as if I always appeared at his bar in army combat camouflage. "Beer or bourbon, Alex?" So much for disguise. I opted for bourbon over ice and turned around on the stool to survey the crowd.

As my barstool spun, I felt slightly off-balance and reached back to grab the bar. I missed and knocked over the beer of the man next to me. Joe quickly mopped it up and gave the man another, just shaking his hands negatively when I offered to pay for it. This really was beginning to bug me. I have never been a ballerina . . . but I've never been a trained elephant either. Resolutely, I refused to worry about it and crowd-watched.

Two queens in matching light orange silk sheathes split up to mid-thigh sat at one table. Killer looks . . . gorgeous legs, short black sculpted curls, kewpie doll makeup, long cigarette holders. Very nineteen twenties, very good!

Somebody had stocked the old-fashioned bubbling neon juke box that played only golden oldies, which I really like. The Beatles came on with *Michelle* and that unique haunting harmony. The '20s girls got up to dance with their tuxedoed escorts. I heard Mather call for a refill in a sour voice.

A table of two straight couples were near me. Apparently tourists, they had no costumes but had wanted to join the fun and had somewhere found party hats and noisemakers. I liked their attitude. The music switched to Nina Simone, and two young girls joined the dancers, staring soulfully at each other with that first-love look that actually vibrates with the certainty it will last forever.

I'd never cared much for Simone's style, but I liked what I had heard about the woman. She'd got her first real professional break at the Atlantic House here. And for years afterward—long after the A-House would have been professionally "beneath" her—she had returned each season as a thank-you. Maybe I liked her style, after all.

I turned back to my drink and a pair of hands touched my shoulders, massaging them lightly. A liquor-laden voice whispered sibilantly in my ear. "Oh, you delicious macho thing, you! You look just *scrumptious!*" It was dear boy, with two cronies in tow, all of them obviously loaded.

I swung around, knocked his arms away and jammed three fingers far enough into his solar plexus to make him gasp and bend over. "Dear boy," I oozed back at him, "if you ever put your fuck-

54

ing hands anywhere near me again, I'll put a nine millimeter bullet up your nose."

Of course, I wasn't carrying, but he didn't know that. He spun away, white faced, and joined his pals, a couple of stools down. As I went back to people watching, I heard him order a drink and saw him pull out a well-stuffed wallet. Unless they were all ones, the wages of sheet-shaking and a little discreet sin were well over the minimum.

I floated with the music and the background noise and the second bourbon Joe had poured without asking. It was all pleasant and familiar. And I felt content enough. That scared me a little. Was I one of those people who were really *meant* to be alone? Forever? Enjoying my family. Enjoying much-loved friends like Lainey and Cassie, Vance and Charlie. Loving Fargo. But alone? Was I simply lazy, or careless about opportunities? Was there the perfect life partner here just waiting for my hello?

I looked keenly around the room. Not so you'd notice.

But I did notice that dear boy Lewis did not seem to be enjoying himself. He drained his glass and set it down sharply, looked at his watch with a scowl and growled to his companions, "I'm splitting. I'll catch you later."

One of his companions asked coyly, "You got a sweet trick you haven't told us about?"

"Nah," Lewis replied. "Going over to the Rev's. They'll still be having dinner. I'll trade a couple of hallelujahs for a good free home-cooked meal, anytime." He walked out, staring ahead, with that careful march-step you use when you're afraid you're going to stagger.

I had no trouble translating his cryptic comments. There was a born-again preacher man and his wife over near Shank Painter Road with a little storefront church and some sort of rambling quarters behind it. The Rev and his mousy spousy made an effort to feed some of Ptown's young drifters. They had some rooms the girls could sleep in, and boys were quartered in a loft over the garage.

Presumably they were fed and safe, at least for the nights they were there. I hoped this was as true as their local supporters assumed. So often, I thought, the fox is the concierge of the henhouse. Perhaps I tend to be a little cynical. Actually, my Aunt Mae rather likes the Rev and his wife. But then, my Aunt Mae rather likes most everyone.

Anyway, giving the Rev the benefit of the doubt, I wondered why Lewis, with that fat wallet, felt the need of a free meal with religious overtones. From what I'd seen of him, it didn't seem like his type of hangout. Suddenly, I sensed someone at my side and looked up sharply, half expecting dear boy had returned for a noisy confrontation. It was ex-Chief Mather.

"Good work with that little pansy, soldier! Got to keep those faggots in their place!" He gave me a snappy salute, turned and left.

I was flabbergasted. Well, at least my costume fooled somebody! Or had it? Surely he hadn't thought I was a male. Was it some sort of sardonic tease? Had I seen just the suggestion of a smile on Mather's face? Maybe he had some glimmer of humor after all. Although . . . maybe he *had* thought I was for real. Why else the offensive language? I shrugged. Who knew with him?

It was getting to be parade time, so I polished off my drink and left. As I came up the alley onto Commercial Street, I saw Lewis and Mather a few yards up the street, exchanging words. I wondered what they could possibly have to say to each other. Lewis was standing with his weight on one leg, pelvis forward in a come-on pose. Mather looked stiff and pained.

Well he might. Jared Mather had years ago relegated himself to a life of pure, excruciating emotional torture. As far as I knew, I was the only person in town who was aware of it, and I had kept the secret so deeply buried, I often forgot it myself. I had learned of it completely innocently.

About five years ago my aunt Barbara was in a serious car accident. Mom and Aunt Mae flew to Delaware to be with her, and I kept an eye on their respective houses. One day after a storm, I went by Mom's place and found no damage, but Aunt Mae hadn't been so lucky. A limb had come down, taking out a bathroom window on its way. I looked around for something to board it up with but found nothing. I stood in the yard, pondering what to do, when I realized I was staring at Mather's house down the hill. If anybody could effect repairs, it would be he.

The day was pleasant and I walked across the fields. Over on the road, a convoy passed, horns blowing, streamers flying. I remembered a long-engaged couple who had tied the knot today and were probably on their way to the airport after the reception. I recalled she was some distant kin to Mather and wondered if he would be home.

As I walked silently up the grassy center of his driveway I heard someone groan. Was he ill? I took a few steps forward toward the window I thought the sound had come from and heard more groans . . . the unmistakable groans of a male in rut. I froze.

Then I heard a voice. "Oh, oh . . . oh, God, Jared that was good." The voice was male, and not Mather.

"Yes, yes . . . but I shouldn't have . . . swore I wouldn't ever do it again! Sweet Jesus! What have I done?" It was Mather now, sounding agonized. "Oh, Lord, what terrible wrong have I done against You? I promised I would never do it again. But I did, I did. And— oh, it felt so good." He sounded almost in tears. I couldn't believe it—could this be the stern, emotionless figure I had known for years?

The other man laughed. "Jared, the only one you did anything *against* was me! And you did nothing wrong. We both enjoyed it, didn't we? That makes it okay in my book."

Mather's anguish exploded into anger. "Anything is okay in your book! Why in hell did I drink champagne at that double-damned wedding? I know better than to drink too much! Why, oh, God, why? Can You forgive me? I repent, I will never, ever do this again. Jesus, save me." He sobbed the deep, racking sobs of a heartbroken child.

The other man now sounded irritated. "Jared, don't go on a crying jag with Jesus. Obviously you wanted this as much as I did.

We're both single. What's the big deal? I'm dying of thirst," he added practically. "What have you got to drink? Beer, I hope."

It suddenly occurred to me that when they got up—which would be any second—they would see me through the window. I couldn't have that. Mather would never believe I hadn't been deliberately eavesdropping for God-knows how long!

Quickly I ran halfway back down the grassy path. If I hadn't been worried that animals of some variety would get into Aunt Mae's house, I'd have kept right on going back to my car. Instead, I stepped onto the crunchy gravel and walked noisily back toward the house. And I sang. When I sing, people listen. Sonny says my voice has the deep resonant beauty of a water buffalo with strep throat.

Sure enough, by the time I reached the back porch, Mather was already coming through the door, wearing jeans and a T-shirt. He was barefooted, tousle-haired and red-eyed. And he looked as guilty as any criminal he had ever arrested. "Alexandra! I—I'm surprised to see you. Can I do something for you?"

I told him what had happened and asked him if he could board up the window.

He agreed to go "right over" and stood in the doorway, waiting for me to leave. There was no evidence of his guest.

I was shaken. I couldn't get it off my mind. Two single adult men get a little blitzed at a wedding. They have sex. What harm? To whom? Yet Jared Mather was a soul in torment. And how many years had he been like this? I wished I could offer him comfort. I knew no one could. No gay person could, nor any straight person either. And certainly not his God. Obviously, Jared was gay, and knew it and could not abide it. Every day must be torture. Those most basic desires—for human contact and affection and physical pleasure were to him, unforgivable crimes.

I made a vow. If anyone ever found out Jared Mather was gay, it would not be from me. This would not become a funny story on the cocktail circuit. It would not become grist for the Ladies' Aid Society gossip mill. And it would never be good for backroom laughs at Police Headquarters.

Jared would not be outed by Alex. I didn't much like him. I thought his religion was hateful, dangerous and false. I thought he was smart enough to know he should have had professional help years ago. And I never felt sorrier for anyone in my life. Talk about ambivalence!

I realized I had unthinkingly turned down toward the parade route and heard music coming toward me. I put thoughts of Mather behind me and let the holiday eve take over. The lead-off band was the Ptown Gay Men's Fife and Drum Corps, with a really accomplished version of the "Colonel Bogey March." They looked good, too, in their Revolutionary War–styled uniforms, with the white stockings that showed off their shapely legs and the tight, tight breeches that showed off everything else.

Hard on their heels was the Lesbian Mothers' Association. Kids not strapped or tethered were being herded along with modest success at staying in step. Then came hordes of people in fantastic costumes, and behind them a pink VW beetle with lots of clowns in, on and around it. They had their routine down pat, so that it looked as if all the people really came out of the car.

A flatbed truck with some hay bales for décor and six women playing down home bluegrass music followed. A banjo, a guitar, three fiddles and a bass were twanging out a real shit-kickin' hoe-down. They were superb, and I hoped they might be playing someplace in town for a while. Maybe Cassie and I could catch them—we both love bluegrass, in small doses, anyway.

Next we were favored by the Bare-Breasted Broncos, a lesbian motorcycle club from New York. Despite the fact that most of them were magnificently endowed and set the ol' gonads to snapping in high-speed bluegrass rhythm, many of us wished fervently that these ladies would not tire themselves out coming so far to visit. But they were ever faithful. By morning at least three of them would be in the medical clinic, four would be detained in local cells and most would have been in fights for making improper advances to other women's partners . . . some of which would be surreptitiously accepted.

Suddenly, across the street, I thought I saw my witch waving and shouting at passersby. Behind the Broncos, and in front of a group billed as the Queens from Queens, I nipped across the street. Now where the hell was she? She had disappeared again! Of course, I wasn't really sure it was *my* witch, and I had no idea what I would have said if I had caught up with her.

Chagrined, I turned down the walkway to see what was going on at the Atlantic House. Mayhem was going on, with wall-to-wall people, hyper-decibel music, and frenzied fun in and out of costume. I tried unsuccessfully to fight my way to the bar. The floor vibrated so badly I really wondered if we all might spill into the basement. Somebody handed me back a bourbon and ice. I wasn't even sure who had bought it for me, until I saw my friends Dan and Mike waving. I had no hope of approaching them and just waved my thanks.

I fought back the way I had come and took my drink (illegally) outdoors to join a smaller crowd, where I at least had air to breathe. It was getting time for the show at the Crown and Anchor, so I downed the drink—I'd better watch that—left the glass on a rock wall and retraced my steps up the alley.

The Crown was busy but not frantic. It was a largely male crowd, and somewhat older, or at least more conservatively behaved than those at the A-House. I found a small table and sat down at the banquette behind it. A waiter brought me a drink, took some money and I settled down to wait. If they were running on time, Ms. Garland would soon come tripping down that yellow brick road. Meanwhile, the band played Cole Porter songs, and I wondered what the gay world would have done without him.

"Excuse me." A pleasant-looking man somewhere in his fifties stood in front of my table. "There's not a seat left in the place, and I wondered if I might share your banquette?"

"Why not? I'm Alex."

"Marc." He put out his hand. Shortly, a waiter appeared and took his order for a scotch and water, "plus whatever the lady is having."

"The lady is having a very light bourbon and water, please."
Then I laughed. "Well, congratulations, sir! You are the one millionth person not to be fooled by my disguise tonight."

"As bad as that?" He smiled.

"Actually, an acquaintance of mine let on earlier that he thought I was a man. I realize now he was just teasing." I moved the ashtray closer to me.

"Sorry." He shrugged. "Maybe it's the lack of a beard. That's probably the reason I don't wear costumes anymore . . . everybody always knew me anyway."

"I'm with you," I agreed. "Unfortunately I'm going to a party later where costumes are required—like tiaras or medals or something. Frankly, it's a pain." The waiter set the drinks down and stood there until Marc paid him. No tabs on a busy night like this.

Marc stirred his drink and looked around. "I haven't missed Judy Garland, have I?"

As if on cue, the band stopped playing and the lights went black. The noise in the room faltered and twittered into silence. I hoped this wouldn't be either an embarrassing failure or a tasteless parody. One or the other seemed likely, and I thought both Judy and Peter deserved better.

There was a fanfare . . . a drum roll . . . moving spots that circled, crossed and then stopped on a barstool that held . . . Judy Garland.

Peter actually looked like her. He wore a long black skirt with a discreet slit, a white cotton shirt with cuffed back sleeves and a stand-up collar, several gold chains and a dark, ragged-cut wig that looked real. He had her startled-deer eyes and full lower lip to begin with, and makeup did the rest. I was impressed. He and the band swung energetically into "San Francisco" and I went from impressed to amazed.

Peter must have been well corseted, because he looked no chubbier than I had seen Judy look in some TV clips. He handled the mike well, moved vigorously and gracefully, just as she had done. Maybe there was an extra wrinkle, maybe he took a breath

61

when she would have held the note, maybe he slid into some of the high notes instead of hammering them dead-on. But the energy, the nuance, the timbre, the voice . . . was *there*. The band segued into "Embraceable You," and I simply gave myself to the music.

She did three or four more Garland songs—by now I was thinking of her as *she*—well, you know what I mean. Applause was loud and long, and I was thrilled for Peter. Then she drifted into "The Man That Got Away," with that tearing low-pitched heart-break. They gave her the most sincere accolade an artist can receive: the room was dead quiet when she finished. There must have been a twenty-second time lapse between Peter's last note and the first cheer from the standing audience. I felt tears building against the dams of my lower eyelashes and observed others reaching for napkins or handkerchiefs.

Of course her signature "Over the Rainbow" was the finale, with everyone standing and joining in. Another blackout. And the little stage was empty save for a barstool with a mic lying on the seat. No bows, no clever repartee, no roses thrown and caught. Judy had triumphed . . . and she had gone.

I was drained. I couldn't make immediate small talk. I didn't even say thanks when the waiter delivered another round. It was several moments before Marc spoke. "Did you ever see her before?" he asked.

"No and no," I replied. "As for Peter, I really don't know why not. As for Judy, only movies and clips of some of her appearances. In person, I think she left the planet about the time I was landing."

Marc nodded and sipped his drink. "Yes. I figured that. Well, I can tell you, Peter is damn near as good as she was, certainly better than she was at the end. She got to be a mess. I was a kid in Provincetown when she was last here, just before she died or killed herself or got killed or whatever she did. She was always drunk or stoned, hung out here and at the old Town House Bar. It was sad, demeaning, humiliating. I used to wonder why I went and watched her, night after night. It was like looking at the same train wreck over and over."

He paused, and I could tell he was far away. I waited, and finally he continued. "She would try to sing and slurred the words, or forgot them entirely. Once she fell off the piano. But we gay boys milled around as long as she was there. We still adored her . . . and she us. It was strange how she loved gay men, but virtually ignored any lesbians who tried to become friendly, even just to compliment her. She was often plain rude."

I lit a cigarette and wondered idly what number smoke it was. "Yes, I've heard that. What was her beef with lesbians?"

Marc waved a hand dismissively, or possibly to disperse the smoke. "A dozen theories. Some thought she was straight and didn't like a lesbian making a pass. That's silly. Surely, with all her years in show business, she would simply have laughed it off. Others said she'd had a lesbian experience and found it unpleasant. Most lesbians said she had *not* had a lesbian experience and was afraid she'd like it, thereby making her life even more convoluted. All she would have needed was the same luck with women she had with men."

I took a drag and carefully blew the smoke away. "She sounds a very confused woman who was comfortable around gay men because they were safe, yet made her feel adored and wanted."

"Oh, no doubt." Marc reached for his jacket and began to shrug into it. "I think the problem was Judy and that big devil called *intimacy*. I think the lady probably literally died looking for love, yet afraid of losing herself if she found it."

Now that was food for thought. And possibly indigestion.

Marc finally got his jacket on straight. "Well, I gotta run. I'm due at a party in Truro. It's been pure pleasure, Alex. I hope we meet again." He gave me a light kiss on the cheek and began to weave through the crowd.

I leaned back to finish my drink and wished he hadn't left. For some reason, I didn't want to be alone at that moment. Then I had one of those idiotic thoughts that make you absolutely certain you're going mad. I looked around the hundred-plus people in the room and was convinced that each of them was with a partner, that

I was the only soul there who was single. Everyone would go home with that partner, wake up together, live out their lives together. I was the only person in the place who would go home to a partner with four legs and a tail.

If I could carry a tune, I'd go on the road as Judy Garland looking for love in all the wrong places. Where the hell were the right places? What the hell was love? Why had I found so many women exciting in bed and so deadly dull out of it? Why did I always feel smothered at the thought of living with someone? And why did my lovers always accuse me of becoming distant and withdrawn?

I thought of Cassie and Lainey. They didn't seem the least bored or suffocated. Of course Cassie flew all over the place, and Lainey nursed at all hours. Sometimes they actually spent days apart. Because of their crazy hours they often used two bedrooms, yet they were very much a faithful and loving couple. They just weren't joined at the hip.

Maybe I should advertise in one of those personal mags. *Gay, 30-ish female private investigator desires female pilot or nurse for intermittent romance.* That should get me enough lunatic replies for a lifetime of entertainment. I raised my arm for another drink and quickly lowered it. Not wise.

Chapter 7

When I walked outside, the cold air gave me a jolt. Obviously, I had had a bit to drink . . . or two. As I walked to Cassie's and Lainey's house I was not sorry it was some eight blocks away. I could smell rain in the air, but at least the parade had managed to complete its course ahead of it. I hoped I could, too. One miserable soaking a day was more than enough.

I heard the party before I got to the house. It seemed in full swing as I walked around the side and onto the deck. There, Peter Pan sat on a railing singing "I Won't Grow Up" in a rather appealing girlish soprano. I smiled and applauded. At least she looked genuine in *her* costume. As I slid back the screen door to the living room, Lainey came through it wearing a coat and carrying a large plastic bag.

"Dull party?" I asked. "Going to try the one up the street? I hear it's better."

"Certainly not!" she bristled. Then, tumbling to the unique

Peres humor, she smiled. "Oh, no. We goofed. We're already running out of ice. I'm going to rob the hospital. Be right back."

I walked through the door into a wall of people, noise, music and smoke . . . at least some of the latter, illegal. Dan and Mike had beat me here, so I had a chance to thank them for their generosity at the A-House. I chatted for a moment with Katie and Marian, enjoyed a moment of triumph with Cherie, one of the other artists whose paintings had been selected by the bank, and carefully avoided eye contact with Mary Sloan. I made my way to the bar, where Cassie was keeping busy. Finally, it was my turn. She gave me a welcoming grin.

"Glad you made it, ol' buddy. We were beginning to think you'd succumbed to the curse of the gypsies or whatever. Now, here"—she pointed—"we have a bowl of vodka punch. And here, a bowl of some nonalcoholic punch that no one seems to like. We have several bottles of fairly bad white wine. But for you, soldier, may I say . . ." She reached under the bar. "This Bud's for you!"

I took it with a smile for her thoughtfulness and a slight worry as to how it would mix with bourbon. I noticed Cassie was drinking O'Douls and raised an eyebrow. "Flying at noon tomorrow," she explained. "I switched to this a while ago. I like a good amount of time with no booze before takeoff." Tomorrow I would probably wish I had done the same.

The CD player moved to something slow, and a tall blonde tapped me on the shoulder to ask if I would like to dance. I liked very much, and turned away from Cassie with a wink. The blonde and I moved easily across the floor, and she felt very good in my arms.

Her name, she said, was Kerry. Mine, she said she'd heard, was Alex. I agreed to that and asked if her last name were Blue. She said no, it was Morris. Obviously, she had not followed my clever Kerry Blue Terrier train of thought, so I concentrated on my dancing. As we turned, I noticed her nod and give a half-smile to a hefty woman standing with two men. Was she Kerry's lover? I knew the woman worked in the office at the clinic where Lainey nursed, but

I didn't know her name. I decided to approach the subject obliquely.

"Kerry, you're not from Ptown, are you?"

"No, uh, I'm visiting friends of some guys who know the women giving the party."

"Ah." That sounded about right for Ptown. "Having a nice visit?"

"Now I am." She moved even closer against me, and I began to think the evening might end on a very up note. A moment later the music switched again, and we stood for a minute, looking hesitant.

Then Kerry said, "Look, there's a chair near the fire. Grab it and I'll get us a drink."

I yelled, "Budweiser! There's one on the bar that's mine." I turned to nab the chair.

Kerry returned swiftly and sank gracefully to the floor, leaning her head against my leg. I stroked her hair and thought we looked like one of those TV commercials with the handsome couple sitting before the fire drinking expensive wine, while outside a Jaguar with a big red ribbon is being silently delivered in the snowy driveway. I started to mention my thoughts, but Kerry didn't seem attuned to some of my offbeat comments, so I let it go.

She had one arm around my lower leg—not the scraped one, fortunately—and was sort of caressing my ankle and the top of my foot. It was different and kind of exciting. My fingers moved from her hair to the back of her neck, ventured lightly over to her collarbone and finally down just to the beginning of her cleavage. She leaned closer as if inviting further explorations, and I was just about to suggest we have a private party at my house, when something out on the deck caught my eye.

Peter Pan was walking with precarious balance along the top railing of the deck, and I could hear the small voice faintly caroling "I'm flying!" I knew it was quite a way to the ground, flying or not, and felt it would be a simple kindness to convince the elf to get the hell down.

"I'll be right back." I kissed the top of Kerry's head and stood up. I took a step, crashed over the coffee table and re-skinned my shin, landed on my left wrist and felt something give, and finally rolled elegantly onto my back with a yelp.

Kerry . . . Kerry Blue Bitch had tied my damned shoelaces together.

A cast of thousands arrived to offer assistance. I was mortified and kept saying I was fine, though my leg and arm were telling me I wasn't. Through the crowd I saw Kerry and Hefty holding each other up through their fits of laughter. First that slimy Lewis and now this pair—I'd have liked to put the bunch of them on their asses. I wondered what on earth had prompted Kerry's little trick, it had to have been a set-up. Somebody finally got my shoelaces untied and retied and attempted to give me a hand up. I yelped again and Lainey took over.

She got me into the bedroom, pronounced my leg a lovely mess and smeared something on it that felt wonderfully cool. She checked my swelling wrist and asked if I could make a fist. Yes, but it hurt. Could I wiggle my fingers? Yes, it hurt. She diagnosed probable sprain and gently taped a washcloth-wrapped baggie of ice around my wrist. "Sleep with that," she said, and tucked an Ace bandage into my pocket. "That's for tomorrow. If the swelling and the pain haven't decreased by then, check with the clinic."

Cassie insisted on driving me home. As I limped across the deck, I heard a soft voice calling, "I can't get up."

"Cassie, I hate to mention this, but I think Peter Pan has flown into your roses."

"Sweet Jesus in the foothills!" Cassie snarled. "That witch of yours make house calls? What next?" She turned to the house calling, "Lainey! You got another effing casualty here!"

While various people assisted in Peter Pan's rescue, I leaned against Cassie's car, feeling slightly sick. Kerry came out, looking shamefaced. "I'm sorry," she said sweetly, "It never occurred to me you'd get hurt. Nell put me up to it. But I really apologize. I'm sorry," she said again.

"So am I," I said. "I've got a business appointment Monday that

68

this will not make any easier. I guess I accept your apology. But, tell me, I don't even know Nell. What the hell has she got against me?"

Kerry looked as if she thought I should know. "Your brother. He's a cop, right? Last week the cops gave her a parking ticket *and* a speeding ticket. She said she didn't deserve either of them, and she's mad as hell."

I opened the car door and shook my head in disbelief. "Tell her she'll really be thrilled at what he gives her when I tell him she tried to kill me." While Kerry was digesting that thought, Cassie came out and we drove away.

I told Cassie the reason for my own crash landing over the coffee table and she shook her head. "Nell is probably just drunk. Lainey can't stand her. I don't really know her."

"Then why did you invite her?"

"I don't think we did."

I was awfully glad to get home, and Fargo was just as glad to see me. He looked concerned, whuffled all over me, checking out aromas of people, places and medications. I let him out, and he was back whining at the door in record time. As I let him in, I saw why: it had started to rain. Fargo is convinced he is made of spun sugar and will melt in rain.

We were about equally happy to climb into bed. Out of habit, I switched on CNN and got a couple of talking heads discussing whether or not the Fed would raise rates on Thursday. That and the booze and the sound of the rain drumming on the windows was all it took. We had survived Halloween, Fargo and I.

Hopefully the curse had expired at midnight.

Chapter 8

I'd been dreaming something about Judy Garland and "The Trolley Song," when it dawned on me the bells were not in a song, but my telephone. And *dawned* was the operative word. Unbelievably, my clock said 7:08 a.m.

At some point in the night I'd obviously clicked off the TV, because I rolled over onto the remote control. In an effort not to lie on the remote, I dislodged the now-thawed icebag from my wrist and got it wedged under my elbow. As I picked up the phone, I leaned on the baggie, and because it was Sunday and I was hung over, God made it break. Cold water seemed immediately to fill the entire bed. I yelled, "Shit!" and from far away a tinny voice agreed, "You got that right." I was holding the phone wrong-way, too.

I finally got the phone straight and that left me too exhausted to do anything about the water; I just lay in it. I croaked, "Who's this?"

"It's Mitch. Where's Sonny?"

"How the hell do I know? Do you know what time it is?" I counted thirty trolleys clanging in my head. My tongue kept sticking to the roof of my mouth, and nausea was nearby just over the rainbow.

"What's his number?"

Unthinking, I rattled off Sonny's home number.

"Not that one. The hotel."

"What hotel?" Then I remembered. "He said not to give it to you."

"Alex, you've got to." Persistent little bastard.

"No. I don't. It is seven-oh-nine in the morning. Get a life, Mitch. You got a problem, call the Chief."

"I got a problem, all right. We got a murder here. The chief is gone."

"Chief Franks was murdered!" I shrieked and felt my skull split. "My God, how?"

"Clubbed. The boy, I mean. The chief went out on Med-Evac. Well, actually, Cassie flew them out."

"*Them?* Cassie? Cassie flew who? Whom?"

"Yeah, his wife collapsed."

"When she heard the news, you mean?"

"What news?"

"Mitch," I said slowly, "I am in no mood to practice our Abbott and Costello act. Start over and make sense."

"I'll be there in ten minutes."

"I said start over, not *come* over." But I was speaking to a dead line.

Fargo whimpered to go out. I didn't blame him. I didn't want to be here either. We started toward the kitchen. I moved like the Tin Man before Dorothy got the oilcan—bent, limping, groaning, hanging on to chairs and tables and doorknobs as I passed them. I let him out into the cool foggy air and wished I could just go out and lie in the grass myself. Instead I put on the coffee and headed back for two Tylenol and a shower.

71

The shower didn't really help except to make me aware of everything that hurt. As yet the Tylenol weren't doing much either. I sat down and gently applied antibiotic ointment to my smarting shin. As I replaced the cap on the little tube, I noticed the label said *Panalog*. Panalog was Fargo's ointment, given him by the vet last summer for a cut on his ear. What—if anything—I should do about this medical mixup was beyond me. If my leg started growing fur, I'd call the doctor. Or the vet.

I wrapped my wrist in the Ace bandage. There didn't seem to be much swelling, though it ached. I took two more Tylenol, just to be safe. I managed to get dressed okay, although I did opt for slip-on mocs. There were several reasons I avoided shoelaces.

By the time I poured two mugs of coffee, Mitch was walking up the path. I motioned him in and sat down; standing up was not good. He tromped loudly in, took off his damp rain hat and coat and hung them on the back-hall pegs. He looked tired and worried and very young. Detective Sergeant Andrew Mitchell was twenty-six or -seven and looked about eighteen, but his boyish charm held no appeal for me this day.

"All right, Mitch, slow and easy does it."

He took a swallow of coffee. "We really have to get Sonny back here right now, Alex. I've got a bad feeling about this one."

It sounded so much like a line from a made-for-TV movie that I laughed. But Mitch looked like he might cry, and I thought I'd better be nice. "I couldn't call Sonny right now if I wanted to," I said gently. "They are traveling all day en route to . . . to their planned destination. I'll try to reach him tonight and tell him what happened—if you ever tell me—and let him decide how he wants to handle it. Okay? Now what is going on?"

"Well, we all pulled extra duty last night on account of it being Halloween. Nothing really happened—a few fights, a couple of DWI's. Some fool woman fell off the railing of a deck and broke her ankle."

"Probably thought she was Peter Pan," I said innocently.

Mitch looked at me strangely, but went on. "I went home about one and was just asleep when Santos called and said I better get back to the station. He told me Chief Franks' wife had got sick again with her heart—tachycardia, chest pain, I don't know what all. They had her at the clinic and got her stabilized some, but wanted to Med-Evac her to Boston, to Mass General where she sees a specialist. Time counted, they said."

I debated whether a cigarette would help or finish me off. Mitch continued before I could decide.

"When Santos called for the Med-Evac chopper up at Hyannis, they told him, they could get out of Hyannis if they had to, but could never land in the rain and fog here at Provincetown. She would have to be driven to Hyannis. And the clinic doc said that was a real bad idea. I told Santos to start looking up our emergency numbers for people at Offshore Air here in Ptown, and I started getting dressed."

"Do any Offshore Air pilots live here?" I asked.

"Two, plus another was on RON status to start ferrying people out this morning—that is, if this damn fog ever lifts. It's supposed to start clearing around nine or—"

"Good," I interrupted and finally lit the cigarette. "What happened with Offshore?"

"No joy there! One pilot said no way could he fly, he'd been drinking till one. Another said they'd have to take seats out to fit a stretcher in and he had no authority to have that done, even if he could find a mechanic to do it. I called the remain-overnight guy. He asked me if I'd looked out the window lately and hung up. The passenger agent didn't answer at all. I was frantic. The Chief was calling every two minutes. They had his wife all ready to transport and might have to try for Hyannis if I couldn't come up with something. Finally, I thought of Cassie."

"Cassie!" Of course! It made sense, but my good buddy—flying in pea soup, with no sleep. Oh, God.

"Right. She said come and get her. So we picked her up and met the ambulance at the airport. Cassie and Santos and I got three seats ripped out pronto and Mrs. Franks and the Chief and an

EMT shoveled in. Alex, you wouldn't believe the rain and fog! You could only see about two lights down the runway. That's only— what?—a hundred yards?"

"About. How did Cassie do? I take it she got off."

Mitch reached for my cigarettes and lighter, a custom learned from Sonny, no doubt. "Oh, yeah. She lined the plane up, revved and just . . . disappeared. I held my breath waiting for the crash, but she got the mother off. I tell you, Alex, that girl's got two big ones!"

He said it with such pure admiration I didn't even refer to his calling her a girl. "Do you know if they got to Logan all right?" I was almost afraid of the answer.

"Yes, Cassie called. And the hospital chopper was there to meet them. Cassie was going to find a couch and nap till the weather broke. She told me to call Lainey." He laughed. "I told her she'd better make the call herself. If Lainey heard my voice on the phone, we'd have another heart attack victim."

I sent up a little silent thank you. Cassie did indeed have two big ones, and a heart to match. "So much for that little drama. You seem to have solved the problem well without my esteemed brother. Now what's this about a murder?"

"Would you believe it? I just got home and dozed off again, when here's Santos back on the line. He says Harmon just came in, yelling and shaking and pointing and swearing he just almost got himself killed and there's a body out at the amphitheater."

"Harmon finally got the DT's?"

"That thought crossed my mind. It also crossed my mind to kill him and Santos. I tried telling Santos to call Captain Anders, and he said he already did, but Anders told him I was the *detective* that *Sonny* trusted so much, so he should call me. Anyway, back I went."

"Poor Mitch." I got up stiffly to let the dog in. He looked hopefully at his dish, but I figured he would survive until I heard the rest of this. He curled up in his bed with a peevish flop, obviously weak from hunger.

"You got it. When I arrived, Harmon was still half-drunk,

74

having coffee and raving on. He said he had stayed up till around three when the tide was almost in, and gone out to Race Point to see what had come in on the storm earlier in the night. You know, he collects stuff. Lobster pots, buoys, driftwood, all kinds of debris that washes ashore."

"I know, my Aunt Mae sometimes buys driftwood from him to make fancy planters for herbs to sell in her shop. But why go out in the middle of the night?"

"Wanted to be the first one there, he told me. He's right, actually, a lot of people scrounge around on the beaches after a big rain. Anyway, he says he starts down the hill in his truck, coming home, and a big light-colored SUV with no headlights comes flying out of the side road and almost runs him into the ditch. Of course he couldn't get a plate number, or even see what state it was registered in."

"Some kind of hit-and-run thing?" None of this was making much sense.

"No. It being Harmon, he decided the SUV driver was a drug runner. He figured someone had brought drugs ashore and for some reason set up the rendezvous with the local dealer over at the amphitheater. He thought the guy in the SUV was hurrying to get out of town before daylight, but thought the supplier might still be up there and he could capture him. He had decided they had come ashore from a cigarette boat. How they got to the amphitheater I don't know. He had enough booze in him to be feeling brave—for the moment."

"What was Harmon going to do, point a piece of driftwood at them?"

"That's what I asked. He reminded me that he carries an old shotgun in a rack in his truck. Prob'ly blow up in his face." Mitch got up and refilled his mug and mine. I waved toward the refrigerator, and he helped himself to milk. "Anyway, he goes over to the amphitheater, and there on stage lies a body. I asked him if he was sure it was a body, and he said he hadn't gone near it, just saw someone lying on stage, but they looked dead to him. Well, I

75

thought it could be anything. People do strange things out here. Maybe someone was communing with nature or the rain god or maybe somebody was passed out from booze. Even a mannequin could have been put out there for a bad Halloween joke, you know."

I did know. Anything was possible in Ptown, Halloween or no. "But it really was a body?" I asked.

"Sure enough. A young, smallish guy, dark, but Caucasian. Had the back of his head and shoulders badly beaten. And it looked like he'd been kind of laid out on the concrete stage. Legs straight, on his back with his arms down along his sides."

"It sounds like he may have been killed elsewhere."

"I thought so, too. Still do. There wasn't much blood, although the rain may have taken care of that. Well, I got Anders out of bed and out there. By the time he got there, we had ascertained the wallet was missing. Empty pockets, no watch or rings. No murder weapon at the immediate scene. Anders took one look and pronounced it simple robbery. Says the dead guy was a transient, robbed by another transient that we'll never find. Just put out a bulletin to the State Police and forget it."

"Good old Captain Anders." I sighed. "How I look forward to attending his retirement party. I can understand a robbery victim being found in an alley, or a vacant lot, even thrown from a car, but I can't understand taking him all the way out there, beating him to death and arranging him to lie in state."

"Not only that, Alex, if it's simple robbery, your victim is usually stabbed or shot or maybe bopped on the head; but this guy was really *beaten*. Looks like a baseball bat or something like that—two-by-four maybe. Anyway, I got to get back. Right now the victim is still in the EMT van, I've got to send him on down to Hyannis to the medical examiner."

"Why are you holding him here at all?"

Mitch looked like a kid caught in the cookie jar. "Well, er, Sonny always has old Doc Marsten take a look at things, says he knows things the new-fangled docs don't. So—ah, I figured it wouldn't hurt if he just gave this guy the once-over. He should be there anytime now."

Marsten could sew up a cut neater and with less scarring than anyone I had ever seen. I had living proof of that just above my eyebrow. Marsten would not have ordered a CAT scan, an MRI, an X-ray and four blood tests for my skinned leg, as many doctors would. But there came a point, I felt, when modern techniques were preferable. However, Marsten did sometimes offer some helpful information long ahead of the coroner's report and if he made Sonny and Mitch feel better, who was I to argue?

"Well, I repeat, Mitch, there's no way I can reach Sonny till evening. I'll call him around six and tell him what's going on. But I agree with him, you're perfectly capable of handling this yourself."

He looked at me so gratefully I wanted to pat him on the head and give him a biscuit. "Thanks, Alex, that helps. I guess I'm doing everything. I have a couple of people searching the area for his wallet and for the weapon. So far no light-colored SUVs reported stolen in this end of Massachusetts. We're going to run his finger-prints to see if we get a hit. We took some photos. His face isn't badly disfigured. We'll show them around if we don't get an ID soon. He may not have been transient. I tend to think not. If he worked here, somebody will miss him at some point." He donned his rain gear. "Thanks for the coffee, and I'm sorry I woke you up."

"I can't be too nasty about it after the night you put in. Call me if anything turns up, so I can tell Sonny." I stood up to walk him to the door, but a throbbing in my leg deterred me. Panalog poisoning?

Another coffee and cigarette made me feel that life might be sustained. It was Sunday, which meant the *New York Times* cross-word puzzle. I'm not a masochist in any other way, but weekly I subject myself to reading almost all four pounds of the *Times* and then doing the puzzle. The worse it is, the more I love to wrestle with it.

So Fargo and I moved slowly down the bayside beach toward a convenience store that carries both out-of-town papers and yummy homemade pastries.

When we got down by the Old Boat Dock Motel, there was a flurry of sand and a cacophony of wild yips. Toby the terrible mini dachshund was upon us. He was madly in love with Fargo and showed his affection by running in circles, leaping at Fargo's shoulder and barking incessantly. Fargo actually liked the little brat and encouraged his performance with occasional head-butts, growls and feints. Finally, Toby tired, or got as far from home as he dared, and turned back. He trotted home, round little belly barely clearing the sand, ears cocked, tail up and saucy little bottom a-bounce with every step. I rather liked Toby—he had pizzazz.

I liked the scones I took home, too. I felt infinitely better after ingesting what Fargo didn't weasel away from me, even though there was now food in his dish. I finished the puzzle and felt so renewed I did some laundry, mainly so I could return Peter's socks before I left tomorrow. I thought about packing, but knew the sight of the suitcase would send Fargo into clinical depression, so I put that off for a while.

Eventually, the dryer spat out a bunch of clothes, including the borrowed socks. As a child, it had been drummed into me to return borrowed items promptly, so I folded them neatly into a plastic supermarket bag, saddled up Fargo and set off.

Chapter 9

"Alex! Fargo! How nice to see you both! Come in." Wolf opened the door wide.

"I don't want to bother you. I just thought Peter might need his socks." I handed Wolf the plastic bag.

"Nonsense! He's probably already forgotten them. But I'm glad you remembered, because we've now got the pleasure of your company. Peter!" he called, "Alex and Fargo are here!"

Peter bustled in, wearing a large chef's apron and followed by Pewter. Fargo sat up and cocked his ears. Pewter strolled past him as if he weren't there and sat down at Wolf's feet, facing Fargo. I wondered how long they would sit and stare at each other.

I gave Peter a hug. "You were so wonderful last night, I'm afraid anything I say will sound phony. Really, I've never had more pleasure from or been more moved by a performance. Forgive me if I say I never knew you were so talented."

"Oh, a thousand, *thousand* thanks! I'm so glad you made it. I didn't see you afterward and was afraid you hadn't been there. It did go well, didn't it? Thank God *something* went well! What a taradiddle this weekend has been! Forgive my appearance, but we are houseboy-less and I'm cleaning up after breakfast for a dozen hungry, messy queens. Thank God, they have nearly all gone home, or back to whatever rocks they live under."

"What happened?" I asked.

"My dear, I can't even think of it without something to calm my nerves. Like—let's see—a tequila sunrise?" He smiled and raised a finger to his chin.

"My nerves could just use a bit of calming, too. Sounds perfect if you'll please make mine mostly sunrise, little tequila." I looked questioningly at Wolf as Peter went back into the kitchen.

"He's not exaggerating." Wolf shrugged. "It really has been awful. It started yesterday morning right after you left. Peter took the tea tray out into the kitchen, mainly to ask Lewis why on earth he had used a silver tea service and cheap clay mugs."

He spread his hands as if at the horror of it all. "Peter came flying back out, saying that Lewis was nowhere to be seen and the kitchen was a shambles, every dish, every glass, every cup—dirty. Nothing cleaned up from the last night's snacks or the morning's brunch. You see, every night late, we put out a few goodies for people who might feel peckish, or who check in late and maybe missed dinner. Then in the morning we serve coffee and tea, biscuits, rolls, maybe some ham or bacon and fresh fruit and cereals. We don't serve eggs—just stuff we can put on the buffet and sort of forget."

He paused to stroke Pewter and continued. "We hollered upstairs, but Lewis didn't answer, so I went up to start straightening the bathrooms and making beds. Peter went out to check if he had gone to his room for some reason."

Peter arrived with the drinks tray. "Are you telling Alex about that miserable little prick?" Goodness me, I wondered, what ever happened to *Dear Boy?*

"You should have seen that kitchen," Peter continued. "It looked like the last meal off the *Titanic!* So here I go out to his room over the garage, like a clucking mother hen, thinking perhaps he was taken ill or hurt himself in some way. And how do you think I was rewarded for my loving kindness?"

"Ah, delicious! Thank you." I lifted my glass toward Peter. "I take it your loving kindness was not reciprocated."

"Hardly!" Peter was thoroughly incensed. "I just get out the back door and here comes the slimy little bastard down the driveway, carrying a suitcase. I guess he figured you would stay awhile and he could be gone before we realized it. I asked him where the hell he was going and he said he was leaving. He'd had enough cleaning up after a bunch of demanding, prissy people and . . . ah, *catering* to a bunch of old queens. He said he was going to the Coast, where they appreciate beauty, whatever that meant."

I laughed. "He probably figured either on becoming a movie star or at least shacking up with one."

"No doubt," Peter agreed sourly. "He spent enough time in front of mirrors. Anyway, I was babbling on that he couldn't leave us in a lurch like this, that we needed him to help us close down for the season, etc. He just kept shaking his head and walking, with me trailing along after him like a fool. And then, I saw that he was wearing *my watch!* Not only is it mine, and valuable and old—but my *father* gave it to me just before he died. Alex, I treasure it! It's all of his I have left, and I loved him . . . a lot." Peter's voice broke. He grabbed the tray and glasses and ran from the room.

"I'm so sorry," I said to Wolf.

"It was about the worst thing the effing little thief could have taken," Wolf grumbled. "It would break Peter's heart to lose it."

"What did he do?"

"I *demanded* he give it back." Peter had returned with refills. "He laughed at me, *laughed*. And called me a sentimental old queer. Then he unstrapped the watch and held it out as if he were going to give it to me. When I reached for it, he just let it fall onto the concrete driveway. I picked it up, and saw that the crystal was smashed and the second hand wasn't moving. I don't know what on earth got into me, but I hit him."

In any other circumstances, the thought of Peter Mellon hitting

81

anyone would have been funny. But heartbreak and outrage can do strange things to all of us. "I don't blame you." I reached across for his hand.

He gave me a squeeze and went on in a pained voice. "Well, it wasn't much of a knock-out blow." He chuckled ruefully. "I missed his jaw and hit his shoulder. Lewis laughed and hauled off and *really* hit me on the cheek. God, it hurt! I was so furious, I actually was going to fight him, Alex, I don't know *how*, but I was going to *try!* Then he said, 'Stay away from me you poor pitiful faggot, or you'll be singing tonight without your front teeth.' And he gave me a shove, and I sat down hard, and he walked away and I—I just sat there. Like a poor p-p-pitiful f-f-faggot." He buried his face in his hands.

Wolf took Peter in his arms and tried to comfort him. "Now, now, you were very brave to hit him at all! And you had a performance that night . . . hundreds were counting on you. You had a terrible time covering your bruised cheek with makeup, as it was. He could have hurt you badly if you'd gone after him. Peter, there was nothing anyone could have done at that time!" He looked at me as if asking for confirmation, and I gave it.

"Wolf is right, Peter. Your performance last night was worth a thousand Lewises—to me alone, never mind everybody else! He's not worth your getting hurt over. He's not worth the powder to blow him to hell. Forget him. His type always gets it in the end. Have your watch repaired and forget he ever lived. Good riddance!"

"Good riddance!" They lifted their glasses and echoed.

I managed a small laugh. "Look, Peter, even the brats have forgotten their feud and want to cheer you up." Pewter had jumped into Peter's lap and Fargo sat beside his leg, looking up with a concerned frown.

Peter smiled weakly. "I'm lucky . . . my lover, my friends . . . even the four-legged ones. Wolf, we need another tray. Don't start shaking your head, Alex, if you weren't here you'd be at the Rat drinking cheap beer." Peter was recovering.

I didn't argue but had no intention of finishing the drink. When

Wolf returned, I told them about my pictures being displayed at the bank. Their compliments may have been a little fulsome, but I was enjoying them anyway, when the doorbell rang. Wolf went, and I heard male voices at the door. I turned around as Wolf, Mitch and Officer Pete Santos walked into the living room.

When Mitch saw me, he blurted, "Alex, what the hell are you doing here?"

It was my turn to be surprised, not to mention irritated. "*I'm* having a drink with two old friends, Mitch. I was invited. How about you?"

Wolf hastened to pour oil on what were becoming troubled waters. "Gentlemen, have a seat. What may I offer you? Coffee? Something cold?"

From a room filled with chairs and sofas Mitch and Santos had elected to sit together on the piano bench, where they looked uncomfortable and slightly ludicrous. My humor improved at once. Pete Santos opened his mouth to accept one of Wolf's offers, but Mitch closed it for him.

"Nothing, thank you, Mr. Wolfman. I wonder if you or Mr. Mellon could help us with an inquiry. Do you employ a young man with the first or last name of Lewis?" Suddenly, I knew why they were here, and as Mitch had said earlier in the day, I got a bad feeling about this one.

"We *did*," Peter retorted. "What's the wretched little thief done, now, robbed an orphanage?" I wished I could caution Peter to watch his mouth, but obviously I couldn't interfere. It was a police investigation, and I had absolutely no connection to it. I glanced warningly at Wolf and got an understanding look back. He, at least, would be careful how he phrased his answers.

Mitch may have been lacking sleep, but his mind was awake. "You say you *did* employ him, sir, indicating the past tense. Was he no longer in your employ? Had he stolen something from you? Did you fire him for stealing? Did you report the theft to our department? When did you last see him? By the way, what *was* his full name?"

Wolf took over. I had to admire his nerve. "You're also using

83

the past tense, Sergeant, whatever *you* may mean. Lewis's name is Lewis Schley. He is from somewhere in Indiana. I'll be glad to get you his full address and Social Security number if they will help you." Mitch nodded. "No, we did not fire him. Yesterday morning he walked out, despite our protests that we needed him for another couple of weeks. He said he was tired of working and was going to the West Coast. As he started to leave the property, Peter noticed Lewis was wearing an antique watch belonging to him. He demanded it back and Lewis—returned it and left." It was a masterpiece of understatement, without a single lie—exactly.

As Mitch nodded and told Santos to go with Wolf and get Lewis's home address, I reflected silently that Wolf was clever with words. A few minutes earlier he'd said that Peter's little dust-up with Lewis was all that could be done "at the time." Dear God, could he have been reminding Peter that a fuller retribution had been accomplished later? While we waited for Santos and Wolf's return, Mitch turned to Peter.

"Have either of you seen Mr. Schley since that incident, Mr. Mellon?"

"No, and I don't want to. Slimy little bastard's gotten everything from us he's going to get."

I cringed inwardly as Mitch went coolly on. "And what has he gotten from you, sir?"

"Clothes, for one thing. When he came here five—six weeks ago—he had what he was wearing . . . period. We gave him stuff to wear, mainly things I had, well, outgrown. Good clothing. And of course, we pay well, and he got good tips. Even if he hadn't saved anything from prior weeks, he walked away from here yesterday with a good four hundred dollars cash. I paid him two hundred yesterday morning, and I know he made at least two hundred more in tips during the week. Ungrateful little bitch!"

Wolf and Pete Santos walked back into the room as Mitch said, "Well, I'm afraid it won't do him much good now. I'm sorry to tell you that sometime last night Lewis Schley was murdered and apparently robbed, possibly at the amphitheater out near Race Point."

I thought Peter might faint. He turned dead white and swayed on the couch. Wolf sat heavily beside him, as if his legs wouldn't hold him any longer. I finally broke the silence. "Mitch, how did you know he worked here?"

"We held four disorderlies overnight. Nacho came in this morning to run them through the computer, make sure there were no outstanding warrants before we let them go. When Doc Marsten finished checking the body, Nacho drove it over to the clinic. She got a look at it as they removed him from the ambulance. She recognized him and had heard somebody call him Lewis. I understand she lives right across the street?" He made it a question and looked at Wolf, who nodded.

"I see," I said. "Well, I saw Lewis flashing a well-filled wallet at the Wharf Rat last night, probably around eight. I had no idea it held so much money. Maybe Captain Anders is right. A simple robbery somehow got out of hand."

"Maybe." Mitch didn't sound sold on my idea. He turned to the two men. "Is that your tan Explorer out in the driveway?" I grinned to myself. Mitch would have given his left nut to get his forensics people into that van, but—thus far anyway—he had no cause for a warrant.

"Technically, it belongs to the business," Wolf explained. "But, yes, it's ours. Why?"

"Mind telling me where you both were about four or five this morning?"

"We were both in bed asleep . . . together. I'll try again. Why?"

"I figured that's where you'd be at that hour. Somebody saw an SUV speeding away from the amphitheater area about that time, thought it might have been tan. Obviously it couldn't have been yours, since you were here." He flipped his notebook closed and stood. "Well, thank you both. We'll be in touch if there are any further questions. See you around, Alex. Fargo, don't take any wooden biscuits." He patted the dog and moved toward the door, Santos dutifully in his wake.

Mitch turned back. "By the way, would you mind if we took a look at Mr. Schley's room?"

Wolf shrugged. "Let me get a jacket and I'll let you in." Mitch and Santos walked out onto the porch to wait. Through the window I saw Mitch stroll over to the broken table I'd noticed yesterday. He stooped and looked closely at the broom handle serving as a leg.

When the threesome was out of earshot, Peter said quietly, "He thinks we did it, Alex."

"He may have some questions, simply because Lewis worked and lived here. But it's early yet, and Mitch's just fishing for any lead. There will be many other things to look into. There's all that cash—somebody has it. There will be other suspects. For example, Lewis came in the Rat last night and started rubbing my back. At least twenty people can testify that I hit him in the stomach and threatened to put a nine-millimeter bullet up his nose. Mitch may well want my story of that event."

Peter clapped his hands. "Brava, brava!"

Wolf came back in and sank onto the couch.

"Anything of interest?" I asked.

"Dirty clothes, dirty ashtrays and dirty magazines. Well, this does it, Peter. We are out of here as soon as can be, and this damned place is listed with a real estate agent on our way out of town! I've had it, anyway, and practically being accused of murder puts a lid on it. Any advice, Alex?"

"I'm a little limited, here, Wolf. You are not my client, and I can't impede a police investigation under any circumstances. I can advise you to tell the truth. Answer what you are asked. Don't elaborate. Don't gossip about this or someone will misquote you. And, for God's sake, don't try to leave until this matter is all cleared up."

"That makes sense," Peter replied quietly. "And we'll try to follow it. But I agree, Wolf, we're out of here as soon as possible. As it is, we've lingered too long at the ball."

"What do you mean?" I asked.

"Oh, things have changed . . . here . . . in the real world, whatever. We came here nearly thirty years ago. And we are now dinosaurs in a *teddibly civilized* world. When we were young and gay," he explained, "you were damn careful who knew it. One slip and you might lose a job or have the neighbors complain or have your parents disown you. Hell, every one of us had a lesbian 'girlfriend' we could trot out for the annual company picnic or a family affair. Now, we have openly gay mayors, senators, athletes, TV personalities. Some companies give us spousal benefits. Some hospitals respect the wishes of the patient's partner. Some states will let us marry and some churches will perform the rites."

"But, that's all good, Peter. Isn't it?" I wasn't following him at all.

"Of course it is," Wolf answered. "But I know what he means. In days of yore, when we got to Ptown or the Hamptons or Fire Island or any place where we could be openly gay, we camped it up. All of us went over the top—swishing around, speaking affectedly, limp wristed—even those of us who weren't naturally like that at all. Now that being gay isn't the disgrace it used to be, we've become pretty mainstream. We're so middle-class respectable, we're deadly dull. We have become the very people we used to laugh at and be just a little afraid of. We join the PTA even if we don't have kids."

He thought for a moment and went on. "We don't live on the edge anymore. There's not that delightful little *frisson* when you meet a guy at work you think may be gay. Nowadays, you just casually ask him if he is. Hell, straight men are wearing clothes to the office today that I wouldn't have dared wear in San Francisco thirty years ago!"

"I'll still take today," I said.

"Oh, so will I in many ways," Peter admitted. "I'm still not making myself clear. It's not that I want to go back to the days of the Inquisition. It's more that I feel like I'm dancing in a disco . . . and wearing a bustle."

I stood up, as did Fargo, earning a low hiss from Pewter. "Well, if you want to live on the edge, you can always move to Idaho or Mississippi. Personally, I'd just as soon not even drive through them."

"My dear, smart gays don't even *fly over* them. I may be old-fashioned but I have no desire to be lynched."

"Scary people still out there," Wolf mused. "I hope one of them hasn't taken up residence in Provincetown."

Chapter 10

I carried the empty suitcase from my office closet into the bedroom and put it on the bed. Fargo was right behind me, tail down and head slightly extended, eyes wary. He knew that a suitcase meant I was going somewhere and that, usually, *somewhere* did not include him. It was at the top of his list of things to dread, ranked right between having his nails clipped and his ears cleaned. As I got out clothes and so forth to take with me, he followed hard on my heels from the bed to the closet, the bureau, the bathroom. I nearly stepped on him a dozen times.

When I began to pack, he jumped on the bed and lay on my clothes. I yelled and he scrambled under the bed, where he emitted disapproving whuffles about once a minute. He would be staying with my mother, where he would be petted, played with, walked, overfed and allowed to sleep on the bed. I hardly thought the SPCA would deem it cruelty. I tried explaining to him that if he was to be kept in expensive rawhides, I had to work. He didn't care.

I finished the chore and checked my watch, which was on my right wrist in deference to my bandaged left one. I hoped I could do without the wrap tomorrow. I didn't like keeping business appointments looking like the walking wounded. Six o'clock and time to see if I could reach Sonny in his little Tennessee love nest.

I popped a beer and sat at the kitchen table. Referring to the card he had given me, I dialed Gatlinburg and got the usual Chatty Cathy computerized voice telling me I had reached the Riverside Crest Hotel in the Heart of the Smokies and to press *one* for reservations, *two* for accounting, *three* for banquet service, *four* for corporate services, or to dial any guest room-number now. For assistance, I was to remain on the line. I did so, and finally got it.

A twangy-voiced but pleasant young woman advised me that she would ring the room for Mr. and Mrs. "Pairs." It rang . . . and rang . . . and finally another disembodied voice informed me that I had reached voice-mail for Room 617 and should leave a message at the beep if I desired. I desired.

"Hi, there," I warbled. "I know you've just arrived and hate to bother you as you get settled, but—wouldn't you know—there's been a bludgeoning murder and Mitch wants to talk with you. A young houseboy for Green Mansions was killed last night and found near Race Point, robbed of a considerable sum. Anders thinks a transient did it. Mitch disagrees. I think it would be a kindness if you would just call Mitch. He's a little shaky. Oh, he feels all alone in this, as Chief Franks had to accompany his wife to Boston for emergency medical treatment. Do call him. Mitch, I mean. Again, sorry for the intrusion. Bye."

As I hung up, the reason for my call pulled into the driveway. I waved him in and offered a beer. Mitch sank into a chair and nodded. "Yes, thanks. If I go to sleep, just punch me if I snore. Hey, sorry about this afternoon, I was just really surprised to see you. I'm so tired I forgot my manners. Sorry."

"No problem. But you came down on them a little hard, didn't you?"

"Well, for one thing," he pointed out, "they are logical sus-

90

pects, with only their word they were home asleep. And I don't think you just up and quit a job and say you're going to California."

I set his beer in front of him, actually remembering a coaster. "You wouldn't. I wouldn't. Lewis would. And while an employer might get pissed because you left them with a messy inn to clean up, I doubt they'd beat you to death for it. Anyway, there's the money. He had a really fat wallet at eight o'clock."

"Yeah." Mitch grinned and looked about fifteen. "And at seven fifty-eight you had punched him in the gut and offered to put a bullet up his nose."

"Exactly right. And if he had rubbed up against me again, I might have done it. Or I might have walloped him with a bat? Could have been more fun than shooting him."

"Not your style, Alex, and—as you say—the money. Either you wouldn't have taken it, or you'd have been out buying drinks all over town."

"Smartass. Seriously, Mitch, do you see something almost ritualistic in this? I mean, wherever he was killed, he was sort of . . . posed out there." I had a sudden vision of a formalistic gay killer or killer-group. If that were the case, the murders would not stop with one. Wasn't that reassuring!

"You mean like he was an actor in a play or something?" Mitch might look like everybody's baby brother, but the pale blue eyes gave him away. Usually warm and merry, they could turn hard and cold swiftly, and they missed nothing.

"Kind of. Maybe if he wanted to be a star, here he was, center stage in a big amphitheater." I found myself immediately wishing I hadn't said that. If Lewis was going to the Coast to have his beauty appreciated by the movie industry, I hoped Wolf or Peter hadn't decided to give him his theatrical debut right here in town.

Mitch's change of subject told me exactly where his mind had gone. "Do you know if Wolf and Peter have any financial troubles?"

"I think the opposite. They've got a condo in South Beach in

91

Miami. Before they knew Lewis was dead, just before you and Santos came, they mentioned maybe canceling a couple of filled weekends and closing the inn early since they had no help in the house. The downstairs and kitchen are in good repair. I assume the rooms and baths are fine or they wouldn't be busy. That Explorer is almost new. I think they are okay. Certainly they wouldn't kill for four hundred dollars."

He continued trolling. "I saw a blanket in the back of the Explorer."

"You'd see one in the back of my car. And Mom's. And in our dear friend Mary Sloan's SUV . . . which, by the way, is light tan. Maybe it was our Mary out carousing in the wee hours. Maybe Lewis leaned against her fender with greasy fingers. That would be sufficient cause for homicide." He managed a weak grin and I noted, with guilt, his pale, tired face.

"Mitch, you're exhausted. I'm sorry I teased you. By the way, I just called Sonny. They haven't checked in yet, but I left a voice mail asking him to call you. I'm sure he'll get back to you tonight. Go home. Go to bed."

"Great. Thanks, Alex." He yawned. "I'm going, I'm going."

Just looking at Mitch had tired me out. Cooking dinner was not on my agenda, nor was going out, so I fell back on that fine old American tradition and phoned for a meatball pizza and small salad. Fargo and I watched an old Cary Grant movie for lack of a better. Fargo forgot his depression and chomped happily on the crusts, plus tidbits of meatball. I checked my briefcase, took a shower and went early to bed. Tomorrow would be long.

It began early. I tried to cram all the last-minute items into my suitcase while Fargo went out on first patrol. But there was no fooling him—he was back in seconds. I drove to Mom's with his head resting on my knee, eyes gazing up at me in great sadness. I felt an overwhelming guilt coupled with a strong desire to wring his neck.

Mom's toast and coffee helped, and I left. Fargo's depression had abated sufficiently for him to be chomping down oatmeal as I closed the door. Driving to the airport, I wondered which of Offshore Air's uncooperative pilots I'd be flying with and decided it didn't matter. No seats needed moving, there wasn't a cloud in the sky and I presumed the one who said he'd been drinking would have sobered up by now. Whoever it was, he set us down at Logan/Boston without incident. I picked up my rental and was on my way into the city.

Since I was north of the tunnel, I figured I'd go over to Wellington and see how squeaky-clean Nancy Whitfield Baker had fared at prestigious Rolles University. I cooled my heels for a half hour looking at murals of the campus. Dean Pennycamp, a short, bespectacled man, at last appeared, holding my business card as if it were covered with some unidentified sticky substance. There was no invitation to his office, nor even to sit in the lobby. We stood, while I explained why I was there and showed him Ellis's letter of authorization and my license. He looked at both as if I had printed them in the cellar. I asked him if by chance he remembered Ms Baker.

"No."

Did he think I might locate one of her professors who did?

"No."

He handed me a copy of her transcript and turned to leave. I asked, "How do you feel about her capability to handle the job in question?"

He looked at me with pitying superiority. "She graduated Rolles. She can certainly handle any job Provincetown has to offer."

"Thanks ever so!" I enthused. "Mr. Ellis will be thrilled to know that, and if Ms. Baker gets the job, based on your exuberant recommendation, I'll tell her to write you a thank-you note."

In the car I looked over the transcript and found almost all A-minuses with a sprinkling of A's and one B. Comments included words like *bright, smart, hard-working, fast on the uptake* and *thor-*

ough. One instructor added that he found her "somewhat brittle." Another went so far as to write that she was "not a people person." All told, though, it was impressive.

My experience at BostonU, Nancy's undergraduate college, was a one-eighty from Rolles. Dean Sheldon was large, gregarious and helpful. Looking over Nancy's transcript before he handed it to me, he commented on the high grades and complimentary remarks.

I asked if there were any notes on Nancy's social life.

"Fortunately, no," he laughed. "Those are only included if she felt compelled to go skinny-dipping in the fountain or run her car over the president's bicycle. And *that* I would remember without a computer."

I began to enter the gist, if not the words, of his reply in my notebook. In mid-scribble the pen went dry. The dean waited patiently while I dug in my briefcase for another. Thank you, witch!

In conclusion, I questioned if he felt she could handle the job at the bank. He thought a moment and indicated the transcript. "From what I see there, and what you've told me about her, I'd say a definite yes. My only hesitation is that—although I don't remember her—she seems like a fast-track big city, corporate type. I'd like a little more feedback on why she wants to move to Provincetown."

I concurred with that need, wondered how to get it, and after some brief chitchat, I left feeling better about those who grazed the groves of Academe.

It was way past my usual lunch hour, and Mom's toast seemed far, far away. The Quincy Market was fairly near and I treated myself to a lobster salad, regretfully bypassing cold, bitter ale for a Diet Coke.

That left me within walking distance of Nancy's next-to-last employer, and it felt good to stretch my legs. My scraped shin was on the mend, sore but not painful. Panalog had surely done the trick. I thought briefly about writing them of their product's wider application, but I recalled a notation on the tube that it was licensed for veterinary use only. I had probably broken some law just using it. That would figure.

By now I had reached Nancy's old office building. After a couple of calls by the receptionist, it was decided I should speak with a Carlton McCallie, who would be with me shortly. I found myself in no rush. I was fascinated by a ceiling-high aquarium, lit only by natural sunlight from an upper area. Various fish swam here and there. Crabs, starfish and a few cousins of my lunch prowled about the sandy, rock-strewn bottom.

A pleasant male voice beside me said, "Every bit of marine life you see in there lives—or at least, once upon a time lived—in Boston harbor."

"It's fabulous! It's got it all over goldfish swimming in and out of little pink plastic castles." I turned to see a ruddy-faced, sandy-haired man in his late thirties, about my height.

"I agree. I suggested including a boot, a beer can and an old license plate for added realism. I was told not to be frivolous. Never be frivolous in a brokerage house. I'm Carl McCallie. Come on back."

We settled into his luxurious office and he leaned back, tenting his fingers. "Now, P.I. Peres, what can I do for you? Are you chasing a con man preying on old ladies? Is my secretary blackmailing a playful vice-president?"

"Nothing half so much fun, but please keep my card handy in case anything like that turns up." I told him why I was there and ended with a question. "So why did Ms. Baker leave your employ?"

"Because of me."

"I see," I said coolly, although I imagine my eyes looked like Orphan Annie's.

He gestured around the room. "When the guy who had this before me decided to retire, Nancy thought she should get it—and with some reason. Instead, they brought me in from the outside. *Angry* doesn't cover it. She was plain pissed. She left shortly after I got here."

95

"Glass ceiling?" It seemed the most plausible reason.

"No," he answered, "that really doesn't seem to apply here. And she is extremely capable. She has a knack for spotting trends, and she's an excellent analyst. If there is money to be made out there, she will find it."

"So why have you got the double windows instead of Nancy?"

"Because the minute people invest their money, they become afraid it's going to disappear." He made a vague gesture toward a window, as if money were flying off his desk and across town. "From time to time, they need their hands held. Maybe the market takes a hit. Maybe there's a divorce, a death, a loss of job. Investors need to feel their advisor is genuinely concerned for their well-being, and the less money they have, the deeper their fear. I understand that. I truly feel the responsibility of stewardship, and I'm not averse to trotting out a little tea and sympathy." McCallie had a nice smile.

"Now," he went on, "Nancy is as dedicated to making money for her clients as I am, but she looks upon it differently. She figures if you hire a mechanic to fix your car, you go away and let him do it. You don't lie on one of those little skateboards and roll around in the grease with him, asking what he's doing."

I shook my head. "Wrong. Anytime you hire anybody to do anything, you are entitled to questions. I don't care if it's a doctor or a dog walker."

"I agree, and that's why I'm here. Not Nancy."

"Okay. Now why Provincetown, after a big city like Boston? It's hardly the financial capital of the world, and it's not exactly husband-hunting land. If she's gay, fine. If not, it worries me a little."

"*She* isn't gay." He grinned, and I wondered if he meant he was . . . or I was. Whatever. "There's a fiancé in the background somewhere. Old family, old money—both of them. I don't know either of them well, but I've been told it's more a merger than a love affair. In which case they'll probably live unhappily ever after in a stone and clapboard colonial with two-point-five children, one-point-six golden retrievers, a car and an SUV they don't need or know how to drive."

He shrugged ruefully. "But before Nancy settles in this Utopia, I think she wants to make it as big as she can on her own. You can't blame her. You know, then she can casually say, 'Well, when I was vice-president at Fishermen's Bank . . .' Are you with me?"

"All the way." I laughed. "I imagine you've got it quite right. If she gets the job, I'll bring you my little mutual fund to guard. I'm a tea drinker, and a little sympathy never hurts."

"Anytime we can help, just holler for Carl. I'm serious."

I thanked him and left, feeling that I'd done a pretty good day's work. Now, if I could just remember how to get out of town. I joined two million other people with the same idea, fought my way onto the Mass Turnpike and headed west at about the same speed as the Conestoga wagons that had gone before me. My final target for today was Oak Hill, Connecticut, birthplace of the famous Cynthia Hart.

A few miles down the road my curiosity got the better of me, and I took the Weston turnoff. Consulting my map, I located Chez Baker and noted that the Bakers Senior lived in a split-level colonial of stone and wood. An SUV stood in the driveway. I felt I understood, and maybe even liked Nancy Baker a little better.

Finally I turned onto I-395 and lost most of the traffic as I dropped down into Connecticut to pick up the road to Storrs. I stopped for gas, so I wouldn't have to in the morning, and asked the attendant if Oak Hill was anywhere near. I was in it, he informed me, and, yes, there was a pretty good motel down the road. I explored the little town and found the bookstore Cynthia Hart's parents owned. It was in what looked to have once been a small cottage. Lights shone warm and welcoming through the windows. I thought of going in but decided it was doubtful I'd learn anything important, and I'd probably just make somebody suspicious of my visit.

I drove staunchly on in search of my motel, discovering that one man's "pretty good" is another woman's "pretty mediocre."

But I was tired enough to sleep well, and the next morning—ready to hear about Cynthia—presented myself at the office of the Dean of Women, University of Connecticut. The secretary buzzed

97

her and explained my visit. Hanging up, she said, "Please have a seat. Dean Trinler will be with you shortly." And about ten minutes later I was told to "go on in."

There are deans and there are deans. The one I encountered this particular Tuesday morning at U/Conn had her back to me, watching papers come out of a printer. She wore a silk dress of deep blue that changed to green and back to blue again as she moved, like the ocean on a half-cloudy day. She turned toward me and I put her in her forties, with dark hair just wing-tipped with white, a killer figure and bottomless blue eyes I immediately got lost in.

"Good morning." She smiled. "I'm Mimi Trinler. Just printing out Cynthia's transcript. Won't be a minute. Sit . . . sit." She turned back to the printer.

Suddenly I saw a quiet cottage by a rippling stream. The sapphire sky was echoed in a thick quilt stretched upon soft grass, with groups of white and yellow daisies growing haphazardly nearby. Her dress lay in a shimmering heap beside my rumpled slacks and sweater. Her body was tan and I raised myself on an elbow to stroke her now-loose hair and gently kiss the wide lips. My hand moved unbidden to touch her breasts—full and womanly and welcoming. I kissed each one softly and then with more vigor and felt a tremor stir her body. She pulled me toward her eagerly, her leg moving between mine, pushing upward.

"Now here we are, Ms. Peres, the full transcript. Ah . . . Ms. Peres?"

"Uhh . . . what?" Where was I? What had happened to my babbling brook? The quilt? "Ah. Yes. Here we are. *Here!* The transcript, oh, yes."

She gave me a wide and rather knowing smile, and for one horrified moment I wondered if I had spoken my fantasy aloud.

I managed to collect myself and state my business—as opposed to my daydreams, which had left me perspiring and probably bright red. Dean Trinler next astonished me by remembering Cynthia Hart. When I asked why, she laughed.

"Cynthia was trouble from day one with unauthorized pets in her room. Various animals rescued from some trauma or other. Dogs, cats . . . and I recall a possum and a baby Canada goose. She always found homes for them in the end. In fact, she talked me into taking a dog I still have. Knocked the hell out of me as any kind of authority figure."

"So she's an animal person. How is she with people?" I asked. Cynthia usually got along well with her peers and faculty, the dean advised, although she did not "suffer fools lightly." We finally got around to grades, and I learned that Cynthia was a bright, if not brilliant student, and had only one disciplinary problem aside from animals.

A group of students, including Cynthia, had tied themselves to a big old oak tree in an effort to prevent its being cut down by university authorities.

"The reason it was coming down was that it was old and sick and rotten," Dean Trinler explained. "I was more worried about a limb falling off and braining one of them than anything else. I'm not sure they ever believed us. Are you a tree hugger?"

"Not to the point of tying myself to one. I thought maybe I should try a person first, and I can't seem to do that too well either." Now why had I said that? This woman did strange things to me. I tried to cover my confusion by adding some notes to my book, but now *another* pen did nothing but scratch the paper.

"Maybe you need a longer rope." She gave me that smile again, and I felt that in five minutes she knew me better than my closest friend. I almost asked her to have lunch, but nine-fifteen seemed a little early.

I thanked her and managed to get out with my dignity sorely wounded and the transcript tucked messily under my arm. It wasn't till I got to the car that I noticed the hem in one pants leg was drooping.

There's no easy way to get from Storrs to Norwalk, but I finally did it. The operative word being *finally*. I kept hitting the search button on the radio and in due course came up with a jazz station which improved my humor. Herman, Baker, Coltrane—oh, yes. I wondered why I was so musically out of sync with my peers. I decided to blame my mother. She played a fairly accomplished piano, jazz and classical, so I was brought up with that kind of music. She also loved every Broadway musical ever produced. A few years back Sonny had recorded her LPs onto CDs and made copies for me. I now boasted what was probably the best collection of show tunes east of New York. I even had—from my grandmother—the original *King and I* cast album with Yul Brynner and Gertrude Lawrence. No wonder Iced T didn't do it for me!

The scenic but slow Merritt Parkway eventually spat me out a few blocks from where George Hampton Mills had held his next-to-last job. I finally got through to the office manager and was not amazed to find Dean Pennycamp's spiritual twin.

Once again standing in a lobby, I learned that Mills had worked for them for two years and moved to a smaller company, where he "felt he would be more comfortable." George seemed to be getting littler and littler; I wondered when he would disappear entirely. No reason was given for our George's change in comfort level. My questions regarding his abilities, customer relations and performance were all answered by non-answers, as was my attempt to inquire if he was happily married. I inquired if the manager had any idea why Mills wanted to move to Provincetown and he shrugged, saying, "doubtless a personal decision."

At last I asked the manager if he knew Mills might have a drinking problem and was told, "We do not socialize among our employees and do not inquire into their personal lives." Thank you, Your Majesty.

I knew when I was licked. I might snoop around and dig up a little more but probably nothing important. I had the feeling anyone I spoke with would be bound by the old *nil nisi bonum* reticence to dish a guy who was already well on his way down. I almost felt the same myself.

Walking back to my car I felt light-headed. Probably I needed food, although I really didn't feel hungry. Was the curse still in effect? Damn that old woman, anyway. I drove a few hundred yards down Route 7 and spotted a Chinese restaurant. I lucked out; the food was quite good. Then there was the fortune cookie. *A successful career buys more food than romance.* But does it warm you on a winter's night, Confucius?

I got back into the dreaded vee-hicle and wended my now weary way to I-95 and started northeast once again, hoping to make Providence before I succumbed to battle fatigue. My wrist hurt and I felt like I'd been driving for a month, but it was the only way I could complete this trip in three days.

I really wanted to get home on schedule. Already I badly missed Fargo. I missed my house . . . the Wharf Rat . . . my mother . . . my friends . . . Hell, I missed my enemies. I wanted out of this car. And into one of my delicious grilled cheese and tomato sandwiches with the tomato falling out and the mustard all over my fingers. These happy thoughts got me to the outskirts of Providence and a motel that really was "pretty good."

After the day I'd had, I figured Choate Ellis owed me a lobster dinner. I enjoyed it without remorse. Returning to my room, I called Mom and learned that she and Fargo were fine, my house was standing last she knew and she would look forward to my early return. Duty performed.

Later, I found the bed firm, the sheets crisp, the pillows ample, yet I tossed and turned long into the night with visions of Mimi Trinler dancing through my half-dreams. In my waking moments, I wondered if there might be any way at all to make them come true. I realized there was not, and felt absolutely no better. I thought of her comment about my needing a longer rope and appreciated what she meant. I decided I was sort of like a paraphrased Saint Augustine: Tie me to someone, Lord, but not too close.

Finally, I slept. So, of course, the next morning I resented getting up. But I turned off my alarm and grumpily arose. Unsurprisingly, I got shampoo in my eyes and managed to put my finger through my hose as I dressed. I must say I have never given

101

much thought to witches in my young life, but I never thought *unkindly* of them. Why was all this happening to me?

I always get lost in Providence, today being no exception. When I finally found the campus and finally found the dean's office, my reception was neutral. Cynthia was a bright student. Yes, I could have the transcript. No, the dean did not remember her. Further, she felt it would be a waste of my time and the faculty's for me to "wander around trying to ferret out some instructor who did recall the young lady." Thank you and good morning.

On to Kudlow Securities, where I was shown into the office of Mrs. Kudlow herself. She was a midsize model with graying blonde hair pulled into a severe bun, but with those classic middle European features that let her get away with it. She was attractive, warm, charming, and in the ring with a gorilla, my money would have been on her.

"I'm so glad you're here." She smiled warmly. "My husband and I have been very hopeful that this Fishermen's job would work out for Cynthia."

"Sounds like you're trying to get rid of her." I smiled back.

"I am . . . but only because she deserves to be rid of us at this point. Let me explain. We are not a large company—we're family-run and owned. My daughter is in graduate school but will join us next year. My husband and I would like to retire while we have breath, and had figured on Cynthia to be ready to take over by then."

She fiddled with a pencil on her desk and frowned slightly. "What we had *not* figured on was our son," Mrs. Kudlow continued. "He had decided on a military career rather than finance. However, he was badly wounded in Iraq and will be unable to resume an active role in the military. He has decided to join the firm. Of course we could not say—had no wish to say—*no* to him under the circumstances."

I nodded. "And with two children in the company, there isn't room for Cynthia."

"Not at the level she deserves. We talked it over with her at once. It would be to our benefit to keep her as long as possible, but it wouldn't be fair. She has worked too hard and been too valuable. The sooner she gets her career on the climb again, the better. Fishermen's sounds perfect for her. She is capable. Handles subordinates well and deals well with customers. Should I call this Mr. Ellis and talk with him? I could fill in any details her resumé may have missed."

I suggested that I have Ellis call her when I got back. We talked a bit more, but I couldn't punch any holes in the story. I did ask casually if she knew anything about Cynthia having a misunderstanding with a police officer regarding an injured cat.

Mrs. Kudlow allowed herself a small laugh. "You phrase it very delicately, Ms. Peres, but I think I'll let Cynthia tell that story herself."

That was all I was going to get, so I thanked her and left.

On the way to the elevators I saw a serious-visaged young woman coming down the hall toward me with a purposeful stride. She was nicely plump, wore a sensible navy blue skirt and lighter blue sweater, and had her hair in a no-nonsense ponytail. It had to be our Cynthia. I'd have loved to ask her about that contempt of court charge, but that was Ellis's purview, not mine.

I couldn't resist. Giving her my friendliest smile, I asked, "Picked up any stray cats lately?" She gave me a startled look and reversed her course quickly. One of those people with no sense of humor, I supposed.

Chapter 11

I sat in a small deli near Kudlow's, savoring a pastrami on rye, chips and a small cucumber salad. Okay. I had done my bit for Ellis. Now how did I go about getting home? As I pondered, weak and weary, there was a nearly soundless *twang!* as a bra strap parted. Ah, my ubiquitous witch! But I was too eager to solve my travel problems to give her much time. I whipped into the ladies' room, yanked off the bra, stuffed it in my purse and hardly missed a thought.

None of my get-home options thrilled me. I could drive to Hyannis, turn in the car and call someone to come and get me. But Mom worked Wednesdays, and Aunt Mae was a reluctant (and terrifying) driver. Sonny was away. Cassie was God knew where—too complicated. I could drive *back* to Boston, turn in the car and catch the afternoon flight, but that meant more driving—in the wrong direction.

There was another possibility. If Offshore Airways had not

switched to their curtailed winter schedule, maybe they had an afternoon flight from Providence to Provincetown, and I could turn the car in at Providence Airport.

I finished my cholesterol special, downed my Diet Coke—God, how I missed the Rat!—and looked around for a pay phone. My cell phone, of course, was safely locked in the compartment of my car at Ptown Airport. Moments later I fed quarters into a wall phone. Offshore assured me they had seats on a 3:15 flight, and I was on my way to the Providence, R.I. Airport. I'd have an hour's wait, but who cared? I wouldn't be in a car!

Fortunately the airport is easily found. I turned in the car without parting sadness and walked into the terminal. About to hand the Offshore agent my credit card, I heard a voice behind me say gruffly, "Now, just come quietly, miss. Don't make me have to use force." I spun around.

"Cassie! Am I glad to see you! What the hell are you doing here?" She was dressed in her uniform of khaki shirt with white ascot, navy slacks, a light blue suede jacket with "Outer Cape Charter" embroidered in gold over the breast pocket. A brimmed officer's cap with gold wings finished the look of a modern-day Amelia Earheart, and the Offshore agent was batting her eyes furiously.

"I just brought four women down to catch a Delta to Atlanta. They're going to some teachers' thing. I'm heading home. Want a ride?"

"Do I ever! I'll ride on the wing. Anything to be going home." I turned to follow her outside.

The agent called after me, "Do I take it you will not be flying Offshore Air this afternoon?" She sounded plaintive. Had I been the only passenger?

I turned back. "Afraid so. I'm sorry. I didn't mean to be rude. See you next time." I waved and left. I caught up with Cassie. "What are you doing at the Offshore terminal?"

"Same as Boston and Hartford. I buy my fuel here, have the plane serviced, etc., and they let me use their facilities. They've cleaned the plane and filled it up. We can leave anytime."

"Let's go." I followed her aboard the neat, sleek little twin-engine plane. It was easy to see why she loved it so.

"Come up and be my copilot, if you promise not to curse my airplane." Cassie grinned. I was delighted to serve. I'd learned a few of those duties and jumped at any opportunity to perform them. If I ever could afford it, flying lessons were on the list. I closed and locked the outside door behind us and followed her into the cockpit. "Close the curtain to the cabin," she said. "That way we can smoke later, without getting the smell into the cabin—I hope."

We fastened seat belts, Cassie started the engines and waved goodbye to the Offshore crewman who'd been standing by with a fire extinguisher. She and I both donned earphones with mouth-piece—me just to listen. I heard her amplified voice, slightly tinny as she began her ritual conversation with the Providence control tower.

Very shortly we clattered and bounced along the taxiway. Strange how planes seemed so clumsy on the ground, as if they knew it was not their milieu. She halted next to the end of the runway as a big 737 flared out and roared past us about thirty feet overhead. Then there was a squeal and puff of smoke from the tires and it was down.

"Give me twenty degrees flaps," Cassie said, and I carefully set the lever. She spoke into the mike. "Providence Control. This is Outer Cape Charter twin Beech two-one-seven, at the threshold of runway two-three, requesting takeoff instructions."

"Outer Cape, Providence Control. You are number one to take off on runway two-three. Wind is southwest at ten. Barometer is two-niner-niner-four and steady."

Cassie ran up the engines, slipped the brakes and we were rolling. Even in a small plane the power was wondrous to feel. The plane actually seemed to *yearn* to be away, pressing forward into the wind like a woman running pell mell toward her lover's arms. There was a little lurch, the nose went up and Cassie turned toward me. "Wheels up." I reached for the switch and heard the reassuring whine, followed by a solid *thunk* as they settled into the wells.

"Flaps up." I carefully reset the lever.

As we climbed toward the bright fall sun and the crystal blue around it the words came out unasked. " 'Oh, I have slipped the surly bonds of earth and danced the skies on laughter silvered wings.' "

Cassie smiled. "Had to be written by a pilot."

"It was. A fellow named Magee. He was in the RCAF in World War Two."

"Any more to the poem?"

"Quite a bit. I just can't remember it. It ends with something like, 'climbing through grey to brilliant sun, and reaching out to touch the face of God.' Magee was killed in combat right after that. Age nineteen. A bit young to put a lid on it."

Cassie answered softly, "Maybe he'd done all he needed to." I put that away to think about later.

"Straighten out on sixty degrees and level off at three thousand. I'll go get us some coffee from the thermos." She was standing up before I realized she was talking to me.

Then suddenly there I was with my very own airplane! I could understand why Cassie loved to fly. She'd been taught by her Air Force father but had bypassed the military as a career herself—for the obvious reason. She'd gotten into the pilot training course of a large airline but had left it when she discovered how unfairly female pilots were treated. Cassie's dad staked her to the down payment on the sweetheart Beechcraft, and the rest was history.

Cassie returned with two plastic mugs. I was very proud when she simply set the automatic pilot and lit a cigarette. "So how was the trip?"

I told her the generalities. I did mention my reaction to the very attractive Dean Trinler, though I did not go into the lurid details. She shook her head sadly. "That's your problem, Alex. You're too damn careful. You should have invited her to dinner and then gone for it!"

I yawned. I wasn't sleepy but my ears were plugging up. Funny, altitude usually didn't bother me. "She probably has a husband and four kids." I pulled out the ashtray on my side and joined her in a smoke.

"So she says no thanks. You really need to be more assertive."

"Yeah, like with the blonde at your party. I'm making my move and she damn near kills me."

"She—the blonde—whatsername—felt awful about that. She really was put up to it. I'm sure she'd like to see you again."

"So she can break my leg?" I tapped Cassie's arm and indicated another small plane several hundred feet below us on a reciprocal course.

"Thanks," she acknowledged. "Plenty of room. How's your wrist? Lainey says a sprain like that can feel worse than a clean break."

"Sore and achy. I've been driving all over. The bandage helps, but I haven't been wearing it much. Anyway—moving along from homicidal blondes, what's new at home?"

"Same old, same old. Oh, Peter and the Wolf are looking for you. I ran into them at the Wharf Rat, and Lainey saw them at the market. They were asking if we knew how to reach you. Didn't say why. I didn't realize you were so friendly."

"We aren't close, really. It's their houseboy who got killed the other night. They're probably afraid it makes them or their place look bad and just want reassurance. I can't think of any other reason." Actually, I could think of several, the first being that Mitch was all over them, the second being that perhaps he had good reason.

I stared down at the now choppy bay and recalled last Saturday. Wolf had been livid at the memory of how Lewis had insulted Peter by breaking his father's watch. Wolf had started drinking early. He might well have continued into evening, nursing his anger as he went along. What if Lewis had returned to his room for something he'd forgotten? He and Wolf might have met. If the confrontation and taunting had started all over again, I doubted Wolf would have contented himself with a little shove or two and a good cry. Wolf was tall, in good shape. He might have been able to give Lewis a fair pounding. But was he capable of killing him?

"Probably," I sighed. Cassie looked at me questioningly. I just shook my head and she shrugged.

"Okay." She turned off the autopilot. "Start a turn to two-two-oh degrees and begin your descent at three hundred feet per minute. Oh, and see if you can dislodge that witch and her cat from the tail section, will you?"

"Don't laugh." I sighed. "Halloween night I found myself chasing an old lady up Commercial Street, thinking she was the witch. Two hours later your friend Kerry had me tied in knots. It's gone on and on. How do witches pick their victims? Why me?"

"Because you are an innocent at heart." She adjusted the trim slightly.

Soon I was happily involved with the aircraft and forgot about the hapless Lewis. When I had the plane lined up with Runway 22, Cassie took over and greased it in. As she performed shutdown procedures, I asked if she needed a ride. She said no, she had several chores to do.

"Like what? Should I wait for you?" I asked.

"Oh, like vacuuming the plane. Doing the exorcism ritual. You know, routine."

"Oh, bug off about that!" I growled. "I'm getting paranoid as it is."

She laughed and ten minutes later Fargo was licking my face and whining to tell me how mistreated he had been. Then he remembered he was mad at me and sulked under the kitchen table, staying there until Mom put a plate of food in front of me.

She fed me an early dinner of leftover meatloaf, mashed potatoes and little brussels sprouts with butter and caraway seed. It tasted infinitely better than the lobster and steaks I'd been eating. I gave her a rundown of my trip. She told me Sonny, Mitch and Peter and the Wolf were looking for me. The list was growing.

After my warm welcome and hot meal, everything seemed to catch up with me, and I couldn't stop yawning, this time for real. Mom suggested I go home before I fell asleep at the table.

As I got to my feet the small gold buckles on the side of my slip-ons interlocked and I fell against the sink. I managed to grab it, almost hitting my chin, and clumsily pulled myself erect.

"Fucking bitch witch!" I hissed. "I'm sorry, Mom, excuse me."

"Are you hurt?" Mother leaned down and disentangled my shoes.

"Only my dignity . . . for the twentieth time." I was so angry my head was spinning.

"Alexandra, you worry me a little. Are you really letting this so-called witch's curse bother you? Surely you don't believe it?"

I sighed. "Oh, of course not. Not really. But crazy things keep happening—all in a row, it seems. I scraped my shin on Mary's boat. Spilled tea all over Wolf's living room and made a fool of myself in front of Sonny's girl. Knocked a guy's beer over in the Rat. I hurt my wrist at Cassie's, had not one but two pens dry up on me during an interview and lost a bra strap in Providence. I don't know—I seem to be falling apart. I'm just tired . . . and my ear hurts, it plugged up on the plane. It's nothing, Mom. I'm just frazzled. And everybody teases me—well, Joe and Cassie." I sounded so childishly piqued even I had to laugh.

"Darling, crazy things happen to all of us all the time." Mom smiled. "And sometimes they do seem to go in streaks. But witches only count in movies, and I don't think anyone is filming you. Now, darling, go home and rest." She struck a silly pose. "Abracadabra! Presto! Hoot, mon! Faith and begorrah! Holy cow! Ipso facto! Hey, nonny nonny . . . the curse is gone!"

I loved that woman. And I smiled all the way home.

I walked into the house, which seemed a little strange to me, even after so short an absence. Fargo seemed to feel the same. He ran from room to room . . . sniffing . . . whuffling . . . checking. I hiked the thermostat, started a pot of coffee and walked over to the telephone message machine, which was blinking as if it had undergone a nervous breakdown. I hit the replay and sat down to listen.

Peter would appreciate a call. *Click.* Wolf would really like to hear from me. *Click.* Mitch had not heard from Sonny. *Click.* Mitch *had* to reach Sonny. *Click.* Wolf needed to talk to me right away. *Click.* Someone would like to speak to Arthur. *Click.* It was imperative that Mitch speak to Sonny or me. *Click.* Would I please call Sonny at the following number . . . *Click.*

110

I picked up the card that Sonny had left with me, giving his hotel number in Gatlinburg and compared it with the one I had just jotted down from the tape. They were not the same. I dialed the new number and was told I had reached Gatlinburg Towers. It sounded expensive. Paula was obviously not a cheap date. No wonder Sonny was thinking of high-paying jobs. Finally I heard Sonny say hello.

"Where are you?" I asked. "What happened to Riverside Crest?"

His voice was hearty and jovial, as if he were addressing the Kiwanis Club. I knew that meant someone was with him, doubtless the lovely Paula. "Why, ah, we decided to stay here. It's right down-town and it's got an indoor pool, a spa, hairdresser, shops—"

"Sounds like the Kansas City Sheraton."

"Could be for all I know. Paula felt the Riverside was a little, uh, rustic and thought she'd be happier here in more traditional sur-roundings." There was just the slightest accent on *thought* that told me Paula wasn't happy at the Towers, either.

"I see. Look, why haven't you called Mitch? He is about in hys-terics by now."

He sounded surprised. "Why should I call Mitch?"

"Didn't you get my message at the Riverside? A young house-boy who worked for Peter and the Wolf got his head beaten in. He was found at the amphitheater, robbed of a bunch of money."

"No, I didn't get any message." Now he sounded bitter. "I wouldn't have, we never checked in. Paula took one look at the lobby and 'just knew it wasn't our kind of place.' I don't see why Mitch can't handle it, but I'll call him. He probably just needs a boost. Everything else okay? Mom okay? Fargo?"

He sounded lonesome. On vacation? With a pretty compan-ion? "Everything's fine. Mom's good. Fargo's glad to be home. Me, too. Anyway, I won't keep you. Have fun at the Kansas City Sheraton. Or is it the Atlanta Marriott?"

"Who can tell? Maybe the Hong Kong Hilton. Bye."

I decided to let Sonny call Mitch before I did. It would doubt-less be a much happier conversation that way. There wasn't much

I could do for whoever was looking for Arthur, whoever he might be. So, reluctantly, I looked up the number for Peter and the Wolf.

As I started to dial, I thought back to my conversation with Sonny. He and Paula had never checked in at the Riverside, so they never got my voice-mail message. I wondered who did, and suddenly a heartwarming, wicked scenario rolled before me. The bridegroom carries his bride across the threshold of Room 617 at the Riverside Crest. "Alone at last!" he cries.

"Not quite," says the lovely bride. "Our phone is blinking. It must be voice-mail."

"Odd. Who'd be calling us *now*? Well, dear, check it. I'll I open the champagne."

The bride picks up the phone, listens, " . . . sorry to bother you when you've just arrived, but . . . there's been a bludgeoning murder . . ." Shriek. *Thud.*

Once in a while I come down with acute *schadenfreude*, so I was smiling broadly as I dialed the phone. I hoped Wolf would answer. I really didn't feel up to Peter's high drama—luck was with me.

"Thank God, Alex, we thought you'd disappeared." Wolf sounded a bit dramatic himself.

"I was away on business, as I mentioned. What's up?"

"I think we're going to be arrested for that little bastard's murder."

"Oh, Wolf! Just because the cops ask you a few questions does not mean imminent arrest! Mitch may be sounding tough because he's a little unsure, working the case without Sonny as fallback. I don't think there's anything to worry about unless, of course, you did it." I made it a question.

"Of course not. But old lady Ethel Winger lives next door, and you know her. She saw the tiff between Peter and Lewis and told the cops. By now it sounds like something between a young Ali and a demented Tyson. And Peter's watch—Mitch asked to borrow it, said we'd get it back and provided a receipt, but I don't like it. I don't understand."

"I don't either, but I wouldn't worry. As far as the fight . . . well, you didn't lie. You just weren't completely forthcoming. And there's no real reason you should have been at that time. Just let this play itself out, Wolf."

"Well, we do worry. We want to hire you, Alex. With Sonny and the Chief away and that idiot Anders in charge, God knows what could happen. Obviously *somebody* had it in for Lewis. We were pissed at him for walking out, and what he did to Peter was unforgivable. But we didn't kill him. However, if the police just keep looking at us, they're never going to find anybody else. You have to find that somebody else, Alex. We did not do it!"

I wished he would stop saying *we*. Did he mean *neither* of them did it, or did he mean that only *one* of them did it, without the assistance of the other? "Wolf, I'm really tired. I just got in. I'll see you around ten tomorrow, okay? We'll decide then if I can help you in some way, although I really don't imagine you need me. We'll talk."

After dragging a few more reassuring remarks out of me, he finally hung up.

Bed. What I needed was my own familiar, beloved bed. I yawned and went to let Fargo out. I got halfway to the back door and the front doorbell rang. Fargo gave two or three ferocious barks and then quit. It must be someone he knew.

"Listen, Fargo, if this isn't somebody with a million in cash and two filets mignon, take 'em out! You hear me? I want company like you want your ears cleaned." He wagged his tail and grinned and I opened the door.

It was Mitch, looking cool, collected . . . and rested, dammit. Obviously, Sonny had calmed him down and made him feel like Hercule Poirot.

"Sorry to bother you, Alex. I know you're tired. But Sonny thought I should update you right away. He thought you might want casually to suggest to Peter and the Wolf that they retain a lawyer."

God, I hate nights like this.

113

Chapter 12

Mitch sat at the kitchen table while I put on fresh coffee. I sat across from him and lit a cigarette, and don't ask me the number— I had stopped counting somewhere over Rhode Island.

"Now what is this? Sonny thinks Peter and the Wolf should get a lawyer? What on earth did you tell him to warrant that suggestion?"

"I'm going to start at the beginning, Alex, and you can decide for yourself. Okay?" He took a battered notebook from his shirt pocket and searched for the page he wanted. Was this murder so complicated? He'd written notes the length of *War and Peace*.

"Here we go. Early Sunday morning Lewis Schley was found at the amphitheater, beaten to death and laid out, if you will, on the stage. Because of the chilly night and heavy rain, time of death was difficult to establish, but both Doc Marsten and the medical examiner estimate between nine p.m. Saturday and two a.m. Sunday. Both believe it was probably early rather than late within that time frame. They both also think he was probably killed elsewhere and moved, though again the rain makes it uncertain."

"He was alive and well at eight p.m.," I reminded him.

"Yes. Several people at the Wharf Rat corroborate that. But nobody claims to have seen him—"

"Mitch," I interrupted. "I forgot to mention it, but I saw Jared Mather talking to him outside the Rat as I was leaving. Maybe Lewis said something to him that would help. Sorry I didn't say something earlier. I've been rather . . . preoccupied."

"Uh-huh, I know. The Wicked Witch of the Wat."

"The what?"

The Wat . . . you know, like wabbit."

"Very funny. Who told you about that?" My coffee was suddenly bitter.

"Oh, Joe, Lainey, Cassie. Anyway, I ran into Mather at Roy's Café having lunch. He mentioned seeing Lewis, but no help there." Mitch laughed. "He said he caught up with Lewis at the end of the alley. It looked like it was about to pour and he felt it his 'Christian duty to offer the boy a ride.' Lewis told him riding with queer haters made him nervous, he'd rather get wet. End of conversation. So much for détente."

I smiled. "I bet Mather loved that." Secretly I wondered if Mather and Lewis had had something going—or if Mather wished they did. Even so, Mather was a good investigator. If he knew anything he'd have made it known somehow. And I wasn't going to out him just to take the focus off Wolf and Peter, even if Mitch would have believed me.

"Well, he was laughing when he told me. But later he said he felt kind of bad . . . like maybe if he'd insisted, Lewis would still be alive."

Mitch yawned and I yearned for bed. But he started his speech again. "To continue, we still have not found his wallet. That, plus Mellon's statement that he had over four hundred dollars, plus your statement that he had a full wallet at the Rat, lends credence to the robbery theory." He started flipping through the notebook and making irritating little noises, clicking his tongue against the roof of his mouth.

"Mitch, you sound as if you're on the stand at somebody's trial. We aren't there yet. Here, have some coffee. And speak English, not detecto-babble."

He glared at me and looked embarrassed. "Yeah, sorry. We haven't found the murder weapon yet, but forensics has been some help in telling us what to look for. It's some kind of wooden stick. They found a few splinters in the wound, pine, common pine. And there was some sawdust on his jacket where the rain didn't get to. It was not a baseball bat. The end of it was square, maybe three inches across. There were some funny—strange—bruises on his shoulders and neck, like he was hit with something knobby. Forensics finally decided it was probably a table leg or chair leg, probably square at the top, then round and tapered as it went down. One little knob toward the top and two or three toward the bottom."

Mitch looked up at me meaningfully. "We know where there's at least one table leg missing, don't we?"

"Yes," I agreed. "From a warped beat-up old table that could have lost that leg months ago. Surely you don't think they took it off the table, zonked Lewis with it and then parked the table with three legs on the front porch for the edification of the Provincetown Police Department!" I set my mug down emphatically.

He shrugged. "Whoever said murderers were always smart? Anyway, there's more. Lewis had a recently healed wound on his left hand. The scar tissue was torn open, as if someone had ripped a watch off his wrist and opened up the cut doing it. We found out that so-called *little* Saturday morning confrontation Wolf told us about was really a first-class fistfight over a watch belonging to Peter Mellon. A woman who lives next door to them saw the whole thing. Now maybe Lewis didn't give the watch back to Peter. Maybe Peter yanked it off his arm *later*. Maybe? We've got the watch, with a broken crystal, by the way, to test for any blood." He moved on to another page, still clucking like a damned chicken.

116

"The crystal got broken Saturday morning," I sighed. "Before he knocked Peter down, Lewis teased him with the watch and then deliberately dropped it on the driveway. They told me about it Sunday before you and Pete Santos came by. And I noticed Lewis check a watch in the Rat. I don't recall how it looked, but it wasn't Peter's."

"Why didn't you tell me? Whose side are you on?" Now that query brought me up short. Did he already have them arrested and convicted? Did he know something that made him so certain?

"Truth. Justice. Motherhood and apple pie. Don't be an ass, Mitch. I'm not on anybody's *side*, and neither should you be! Can you visualize Peter Mellon in a fight? He took a dainty swipe at Lewis and missed. Lewis hit him on the cheek and then pushed him, and he fell down and cried over the broken watch. You better have your witness think again. You know old lady Winger would say anything to look important."

"All right, Alex, I guess she could have exaggerated. But there's one other thing. We know where Peter was from about seven-thirty till midnight Saturday . . . the Crown and Anchor. But we can't seem to trace Wolf." He began flipping and clicking again. I wondered idly if he would stop if I threw my coffee in his face.

Finally, he found the page he was looking for. "Wolf says he drove Peter to the Crown and dropped him off with his costume and makeup. He knew there would be no parking spaces, so he took the car home. He walked back down to the A-House for a drink and then went to see Peter sing. He says afterward he walked home *again* and brought the car down to get Peter and his stuff, since it had begun to rain. That is a complicated lot of walking and driving. More to the point, we haven't found anyone who saw him, and he says he can't remember who might recall seeing him at either place."

I sipped my coffee and knew I could fall asleep with the mug in my hand. "The A-House was plain crazy. I'm surprised the fire department didn't shut them down. It would have been easy to miss someone in that crowd. The Crown was not quite as bad, but I admit, I didn't see Wolf. He could have been in the bar."

"Maybe," Mitch conceded. "But the bartender doesn't remember him being around until after eleven p.m., when he came in, soaking wet. And you'd think the barman would remember Wolf being there earlier, with Peter there playing the star."

"He was damn good." For some reason I was getting irritated. I tried to credit it to fatigue.

"I don't doubt it, but see if this makes sense to you. Wolf drives Peter to the Crown. While he is gone, Lewis returns, maybe to get something he forgot from his room. And maybe, seeing the car gone he figures no one is home and goes in the main house to see what's loose and easy to take—maybe from an unlocked guest room. Believe me, I don't see Lewis as a choirboy!"

I got up and poured us coffee. Mitch was reaching toward his notebook again, and I accidentally spilled a few drops of coffee on the back of his hand. He moved it quickly and licked the drops off and continued.

"Wolf returns. Lewis sees the car lights and tries to run away or maybe tries to attack Wolf. Or maybe Wolf sees him moving around in the house and thinks it's an unknown burglar. Wolf grabs the table leg from somewhere in the car or the garage or by the garbage cans—whatever. He belts Lewis—maybe in self-defense—and gets so mad he just loses it and finishes him off. He knows he can't leave the body in his yard, so he takes him to Race Point and lays him out like King Tut on stage. He rips the watch off Lewis's arm and keeps it. He tosses Lewis's wallet out the car window along the way—with or without the money—comes back and collects Peter at the Crown and Anchor."

I was weary. Mitch's theory had some validity, but I felt constrained to defend the two old trouts. I don't know why. The last person I had defended to the police had proved to be a double murderer. I hoped there wasn't a pattern developing here. Maybe I just felt guilty about pouring tea and rum all over their living room furniture.

"You're stretching, Mitch. Whether it was defense or attack, if Wolf saw Lewis before getting out of the car, he could have

118

grabbed the tire iron. If Wolf was already in the house when he became aware of Lewis, he could have grabbed the poker. I cannot see him keeping a table leg in the car or in the garbage can or behind a shrub in the unlikely event he might someday need it as a weapon. And I cannot see him calmly unscrewing a table leg with Lewis about to jump him . . . or with Lewis running away. Next, you have Wolf at Race Point sometime before midnight, and then you have Harmon reporting their car out there around four-thirty a.m. I doubt Wolf took him there at eleven p.m. and went back five hours later to say farewell."

I slumped in my chair, lit a cigarette and sipped my coffee. It was a tossup which tasted worse. I was not happy to hear Mitch prolong his diatribe.

"Oh, come on, Alex. I don't know about you, but *my* tire iron is under a fiberboard floor in the trunk. It would take me ten minutes and plenty of noise to find it. The table leg was only held by two wing-nuts, fast and quiet to remove. And maybe Wolf was afraid the robber or Lewis could get to him before he got to the poker."

I had a great desire to go get my own poker, but I still had some hope of getting Mitch past this sticking point. I had to; there *were* other possibilities.

"Mitch, it's possible Lewis never came back to their house at all," I began.

"Of course it is. It's also possible Wolf lured him there. We only have Peter's claim that he paid Lewis his wages. Maybe they owed him money. Wolf told him to come to the house at ten. He was waiting, table leg in hand. Wolf could have dragged the body behind a shrub and gone back to the Crown to pick up Peter. They could have waited till the town quieted down and taken Lewis out there in the wee hours. Or maybe Wolf did take him out there before midnight, and the SUV Harmon saw later has nothing to do with anything. It works either way." Mitch closed his damn notebook with a snap and a final tongue click.

"Mitch, this is all very iffy and circumstantial." And unfortunately, his last scenario made a lot of sense.

"Agreed. But I want forensics to look at their SUV and that table. I hope to have a warrant for impounding them sometime tomorrow. It's closing in on them, Alex. I think that's what Sonny meant. I think he's just being nice, advising they get legal counsel now, since they're town residents and friends of yours."

Why was everybody insisting that Peter and the Wolf were such close friends of mine? They never had been, not really. Oh, well. I was too tired to argue. "Okay, thanks for the rundown, Mitch. I'm ready to pass out. I'm sure you're tired, too. I really hope it turns out to be someone else. Are you at least *looking* for other possibilities?" I stretched my arms and yawned.

"Sure. We've been checking on transients, which isn't easy on a weekend like this. We've got bartenders looking for anybody with a wad of cash. We're looking for the murder weapon. We're trying to figure where the sawdust came from. And we keep looking for someone who might have seen Lewis between eight and twelve. All we know right now is that he walked out of the Wharf Rat at eight p.m., headed for Reverend Bartles' place and never got there. I don't know much else to do."

I didn't either. I stood up, swayed, and we said a rather grumpy goodnight. Fargo and I quickly got ready for bed. Maybe sleep would help.

Sleep did. When Fargo woke very early Thursday morning with that "I've got to go—I've got to go *now!*" look in his eye, I felt considerably better. And a dawn that promised to become a lovely, warm, sunny fall day didn't hurt. Coffee and that first delightful cigarette improved my already good mood, and I didn't even argue when Fargo started his little song-and-prance routine to go to the beach.

On the way there, I drove by the amphitheater, hoping for inspiration. All I saw was a lot of concrete, damp with morning dew, and some dressing areas and poles with bars for spotlights. There wasn't even any police tape left. Obviously, they, too, felt the locale held nothing more of interest.

At the beach there was a single set of large footprints meandering along just below the high tide mark. I wondered if Harmon had been on early patrol for driftwood and other goodies. And I wondered what he had really seen through his haze of alcohol that rainy night.

Back home, I batted out my report for Mr. Ellis in overdrive, pleased that I would get it to him a day earlier than promised. Fargo and I delivered it. Ellis seemed surprised and happy to get it.

We chatted briefly about the three candidates. While Ellis was impressed by Nancy Baker's expertise, he seemed to feel she might be "somewhat intense" for a small town. He didn't even crack a smile at George Mills's Halloween escapade. When I recounted Cynthia Hart's adventure with the injured cat, however, I got the widest grin Choate Ellis is capable of giving. He said he couldn't wait to learn the details. I got the feeling that Ms. Hart might soon be getting an offer. I was sure Mr. Mills would not. Well, Cynthia looked to be a deserving young woman.

As promised, we arrived at Peter and Wolf's a shade before ten. Wolf let me in and returned to sit beside Peter on the couch. As I looked at them, all I could think of was two terrified white rabbits caught in the glare of oncoming headlights.

"What on earth is wrong?" I asked. "You two look as if you've seen a ghost." It was not a happy choice of words.

"Ooo-oooh!" Peter moaned. "You're right. The ghost of that horrid little creature will haunt us until we die!" He burst into tears.

"Which won't be long," Wolf added shakily, "if the police have their way. They just took away the Explorer. We're finished. And we didn't do it."

"Oh, for God's sake!" I was in no mood to have aging queenly histrionics ruin my so-far great day. "Lewis ran errands in it sometimes, didn't he? I think I've seen him in it. So of course they will find hair and clothing fibers of his in the SUV. All very logical. If that's all they can come up with, actually, it rather lets some air *out* of their balloon. By the way, did you ever haul sawdust in the SUV?"

"Sawdust?" Wolf looked startled. "No, I can't remember ever doing that. Some logs once or twice. But the cops saw a stain on one of the back mats. He pointed at it and told Mitch it looked like blood. That's all they need. We'll be arrested any minute."

"Guys! Get a grip! Nobody's yet proven blood is even there! And if so, it could be yours or anybody else's who's been in the vehicle . . . including a drippy steak!"

"It'll be Lewis'," Wolf projected gloomily. "He was bleeding all over the place the day I picked him up."

"What the hell do you mean?"

"Five—six weeks ago. I'd been to the dentist in Hyannis and was coming home in a drenching rain. Lewis was standing on the side of the road in just shirt and jeans, no jacket or raincoat, soaking wet, thumbing a ride. I stopped. He got in, shivering badly. I told him there was a blanket in back, and he sort of got up and leaned over, pulled it up front and draped it around him. I noticed his left hand was badly cut and bleeding and asked him what had happened."

I couldn't believe this! What else could they come up with to make themselves look guilty? Blood on the mat, blood on the blanket. My God.

Wolf went on. "He said he had slipped in the mud and fallen on a broken bottle. I believed him then. Now I think he was out in the boonies looking for places closed for the winter and easily robbed. I'll bet he accidentally put his hand through a window, set off an alarm and ran. Anyway, he declined when I asked if he wanted to be dropped at the clinic. Said he had no money. I gave him a clean handkerchief to put around the cut."

"So you brought him here?" I guessed.

"Yeah, I felt sorry for him. I patched his hand up—it really should have been stitched—and Peter fed him. Lewis asked if we knew of any jobs. Well, our sheet shaker was leaving shortly to go back to college, so we hired him. One of our more brilliant moves. But, Alex, you know how it is here with houseboys—they almost never have references." He shrugged and raised his hands palm-up. "Hell, half the time the address and Social Security number they give you is bogus. How were we to know what a little louse he was?"

"I understand. It's always that way with summer help unless they happen to be local people. Anyway, blood in the SUV is not going to mean much, there are too many ways it could have got there. Relax." I could have used some coffee. The fact that they hadn't even offered it told me how disturbed they were.

"No," Peter shook his head. "We want to hire you—retain you—whatever the term is. We need your help, Alex. Mitch is determined to frame us for this. He's not doing anything to find the real killer! I mean, what about Reverend Bartles? It's only Bartles' word that Lewis never got to his place. Maybe Lewis did get there. I can think of all sorts of simply *fabulous* scenarios for that little rendezvous!"

So could I. Just because Bartles had *Rev* in front of his name meant little to me. To me, *Rev* did not automatically translate to *sinless*. And Peter was right—Mitch had seemed to skip over Bartles. "Look," I temporized. "I've been away. Let me nose around for a day or so. If I turn anything up, we'll talk about a bill."

I nodded toward the coffee table, which still showed a slight discoloration. "I probably owe you more than you owe me. I still say there will probably be nothing, and in the long run the cops will handle it right. But now, I'd suggest you don't answer any more police questions without a lawyer present."

"Good!" Peter drew himself up dramatically and took a deep breath. He continued haughtily, "If that child Mitch appears *again*, I shall simply send him home to mama! He threw an absolutely juvenile fit over that silly table."

"Why did Mitch make a scene?" I asked. "Didn't you let him take it? Didn't he have a proper warrant?"

Wolf intervened as Peter drew another shuddering breath. "Oh, I guess the warrant was all right."

"Then why not give him the table?"

"Oh, you see, we burned it."

Chapter 13

"You burned it," I echoed. Alice in Wonderland had nothing on Alex in Provincetown. Things were getting curiouser and curiouser here, too. "Might one inquire *why* you burned it? Why you incinerated possible evidence!" I ended in a squeak.

"Now *you're* getting testy about it, too. It was our table. If we want to burn up our furniture who's to say we can't!" Peter sounded a little testy himself.

"Alex," Wolf spoke reasonably. "We had no idea we were doing anything . . . questionable. Since we planned to close the inn earlier than usual this fall, we didn't order extra firewood. The weather was so awful over the weekend, we kept a fire in the fireplace most of the time for the guests, and used up all the logs we had."

Peter picked up the explanation. "Last night we felt so low and lost and alone . . ." He cocked his head and smiled mournfully, obviously appreciating the unplanned alliteration. "So low . . . so lost . . . so alone, we decided a wee nightcap and a fire might cheer us up. There were no logs, so Wolf just knocked the table apart and we enjoyed a little light and comfort in a dark, unfriendly world."

I stood and walked to the guilty fireplace. I was annoyed—no, angry. I felt they were playing with me. Obviously, they knew I liked them. Maybe they thought they could charm me into being their white knight. Well, I had done that once, and my armor still had the dents to show for it. I wasn't buying their damsels in distress act.

"I'm touched. You have that old table sitting around for years and you pick last night to burn it. Either you are truly babes in the woods or very clever killers. And right now, I'd have to toss a coin to make a choice!"

"*Alex!*" they chorused. Peter continued, "*Of course* we aren't killers. How on earth were we to know Mitch would want that damned table? He'd be welcome to it. God knows it was worthless. And it was not old, my dear, we bought it about three weeks ago."

"Three weeks?" I was surprised. The rickety thing had looked like an antique to me. I walked to the window, as if the table were still there for me to re-evaluate. I came back and sat down.

"About," Wolf nodded. "We got a flyer in the mail from Wood's Woods, that unfinished wood furniture shop in Orleans. The table was featured, on sale *very* cheap. I should have remembered my grandmother's warning. Buy cheap, get cheap. Anyway, I took a drive up, and the one Wood had on display looked all right, so I bought one to use in the sun porch. I got it home and out of the carton to assemble it and damned if one leg wasn't missing. On top of that, one of the screws to anchor the top broke off as I started to screw it in. Lewis found an old broom and cut the handle off for a makeshift leg."

He turned to Peter. "Why don't you make some coffee?" Peter nodded and headed for the kitchen, with Pewter and, surprisingly, Fargo following hopefully. Wolf resumed. "We used it on the porch one night with a cookout for the guests and just left it there . . .

forgot it, I guess. It rained overnight. When it got wet, it started to warp so fast you could practically see it curl! Lord, nothing's gone right lately."

It sounded almost too convenient to be true. "Did you call Wood's Woods and complain?" I asked.

"Yes." From the kitchen.

"No." From the couch.

"Keep the stories straight, boys." I'd about had it with these two.

"Wolf," Peter called from the kitchen, sounding genuinely confused. "You were going to call and demand our money back."

"I know. It got busy here, and every time I thought of calling, it was sometime I knew they would be closed. Finally, I decided just to wait till after the weekend when things calmed down. Ha-ha. So, no, I haven't called. What difference does it make?"

"It would be interesting," I answered sourly, "to know if anyone else bought one—or says they bought one—with a leg missing."

"Oh. Oh, yes, of course." Peter returned with three mugs, a carton of milk and a sugar bowl on a tray. The formality of service had certainly changed with Dear Boy's departure. "You see, Alex, it's things like this we need you for! I would never have thought of that. And I'll bet Little Mitchie hasn't either."

I couldn't help grinning. "Better not let him hear you call him that. Anyway, I'll check Wood's Woods. If another leg is missing, and a table leg turns up as the murder weapon, you'd be a little further off the hook. They found pine splinters in the wound, and if they match pieces of other tables, you'd be even further off the hook. Even though you are first-class top-notch assholes for burning that table!"

They looked at the floor like chastened children, as perhaps they were. "Now, Wolf, where the hell were you Saturday night between eight and midnight? And tell the truth. One quibble and I'm out of here."

"Okay. About seven-thirty I drove Peter down to the Crown and Anchor. I dropped him and his costume and makeup kit right at the door. No way could I find a place to park, and the parade was starting, so I drove home and walked back down just ahead of the rain. I stayed in the dressing room with Peter until he went on. Several people can confirm that." Wolf paused and looked uneasy.

"That takes us to about nine o'clock. Then what?" I urged. I didn't want him to take time to think something up. I wanted to hear what was bothering him. "Then what?"

He sighed and looked sadly at Peter. "I'm sorry, darling. I did something awful and I lied to you about it."

Peter turned dead white and clasped his hands to his mouth. I was hard put not to do the same. I really didn't want to hear what I thought I was about to. I cleared my throat and somehow spoke evenly. "What did you do?"

"I knew Peter was a nervous wreck. The dust-up with Lewis, his father's watch, the bruise under his eye, having to pitch in with me and clean rooms when he should have been resting—all these things had left him exhausted and *very* shaky. I . . . I was almost certain he was going to blow the performance. I had visions of his voice failing him. I was afraid he'd forget lyrics. I could just see him tripping on that long skirt and ripping it. I envisioned a total disaster, with the whole audience whooping and laughing him off the stage. I couldn't face it." He paused and wiped his face with his handkerchief. "Just as the show started, I left. I saw you as I went out, Alex. You were sitting with Marc. I didn't know you knew him."

I didn't bother to explain about how I met Marc. I didn't know whether I was relieved by what Wolf had said or not. He was clever—they both were. I found myself wondering if this might be a little play produced solely for me. One of them could have run into Marc, and Marc could have casually mentioned sitting with me. It was almost too perfect as Wolf's throwaway line.

Wolf turned toward Peter but couldn't look him in the eye. "So you see, my dear, I not only had no faith in you, I left you to face your incipient disaster all on your own."

I waited for Peter to become a blubbering mess or a blazing

virago, but he fooled me. He took Wolf's hand and spoke quietly. "I don't blame you. You haven't said a thing I hadn't been thinking all that afternoon. It's almost funny, all day I had been trying to think of a way to get you not to go. I didn't want you to see me make an ass of myself, or faint, or exit sobbing or whatever it would have been. *However,* since I was such a *triumph* . . ." Now he was Peter again. "I confess I had Walter make a video of the whole thing. He promised to burn it if I blew up, but I didn't, and now we can bore everybody silly for *years* making them all watch it. My love, you are forgiven." As stars in a gay soap opera, these two were direct from Central Casting.

"A heartwarming scene," I said. "I'll try again. Wolf, where were you?"

Wolf flashed Peter a radiant and grateful smile, and turned toward me. "I was home, as I said. I walked home from the Crown, feeling pretty despondent. I tossed the two final logs on the fire and sat down. Pewter jumped up to console me. I just sat there, thinking. Things seemed to be coming apart, somehow. I guess I felt . . . old. Like I couldn't really control things anymore. And that I had never really *done* anything with my life."

He sipped some coffee and looked up with a rueful grin. "You know, at some point we all think we're going to be President, or find the cure for cancer or discover Atlantis or whatever. It suddenly occurred to me that when Saint Peter asks me what I've done to pass through those pearly gates, I'll answer, 'Why, good sir, the towels were always fresh and sweet-smelling in my guesthouse.' Somehow, it doesn't have much of a ring to it."

I laughed. "Better than saying they weren't. We can't all be Washington or Salk or Columbus. Somebody has to dump the ashtrays." Against my better judgment, I couldn't dislike these two. But that could be a serious mistake. "Did anyone besides Pewter witness these dark thoughts?"

"Actually, yes." He sighed. "I know, I should have told Mitch, but I was afraid he might let it slip and Peter would find out I skipped the performance."

128

He indicated a chair beside the fireplace. "Sitting there day-dreaming, I heard the back door open. I admit, my first thought was that Lewis had come back to put his sticky little hands on anything loose—the guests are lax as hell about locking doors. But it was one of the guests." He nodded at me before I could interrupt. "I'll give you his name and address. He asked me to cash a check for him, said he had spent more than he had realized. I cashed a fifty-dollar check for him, and we had a drink and talked for a while."

Wolf stretched his legs and accidentally gave Pewter a little kick. He apologized with an ear-scratch and picked up his tale. "I glanced at the clock and was surprised to find it was nearly eleven. I explained to our guest that I had to leave and offered a ride, but he said he had gotten so relaxed, he'd just enjoy the fire for a bit and go to bed. So I left, found a place to park out on the wharf and walked over to get Peter."

I felt at least partially relieved by Wolf's explanation. I could check his stories about Marc and the houseguest, and if they were true, it pretty well accounted for his time between seven-thirty and midnight.

Of course he *might* have encountered Lewis upon arriving home, but I doubted he could have had a casual, coherent conversation with a houseguest if he had just minutes earlier bashed Lewis's head in and stashed him behind a bush for later transport to the beach. Mitch said Lewis had possibly been killed as late as two a.m., but more likely earlier, so it looked as if Peter and Wolf were at least marginally in the clear.

"I say again, Wolf, I don't think you two have anything to worry about. Since Lewis worked and lived here, you come into the spotlight. The fight and burning the table are negatives, but the watch is easily explained and the table is so dumb it almost has to be innocent. Give me your guest's name and phone number . . . and Marc's. Also, I'll see what I can find out about table legs and the righteous Reverend Bartles. We'll talk during the weekend."

"Ah, would you like a small . . . ah, is *retainer* the word?" Peter asked delicately, as Wolf scribbled on a card.

"Absolutely," I said. "A copy of the Judy, Judy, Judy tape for my very own."

"You shall have it, my dear, the *only* duplicate copy."

I left my car parked at Green Mansions, and Fargo and I walked the few hundred feet to the Wharf Rat Bar for the lunch I felt we so richly deserved. I took a seat at the bar and noted that the usual suspects had gathered around the front table. Fish had taken second place and the topic du jour was, of course, murder. The consensus held that Peter and/or the Wolf had done it. The more Harmon drank, the more certain he was that it had been Wolf he saw in the Explorer, that Wolf was the go-between in a drug ring and Lewis was blackmailing him. Others were betting on Peter, that he was jealous of Wolf making a play for Lewis. One or two still voted for the transient robber, but they were few.

I decided to have a little fun. After Joe had taken my luncheon order and brought me a Bud, he asked, as usual, what was new with Ptown's favorite sleuth. I gave him a big wink and answered in a whisper that could have been heard in Wellfleet, "Harmon's footprints were found on the beach this morning. You know what that means. Not only what you're thinking, but also possibly firewood."

"My God!" Joe played along, and the silence at the front table became palpable. "Are they sure, Alex, really sure?"

"Yep. The worn spot on the heel was a dead giveaway." Out of the corner of my eye I could see Harmon lifting one battered boot and then the other while he and his cronies leaned as if in prayer, to examine the soles.

Harmon addressed his companions indignantly, "Well, even if I was there and who says I was, it don't mean nothing. Just walking on a beach don't mean *nothing*! And Mitch ought to know that. No more does picking up a little wood. That ain't illegal. I'm going down there right now and tell him he ain't got one thing on me. Not one." He nearly ran from the bar. I smiled at the thought of the lengthy and many-faceted conversation he and Mitch would enjoy. Then the smile faded, as I realized that once in a while my humor took a dark, twisted turn that reminded me of my father. I had to watch that.

My reflections were short-lived. Just as I had taken Fargo's hamburger and water out to him and returned to my fried clams, Ben Fratos came through the door with his usual swagger. He took a barstool a couple down from me, and we nodded to each other with mutual lack of enthusiasm. Why did Fratos always arrive in time to ruin my lunch?

I turned away from him slightly, but it didn't work. He took a noisy swig of his beer and said, "Well, I understand you got yourself a case. Trying to clear Peter and the Wolf, are you?"

"Not me. I didn't even know they were cloudy."

"They're *under* a cloud. Blood all over their SUV, Wolf with no alibi, a table leg—probably the murder weapon—missing from their place, and even poor little faggy Peter having a fight with the vic. I'd say that's cloudy."

I knew that, as an ex-cop, Fratos was still friendly with one or two men on the force and that they would have passed along information on the case. But it made me mad he would be so irresponsible as to blab it all over the Rat—the equivalent of CNN, or better.

"Gee, Ben." I smiled. "You seem to know an awful lot about the case. You get your info direct from the perp?"

His reaction totally unnerved me. He slammed the beer bottle down on the bar and stood up, red in the face, muscles popping along his neck. "You fucking nosy dyke! You been following me? I'll teach you to trail *me* around!"

He swung at me. I ducked, and suddenly Joe was between us, arms around Fratos.

"Ben, you crazy or something? Alex was just riding you a little, and I gotta say you started it. Looks to me like you already had too much beer somewhere. This one's on the house, but you better get on home and sleep it off. Get on now!" Ben looked like he'd like nothing better than a fight, but finally turned and left.

"Jesus, Alex, I'm sorry. You okay?" Joe patted my shoulder.

"Oh, yeah, he missed. But what on earth did I say? He knows I know he has contacts who'd tell him stuff about a case, especially a murder. Why would he get so upset? He had to know it was just a needle."

"Well, for one thing he was half-drunk. For another, you're not his favorite person." Joe returned to his usual place behind the bar. "I don't know why he blames you for that Keystone Kops act he pulled with that skylight, but he does. Has from the beginning. Anyway, you want me to reheat your lunch?"

"Uh, no, thanks, Joe. I've kind of lost my appetite. Maybe Billie could wrap it up for me. I'll have it later at home."

He was back moments later. "Billie gave you a fresh salad and added some pecan pie for a little comfort, she says. And it's on us, Alex. Billie says you should have punched him while I held him."

"Thanks. Billie is a woman of great ideas." I smiled as I took the package. "But I have a feeling it would take more punch than I've got to shut *that* mouth."

And it did.

Chapter 14

Fargo and I walked to the car. I sat a moment, feeling dizzy and shaken. I was more upset than I wanted to admit. Fratos could have broken my jaw if he had connected. What the *hell* had gotten into him? Okay, he'd had a few. Okay, he didn't like me, but you don't attack everyone you don't care for. Or maybe you do if you're Ben Fratos—he had the reputation of a short fuse.

It went nicely, I suppose, with his long, prying nose. He liked to be in the know about everything and anything going on in town. Who was selling his house, whose car was being repo'd, who was fighting with her husband, who was behind in his mortgage payments, who was cheating, whatever. You were likely to spot Fratos any place at any hour—watching, smirking. I've no idea what purpose this gathering of information served. He had few investigatory cases, I knew that much.

At home I put Billie's package in the refrigerator for later reference. I automatically pulled out a Bud and then put it back. I was edgy. This damn murder was getting to me. Though I couldn't put my finger on anything Mitch was doing wrong, he seemed as centered on blaming Peter and the Wolf as Captain Anders was on blaming some nameless thief.

If Anders was right, there'd probably never be an arrest, much less a conviction, unless the killer was found by sheer luck. One transient in Provincetown on Halloween weekend would stand out about like a seagull at the town dump. Anyway, why would a transient killer who struck opportunistically, having seen Lewis flash big bills, carry him out to the amphitheater and pose him on stage? It almost had to be someone who knew Lewis and had reason to kill him. That left Wolf and Peter, and in my heart, I really didn't want it to be them.

I checked my watch and was surprised to find it only a little after one. "Saddle up, Fargo, let's go see what Mr. Wood has to say about selling legless tables."

There are those who would say that Fargo did not understand my entire sentence. I happen to think Fargo understood every word I ever said. But I am positive he got "Saddle up" and "Let's go." Why else would he have beat me to the back door with a big grin and majestically sweeping tail?

Heed this warning: watch what you say in front of your dog. He knows.

Headed for Orleans, I drove past the dunes, nearly white and blindingly bright in the midday sun, with the intense autumn-blue sky opening as a deep pool behind them. On my right was the bay, lined with all the little cottages and their hopeful signs of *We're Open!* and *Free Heat!* and *Off-Season Rates*. Anything for a few more profitable weekends. A great expanse of pure clean space on one side and crowded commercialism on the other—somehow, in Provincetown, it seemed fit. I loved it all.

As we drove down Route 6, we passed Mr. Ellis, abroad on some errand, no doubt, and looking rather like a benign midget behind the wheel of his cream Lincoln Navigator. He gave a brief, choppy wave and quickly returned his hand to the wheel. I had the feeling Mr. E. was not an SUV man at heart and wondered why he had one—as I wondered why so many people do.

Cream colored. I wondered if Ellis had been careening down the beach road in the small hours of Halloween night, tossing Lewis's wallet and watch out the window, nearly sideswiping poor Harmon. While I found it difficult to picture the dapper Mr. Ellis playing Casey at the Bat with Lewis's head, I thought sustained contact with Lewis might bring out the worst in most of us. But why, for example, would Ellis want to kill him? My whimsical side took over.

Lewis owed money to the bank, so Ellis beaned him, took his cash and laid him out on stage because he knew it was the only funeral Lewis would have. Lewis tried to steal Ellis's pretty Lincoln, and Ellis grabbed a handy chair leg and killed him, not wishing to bother the police with a personal problem. They had a lover's quarrel, and Lewis threatened to blackmail Ellis. Ellis killed him and—in a fit of remorse—laid him on the stage so he would be more comfortable.

Now that scenario appealed to me. Not that I had much serious thought of Ellis being involved in any way with Lewis or his demise, but the words *blackmail* and *Lewis* seemed a likely combination. Whom would Lewis blackmail? Anyone he could, was my first answer.

And that would be? Someone with at least some amount of money. Someone who was doing something naughty or illegal. Someone whose reputation or career would suffer if the knowledge became public. Someone *like* Ellis, actually, although I couldn't imagine his embezzling funds or climbing into the wrong boudoir window. But of course, that would be the whole idea. You are doing something wrong—pay me or I will reveal your criminal or embarrassing secret. So many people could be vulnerable: a banker, a lawyer, a teacher, a cop, a minister . . . a minister. Reverend Bartles?

He did keep popping up, didn't he? Perhaps an unseemly liking for young girls or boys? Perhaps Harmon's favorite evil, some connection to drugs? Possibly money laundering? Probably not stealing from the collection plate; I doubted there was enough in it to steal. There was at least some link between him and Lewis, though. I wondered how far it went and how I could find out what it was.

I was still puzzling over that one when I arrived at Wood's Woods. The business was housed in a small building with a sort of attached lean-to, where I heard an electric saw buzzing. Perhaps Mr. Wood did custom work or repairs. I walked into the "showroom"—an overcrowded room with various pieces of unfinished furniture assembled and displayed in no order I could discern. In one corner I spotted what I thought was the twin of Peter and Wolf's table, albeit with four sound legs.

The noise of the saw stopped and Mr. Wood came into the room. He was a small, skinny man in dusty khakis. He had an advanced case of male pattern baldness, with nearly colorless hair receding almost as I looked. A beaky nose held a pair of sawdust-specked glasses—sawdust! From no clues I was now gathering more clues than I knew what to do with. I must have been staring at him, for he looked at me uneasily, and when he spoke, his voice matched the rest of him, high pitched and unhappy. "Yes, can I help you?"

Some of my best performances are off the cuff. I looked sternly at him. "Mr. Wood?" He nodded. I flashed my private investigator's license, casually placing my thumb over the word *private*, letting the word *investigator* show and allowing the Great Seal of Massachusetts to work its magic. "There's been a problem, sir, with your selling tables much like that one there, with missing legs. Are you aware of that? How many complaints are unanswered? Where were the sales made to? What solutions have you offered?"

He looked stricken. Maybe this was all a surprise to him. Maybe all his tables had four good legs. Maybe it was because most everybody has a slight fear of authority, and I was being very authoritative. Maybe Wolf and Peter had lied like troupers.

"Look, Miss . . . Ms . . . ma'am, none of it was my fault and I am making every one of them good. Every single one. My wife is out now delivering legs." She sounded like a mad midwife. "You see, I got a chance to buy these tables at a closeout, real cheap, you know? I put that sample one together and it seemed okay, maybe a little flimsy and rough cut, but not bad for the price. So I ordered a bunch and sent out fliers advertising them. I sold thirty-four—all but that one there and one still in the carton. How did I know some only had three legs?" His voice rose to a self-justifying whine.

I scribbled some meaningless words on a notepad holding an old grocery list. He looked even more alarmed and continued his screed. "The minute I started getting complaints, I called the company and they promised to send replacement legs, but they took their sweet time . . . only got here yesterday. Right now, my wife is out with them, as I said. She's up in Hyannis and Sandwich and I forget where. Tomorrow she'll go out toward Wellfleet and Truro and all. I'm doing the best I can," he almost whimpered, a slight sheen now coating his extremely high forehead.

"Really? Then why didn't you cannibalize the two you have left? You could have taken care of eight disgruntled customers right there."

He looked at me with the pitying condescension of the expert to the ignorant. "Now, ma'am, I could hardly do that! I might have a chance to sell one—or both—of them, you see?"

"Right, I see." What I saw was why the store was where it was and the size it was and why it always would be. "I have other questions. Did you ever employ, or sell to or know anyone named Lewis Schley?"

He pondered, or at least pretended to, and answered, "No. Don't know him. He might have bought something for cash, but I wouldn't know that."

I doubted Lewis would have bought anything here. If he had done any work for Wood or—unlikely, I thought—had a more personal relationship, Wood wasn't about to say. I would tell Mitch that Wood had a lot of sawdust around and he could do what he

137

liked about it. "All right." I made it sound as if I were doing him a big favor. "We'll let that go for now. Do you have a list of people who complained about missing legs who live in . . . oh, Wellfleet, Truro and Provincetown?" I figured that covered enough area to include anyone Lewis might have known.

"Yes, but I'm not handing out my customers' names and addresses just because you're some consumer protection do-gooder on a spree or something. Why do you care if somebody got a damaged table as long as I'm making it good, anyway?"

He was a fool, but unfortunately he was not a complete fool. Sometimes the only choice is the truth.

"Lewis Schley was killed in Provincetown Saturday night. It is probable that the weapon was a table leg, pine, possibly from one of your tables. If so, the murderer could hardly have used it to beat Schley to death and then simply screwed it back on his table and sat down to breakfast. He may have complained that a leg was missing and asked for a replacement. The fact that legs now seem to be missing all over the Cape is just good luck for him. He may not have known others were missing, probably didn't. But I want to talk to anyone in those three towns who complained to you. Are you with me?"

"Oh, yes, ma'am! The list, I'll get you the list right now." He started exploring his pockets. "It's all written out with addresses. Always like to cooperate with the police, I do." I favored him with a nod and the wintry smile I assumed a police officer might give. "Murdered, you say, maybe with one of my table legs. You don't think my wife is in danger, do you?"

I liked him a little better. "Not at that end of the Cape. We think the killer was local. In fact . . ." I had a sudden bright idea that would give me a good excuse to call on the list of presumably disgruntled customers. "In fact, if you have replacements available, I'll be glad to deliver them for you. That way, your wife won't have to go to the Outer Cape at all. Much safer all around."

"Why, yes. They're right there in the back. Thank you, I really appreciate that."

138

I took the list from his limp hand, placed my car keys in it and said, "Great. Just put them in my trunk and forget all about this." I knew he wouldn't—he'd dine out for a year on this story. As he loaded the legs in my car, I glanced at the list. Two lived in Truro, two in Wellfleet, three in Provincetown. One of the Provincetowners was old Mr. Leander, so crippled by arthritis he could barely get around. One was the ubiquitous Rev. Bartles—I really had to meet that man. The third was—damnation!—my Aunt Mae. Yes, Aunt Mae.

As Fargo and I tooled along toward our Wellfleet deliveries, I tried to visualize Aunt Mae as the Table Leg Killer and failed. She was a vivacious lady with a pouter pigeon build who had no children and was mother to the world. When my Uncle Frank had died, she started fooling around growing herbs, more as a pastime than anything else. But she developed a deep interest and learned much about them and their place in history, as well as the kitchen. She now had a shop in what used to be her garage, where she sold dried herbs and small pots of herb plants which she raised in a little attached greenhouse. She had even published two thin books on the subject. She had quite a following and I loved her to pieces.

Of course, there *had* been the time when two young boys tried to swipe a bunch of her little clay pots, and she had chased them halfway down Bradford Street, belaboring them with a string mop. But I didn't think that really counted.

I turned down a rutted dirt road to my first delivery and figured I was in luck. There was a car in the yard. As Fargo headed for the nearest tree, a young woman came around the corner of the house.

"Hi," I said. "I'm Alex Peres. If you're Mrs. Reismann, I have a table leg from Wood's Woods for you."

"I could say, it's about time, but it's probably not your fault. That's great. We've had it propped up on a broom handle." She turned toward the house, calling, "Ray! The table leg is here. Thank you so much," she continued to me, "for bringing it. I figured we'd have to go get it, and we're really busy. Closing the cottage for the winter."

I picked up this opening. "Quite a job. Have you been at it long?" Her husband had approached and I handed him the leg. "Here you go."

"It seems long. Actually we've only been here since Monday. Parked the kids with my mom and figured we'd have some peace and quiet while we work. You know how it is."

I smiled in agreement and called the dog back. If they were telling the truth—and it would be easily checked—they were out of the picture. We got in the car. They waved and I left. One down.

My second stop was a rough-hewn log cabin beside a two-duck pond. It was almost postcard perfect and I felt a small pang of envy—and an elusive memory of Dean Trinler—as I knocked on the door. It opened to reveal a large man, unshaven, with a beer belly and wearing a none-too-clean T-shirt and gray work pants. My little dream dissipated quickly as my gracious host burped and said a welcoming, "Yeah? Whaddya want?"

"Hi. Are you Mr. Matthew Quinn?"

"Who wants to know?"

"Me. I'm Alex Peres. I'm delivering for Wood's Woods. We have a table leg for you, I believe."

"Been waiting two effing weeks!" he snarled. "I don't know how you people stay in business. Any asshole should know a table needs four legs. I've had it wobbling in there, propped up on a sawed-off broom handle."

There was going to be a great dearth of broom handles before this was all straightened out. By now I had handed him the leg and all I wanted was to find out if he'd been here last Saturday and leave. I managed a smile. "I'm sorry for the problem, Mr. Quinn. I'm just a delivery person and—"

"Delivery person," he mimicked unpleasantly. "God forbid you should be a plain old deliveryman. Into women's lib, huh?"

"Not deeply. I've yet to march on Congress. I won't keep you from your activities. Down here closing up the cabin? It's a lovely place."

"No, I live here, nosy. What's it to you?"

He pissed me off. I collared Fargo, which pisses *him* off, and makes him bare his teeth and look ferocious. "In fact, I was just wondering if you were in Provincetown on Halloween night, using one of your original table legs to beat up Lewis Schley."

"You a cop?"

"Private investigator. Well, were you?"

He treated us to a fierce grin. "I'm a *cop*. From Worcester. Or, I was a cop. Retired on disability. And, no, I haven't killed anybody. And, yes, I was in Ptown Halloween night for a few drinks and a look at the queers' parade."

"How did you know Schley was dead?"

"Think I done him, huh? Actually, it was in the paper, stupid. Now get off my back." He swung the table leg and laughed when Fargo and I backed up. "Don't be dodgy, I can be nice. Maybe I'll see you in the Harbor Bar some night, honey. Although"—he gave me a head-to-toe scan—"I bet you go for the girls, right?"

"Oh, yes. And if I ever have any doubts about continuing to go for the girls, I'll just think of you." I turned and dragged a snarling Fargo back to the car. I burned rubber on the way back to the highway. Bastard! Quinn reminded me of the type who liked rough sex with a young man and then swore how straight he was. He looked like he could give someone a beating just out of meanness. When I turned my list of Wood's customers over to Mitch later, I'd give Quinn a gold star. I stroked Fargo's wide, silky head and apologized. He accepted.

We struck out in Truro. Our first stop was at the house of Dr. W. James Lucia, as confirmed by a neat sign on the lawn. But the house was boarded up solid. There were no nearby neighbors to leave the leg with, so I tucked it behind the screen door and hoped it wouldn't be warped into a right angle by the time the doctor found it. I mentally crossed Dr. Lucia off my list. Not that doctors couldn't murder, just that I assumed he could think of a less athletic method.

We took a one-lane blacktop road up the hill overlooking the beach and found the house belonging to the Misses Jane and Flora Markham. It, too, was closed up, although two ill-fitting shutters gave me a view into the living room. The furniture was heavy 1940s Bauhaus, complete with those little crocheted doily things on the arms and backs. The women must be 1940s vintage themselves! Poison, maybe. Gun, possible. Table leg . . . nah. Propped leg on porch.

I stopped in Ptown's east end, where Mr. Leander lived in the ground floor of a two-family house. As I expected he was home and glad for company. He showed me his table in the kitchen. At least there was no broom handle. He'd propped the corner up on an end table plus two thick books. I screwed the new leg in for him and moved the end table back to the living room. He was embarrassingly grateful. Sweet man—a pleasure to do him a small favor.

I wasn't up to Rev. Bartles or even Aunt Mae. They would have to wait for tomorrow. PI Peres was dragging tail, and even the tireless Fargo was dozing on the car seat. We pulled gladly into *Chez Alex* and called it a day.

Aging improves wine. It does not help salad and it makes fried clams and French fries soggy, and running them through the micro didn't help. The big slab of pecan pie saved the day. I sat down on the couch and propped my feet up.

I had a lot to think about. So I went to sleep.

Chapter 15

My calendar said it was Friday. My mind said it was somewhere around Tuesday. Can you get jet lag driving around New England?

I pulled into Aunt Mae's driveway and was pleased, as always, by the view. She and Uncle Frank had bought their early 1800s salt-box home when they first married, and Aunt Mae still lived there. They had enjoyed maintaining it and always kept it a color of paint that had been available when it was built. These were rather deep shades of blue, yellow, red, green and even orange. White was apparently prohibitively expensive in those post-Colonial days, and pastels came later. Its latest color was barn red with white shutters and doors.

The house stood on a small rise with a large oak as guardian spirit and surrounded by some three acres that sloped away to Shank Painter Pond. A small cottage stood near the pond and the garage/herbal gift shop was positioned to face the town road.

I walked into Aunt Mae's kitchen, which still had the original fireplace, planning to surprise her with the missing table leg. Instead, it was I who was surprised, as I viewed the table, complete with four matching legs and not a broom handle in sight.

"Good morning, favorite aunt. What's this?" I asked. "I thought you were missing a leg here. I got this one from Wood's Woods yesterday. You starting a collection?"

"Of course not. One *was* missing. Sonny sawed off an old broom handle to prop it up for me. But then I got a real one."

And another broom handle bit the dust. "I see. I wonder why Wood didn't tell me? Why did he give me this one to bring to you?" I also wondered why nothing was ever simple.

"Oh. He didn't know I had one." Aunt Mae frowned. "That was thoughtless of me. I should have called and told him. Now I've put him and you to trouble. Oh, I *am* sorry, dear. But how did you come to get my—*a* table leg—from Mr. Wood?"

I explained the entire, by now thoroughly confusing, situation and she gave me a weak smile of understanding . . . or defeat.

"I see." She sighed. "I'll just have to take it back to him. I'll be going up that way at some point." She took the damned leg from me and propped it on the back porch. By now I never wanted to *see* another table leg, and Aunt Mae looked as if she agreed.

"Aunt Mae, I still don't understand. If you originally got only three legs, where the hell did you find a matching fourth?"

"Don't swear, dear. It was through Rev. Bartles, although, of course it was actually Jared Mather."

"Aunt Mae, I am missing something here. What the heck are you saying?"

She was pulling pies out of the refrigerator and putting them into some kind of cake box. Her voice was momentarily muffled, but I got the gist of it.

"It's quite simple, Alex. I took some soup over to Rev. and Mrs. Bartles for their bunch of homeless kids. I noticed their table was just like this one, but with four legs, so I told them my sad tale. Rev. Bartles said they had had the same experience."

She placed the boxes on the table, where I got the full aroma of their contents. I brought my attention back to legs with difficulty, as she continued. "They, too, had called Mr. Wood about getting only three legs, but no fourth leg was sent to them as promised, and there they were with a table propped up on an old rake handle." One broom handle saved, I thought.

"Then the reverend explained that Jared Mather had been there for some reason. He goes to their church sometimes, I think, although it doesn't seem his type. Anyway, Jared told Rev. Bartles to bring one of the legs out to his house—his shop—and he'd make him one just like it. So he did."

"Mather *made* Bartles a table leg? Just like that?"

"That's the way I understood it. Jared is terribly good at that sort of thing."

"Amazing. And he made you one the same way?"

"Not exactly. You see, when I saw Lawrence's—Rev. Bartles'—replacement, I decided to get Jared to make me one. He is a neighbor, and I've known him forever. I even dated him once or twice when I was a girl—he was as serious and solitary then as he is now. But quite the gentleman! No effort at all to get fresh. Rather dull, actually. Of course, then I met your Uncle Frank. Talk about opposites!" She gave a happy reminiscent laugh and brought herself back to the present.

"Anyway. I took one of the legs off my table and went over to Jared's. I told him my sad tale, and he said he'd be happy to make me one. About that time, I noticed what looked like a perfect copy of my table leg tossed on his scrap heap. I asked why I couldn't just have that one. He said it was his first attempt to make one for Lawrence and it wasn't quite right, that those little knobby things weren't spaced quite correctly, and that the piece of wood was flawed. I told him it looked fine to me, and the spot wouldn't show if I put that leg in the back."

I knew why it might have "looked fine" to Aunt Mae—she was very nearsighted, hated to wear her glasses and traveled a fair portion of life in a pleasant haze.

"Well, we had a little argument," she chuckled. "He's such a perfectionist! But I won. Finally Jared laughed and said all right. Anyhow, he picked it up and washed it off with some solvent. The flaw barely even showed. So I thanked him and took it along."

I glanced at the table and saw no difference in the legs. Any imperfection was hidden by the overhang of the tabletop, but then, I was probably not the perfectionist Jared was. "Well, I'll take Bartles his leg anyway, let him know Wood is on the up and up, even belatedly." And get a chance to talk to him, I added silently.

"Oh, if you're going over there you can do me a big favor, dear. Would you take over these two pies I baked for them? It would save me a trip."

"I dunno. Do I get a sample?"

She laughed and cut a slice from one of her already-cut cran-apple pies and poured me a cup of strong coffee. Fargo got the outer crust. We lived pretty good, we two.

I pulled into Bartles' parking area and looked in vain for his ancient, unmistakable van with *The Lord Will Always Help* stenciled crookedly on the side. I figured His help might indeed be all that held the venerable vehicle together. I hoped someone was around. I could leave the leg. I didn't know what to do with the pies. Well, actually I did know, but Aunt Mae would kill me.

Bartles came around the corner. He was a rather effete youngish man wearing a strained expression. "Good morning. May I help you?"

"Good morning. I'm Alex Peres. My aunt, Mrs. Cartwright, sent you these two pies, and here's a table leg from Wood's Woods, which I understand you don't really need."

"Ah." He smiled cordially now. "Mrs. Cartwright, a dear lady, and so generous to us! Her contributions of food are very welcome to us, in every way. And how good of you to make the deliveries."

"My pleasure. I happened to be in Wood's store yesterday, picked up Aunt Mae's replacement leg, plus yours and Mr. Leander's . . . if you know him? Here, I'll carry the leg in for you." I wasn't about to curtsy and drive away.

"Thank you. Come on around to the kitchen, if you don't mind. May I offer you coffee?"

"You're very kind. I'd enjoy a cup." God, I was beginning to sound like him. We went into a kitchen with dishes from breakfast stacked high in the sink, but basically clean. I wondered why part of a free breakfast didn't include helping with the washup. He finished clearing the table and we sat down to mugs of exceptionally good coffee. "The pies, by the way, are cran-apple, her specialty."

He rolled his eyes with pleasure. "Oh, we'll all enjoy them tonight! I do hope you're not delivering them because she's not feeling well." He made it a question.

"Oh, no. She's fine. I just happened to be there and saved her a trip. But I'm curious about your table, sir. Aunt Mae told me Jared Mather made you a replacement leg just sort of off the cuff. That sounds almost impossible, even for Jared."

"Not at all! He was here about a week ago and noticed my makeshift prop. I told him I was giving up hope that Wood would come through for me, and he insisted he could easily duplicate a leg. And, indeed, he did. We went out to his shop and he made a couple of measurements, picked out a piece of lumber and turned on his lathe. He insisted that his first attempt was imperfect in some way and made a second one. Totally unnecessary, as far as I could see. But I wasn't going to argue with the expert."

He glanced around at the loaded sink. "Anyway, thanks again for bringing the other one over. I'll call Wood and tell him I don't need it, in case he wants to pick it up." I think he was ready for the coffee klatch to end.

I wasn't. "You knew Lewis Schley, didn't you?"

Bartles had been treating me as if I were a distant but unquestioned member of the Royal Family. Now he looked at me as if I had delivered a ticking package with the words *Terrorists, Ltd.* featured prominently in the return address. "We-e-ell, I *guess* you could say I knew Lewis. He came here to visit a friend once or twice and stayed to eat. He paid generously for his meals. I talked him into staying for services once. I had hoped to know him better. He was in need of much help."

"I'm glad to hear he wasn't cadging meals. He had a well-paying job and a nice enough room over the garage where he worked—although he made pretty much a mess of it. So why did you think he needed help?"

"There are many kinds of help, Ms. Peres. The life Lewis was leading—"

"Oh, yes, of course. Now I follow you." I didn't want to get off on *that* tangent! "You know Lewis was on his way over here Saturday night—the night he was killed. In fact, I heard him say to a friend that he was going to get a meal at the Rev's. Would that have been surprising to you?"

"Not really. I think he enjoyed the friendly atmosphere around here. He could relax and just be young. I think Lewis tried to act much more sophisticated than he really was. The young people have fun around the table, as well as getting a decent meal. I don't preach at them with every mouthful, you know." He smiled dryly.

"As you know, he presumably never made it."

His reply was sharp and fast. "There was nothing presumable about it! Neither my wife nor I saw Lewis that night—nor since, obviously."

His wife! I had forgotten all about her. Where the hell was she and their toddler, a little girl, I thought. "Oh, yes, Mrs. Bartles. Aunt Mae thinks so highly of her," I fabricated without a qualm. "And your little one. I had hoped to meet them." I looked up at him and knew, as well as I knew it was Friday, that he was about to lie to me.

"Well, another time, I'm sure," he gushed. "Emmy's gone to the supermarket. Sometimes it seems to me one of us is *always* at the supermarket, ha ha. Well, she'll be sorry to have missed you, but I mustn't keep you." He walked to the door, so I really had no choice but to follow. He bowed and thanked me out and closed the door firmly.

As I walked past the garage I noticed a stack of freshly cut logs and, past them, a frost-nipped vegetable garden mulched with sawdust. I got in the car and sat for a moment. I turned to Fargo and scratched that special place on his ribs that makes him kick his back foot.

"Darling dog," I said, "yes, I saw the garden. Now . . . you and I know very little about children, but if you were a mother going grocery shopping, would you prefer to leave your two-year-old at home with daddy or drag her with you?" He wiggled, which may have been a shrug, but I took it as agreement to my own doubts. I started the car and we took what would be the normal route from the Rev's to the market. We did not pass the van headed home. We did not find it in the market parking lot.

Of course, she might have been anywhere, doing other errands or visiting a friend. But I didn't think so. I thought she was gone, as in packed up and gone. That would account for the piled-up dishes and for the lack of baby paraphernalia lying around the kitchen. Why had she gone, and where?

I pondered the possibilities as we headed for Beech Forest and a run. Maybe there had been illness or other emergency in her family. Maybe she just needed a break and was spending a few days with a relative or friend. But any of those would be a perfectly normal reason for her absence, and no reason for Bartles to lie.

Maybe they had a fight and she went home to Mums. That would be normal enough, too, actually. I assumed preachers and their spouses had occasional rows. And probably for the same reasons we all had. I had no reason in the world to think her absence had anything to do with Lewis. I really didn't. But I did. Maybe her body would turn up on Harmon's next driftwood hunt.

Obviously Fargo didn't intend to brood on it. The minute I pulled into the parking lot near the picnic area of the forest and opened his door, he spotted a browsing rabbit and took off. He was a hundred yards down the trail and barking joyously before I was out of the car. I didn't blame him for his joy. It was a lovely place to be this autumn day. Some of the copper leaves had fallen, but most were still attached, rustling in the light air like the skirts of an

Edwardian lady pacing her garden path. I shrugged and began to walk along the quiet way. I would catch up with him sooner or later.

It was later. Fargo circled the entire pond in happy pursuit of anything that moved. Finally, I simply sat on a concrete bench and nabbed him on his second lap.

Chapter 16

When I finally got home, there was a small package inside a supermarket bag tucked in the back screen door. It was beautifully wrapped in lavender flowered paper with a purple bow, and I knew what it was. Sure enough, it was the tape of Peter's performance, with a hand-painted label entitled *Peter Mellon Remembers Judy* and a photo of Peter in costume. I was delighted, and, when I opened the little card that accompanied it, touched. "Peter and Wolf will remember Alex with fondness and gratitude."

I reminded myself not to get too sentimental. Murderers, I had learned the hard way, did not always have little horns and cloven hooves to make the I.D. easier.

Maybe I'd run the tape tonight. Right now I had to go through a pile of mail so high it was about to spill off the desk, do a little bookkeeping and that sort of fun activity—almost, but not quite, as bad as housekeeping. I turned on MSNBC, more for background noise than any real hope of interesting news at this time of day.

151

I had made some inroads into the paperwork when a commercial penetrated my consciousness—some bank touting its "friendly" ATM service. How could an ATM be friendly, I wondered. Then I jumped. Friendly or not, I'd better get to the one at the bank. I was very nearly out of cash. It was also a good excuse to quit what I was doing. I took the car. I'd had enough walking pursuing the damn dog around miles of trail this morning. When I got to the bank parking lot, I saw that the ATM had a line—either it had eaten someone's card again or it was into its sulky mode, repeatedly flashing, "That is not a valid command." I went inside.

After I completed my brief business with a teller and turned to leave, I heard Mr. Ellis's fruity voice. "Alexandra, my dear, wait up and meet Cynthia Hart, our new Financial Services Manager."

I put on my official welcoming smile and turned to meet again the blonde, serious young woman I had last seen at Kudlow Securities in Providence. Instead, I faced a petite young woman with crisp dark curls and a wide mobile mouth beneath a nose that just missed being Roman, and brown eyes that were right up there with Fargo's for warmth and expression. My smile became quite genuine, as I realized that whomever I had teased in Kudlow's hallway, it had *not* been Cynthia Hart!

"Ms. Hart," Ellis continued, "meet Alexandra Peres, not only a valued client of our bank, but also an outstanding nature photographer, whose work we plan to exhibit in a few months. My dear"—he shook her hand warmly in both of his—"I have some calls backed up. If you will forgive me, I will say goodbye here, and I'll see you a week from Monday."

Cynthia and I stood, smiling at each other, but seemingly with nothing to say. Finally, I indicated the side door. "Are you parked out here?" She nodded, so I said, "Okay, I'll walk you out."

We got to my car first and Fargo stuck his head out the window. Cynthia reached out and began gently to scratch his cheek. His neck stretched and his nose went up in ecstasy. "Oh, yes, lovely boy, that's a great spot, isn't it?" she asked.

"Fargo, meet Cynthia."

"Oh, call me Cindy, please. Cynthia makes me think I'm back in school."

"Ah, then I can revert to Alex. Thank God we've cleared that hurdle. May I buy you a drink or coffee?"

"I'd love it. But right now, I'm on sort of a tight timetable, and Mr. Ellis is . . . well." She glanced at her watch. "I'm in kind of a bind," she said. "Perhaps you could help. I was hoping that today or certainly by tomorrow, I might locate—I guess an apartment, although I'd *dearly* love a cottage if it's not too expensive. I need a year-round rental. Am I in trouble? What would you say is my best bet? The paper? A realtor?" She ran out of breath.

I leaned against the fender, trying to come up with a helpful idea—and suddenly I wanted to be *very* helpful, indeed. "Year-round rentals are not always easy. You can make too much money just renting your property in the summer. However, I have a thought. My aunt has a cottage on her property. She said something recently about being sick of summer people. She's had a couple of bad experiences lately."

Fargo looked moonstruck. I tried not to. "Anyway, I know the cottage is in good repair. It has a good-sized living room, a kitchen, bedroom and another little room for a tiny bedroom or an office or whatever and—of course, a bathroom. Would that suit?"

"It sounds perfect. I wonder what she's asking?" By now Fargo had both front paws on the windowsill and was giving her face the occasional lap. How come the dog got all the perks?

"I don't even know if she's renting. But we could go ask. Do you want to leave your car here?"

"Oh, I'd be a little uneasy. Could I just follow you?"

She could and did and fortunately Aunt Mae was at home. I introduced them, explained who Cindy was, and took Fargo out in the yard to give them some privacy. Shortly, they walked across the yard from Aunt Mae's house, past her garage/herb shop and out to the cottage. About fifteen minutes later they came back to the house, both smiling broadly and Aunt Mae with folded check in hand.

As they neared me, Cindy grinned. "I believe you've met my landlady?"

"Frequently," I laughed. "Say, that's great! I'm sure you'll both be happy. Congratulations."

"Thank you so much for thinking of me, dear," Aunt Mae put in.

"A double-edged sword, favorite aunt. I don't want to see you again with a bunch of losers like you had last summer. Anyway, Cindy, are you going back tonight or staying over?" Was I perhaps formulating a plan? Cassie's advice was pounding in my head, and I felt that the curse was fading fast.

"Oh, going back, definitely. I've got a million things to do. I'm *pretty* well packed, I've been living out of boxes forever. And I've got everything ready to turn over to my replacement at Kudlow, but still . . ." She gave an embarrassed little moue. "Do you get the idea that I was really counting on this job?"

"Nothing wrong with being prepared," Aunt Mae murmured.

"Right," Cindy agreed. "But I'll still have quite a push to move down here by Wednesday or Thursday, and I really want to try, because I *would* like a few days to settle in before I start at Fishermen's a week from Monday." She turned and gave the cottage a little smile.

I was stunned. "How can you do that? Leave your job, get out of your apartment and get moved down here in five, six days?"

"Well, the people at Kudlow have known for some time I was looking, and my assistant will be taking over my job there. She's very sharp and up to speed. I told my landlord if I left without notice he could have the security. He's delirious. He'll rent that apartment the day after I leave. So there we are."

"Cindy, I hate to sound negative, but I really doubt you can line up a mover so quickly. They're usually booked weeks in advance." I spread my hands apart.

"Indeed they are. However, if you're the baby sister of the owners, they tend to make allowances."

Aunt Mae favored me with a wry smile. "It would seem,

Alexandra, that Cindy has things well organized. Perhaps you should simply, as the children say, butt out."

I glared at her, feeling rather foolish. "Well, yeah. Okay. Cindy, that leaves us with time for an early dinner. Keep up your strength for the drive back."

"Now that sounds good." She swung her purse over her shoulder, as if ready to march. "Somehow I missed lunch, and I'm starved. A real dinner sounds much better than a greasy burger all by myself somewhere en route. We'll go dutch of course."

"We'll go my treat. You've contributed enough to our family coffers for one day. Aunt Mae, is it okay if we leave Fargo and Cindy's car here?" I was edging into my smooth, suave Cary Grant role.

"Of course. Come on, sweet doggie, I'll give you a drink and a biscuit."

Cindy and I went over to the Sea Bounty. It was one of the better restaurants still open. We had no trouble getting a table so early. It could hardly be called the dinner hour. The waiter asked what we'd like to drink.

Cindy answered immediately. "I'll skip the drink, thank you, and have a glass of wine with dinner. I've got a drive ahead of me."

"Then I'll wait, too. Just bring a wine list along with the menus, please."

We both ordered clams casino to start. Cindy chose crab cakes with a yogurt and diced cucumber and dill sauce, plus saffron rice and a Caesar salad for an entree. I settled for my favorite, broiled sea scallops with curly fries, and sliced tomatoes and cucumbers with fresh basil and olive oil. I looked knowingly at the wine list and—blindly—picked a California Chardonnay I hoped would not disgrace me. Frankly, I like a nice claret with most any food, and know about as much about wines as I do the quantum theory. But nowadays one feels one should be an expert, so I do my best at least to act the part.

The waiter brought the wine and I went into my little charade. I pinched the cork for dampness—I knew not to sniff it. I rolled a bit of wine around in my mouth, swallowed and smacked my lips. "Yes, quite good, really. Elegance well offset by a touch of peasantry. Not overbearing, but a solid, reliable little wine."

The waiter's eyebrows made little half-moons above his eyes, and Cindy looked at me with polite interest. "Could I try a taste, too?"

The waiter pursed his lips and complied. She sniffed the glass, took a sip, swallowed and clicked her tongue several times. "Ah, from one of the less rainy years, I'd say. It has that slight astringent taste, doesn't it? But no bitterness, just a firm statement of presence. Well done, don't you think?" She looked at me straight-faced, and I had the feeling my jaw had dropped. The waiter had poured and left—either terribly impressed or resigned to dealing with lunatics.

I looked at Cindy closely. Her expression was bland but her eyes were dancing. "You rat!" I exclaimed. "You saw right through me, didn't you? My great secret is no more. You realize I'll have to shoot you after dinner? My reputation in this town is finished."

She gave a full-throated laugh. "Then you can't have much of a reputation! Sorry, I just couldn't resist. You were so serious. But I had seen you do just what I do. You checked the cheapest and the most expensive, went about halfway between, crossed your fingers and ordered. My knowledge of wines is bounded by red and white. How about you?"

"Mainly I just settle for claret," I answered glumly.

"Good, we'll stick with that in future. Much less effort." I could no more not have smiled back than I could have quit breathing. And I liked that remark about the future.

Dinner was good. We enjoyed the food and each other. I managed to regain a little ground when Cindy remarked on what a sweet dog Fargo seemed.

"Strange," I answered, "I had you for more of a cat person, maybe wounded cats or even a baby goose."

She peered at me sharply but made no comment.

"In fact," I continued, "I visualize you as a sort of tree-hugger at heart. I can just see you tied to a lovely old tree, daring the authorities to cut it down."

"Okay. How do you know all this? This can no way be considered coincidence. Do you know one of my brothers or something?"

I decided the joke had gone far enough. "No. In point of fact, I'm a private investigator. Sometimes I do a little rundown on people for possible employers. Several people, including you, were on Ellis's short list for the job at the bank. He wanted a background check that covered more than just your resumé, so I took a little swing around three states the beginning of the week and gave him a report on the people he was interested in. Obviously, you were the front runner."

"So now you know all my secrets." She smiled but didn't sound entirely happy. "Did you tell Mr. Ellis about the cat?"

"All I knew of it. What really happened?"

She gave a rueful grin. "There I was, minding my own business, driving home, when the car in front of me clipped a little half-grown cat. Either unaware or uncaring, the driver didn't stop. Well, of course I did, I put the poor dazed thing in the car and hied off toward a veterinary clinic about a mile up the road."

I poured us both a small dividend of wine. "And at what speed were you traveling, ma'am?"

"At a damn good speed, thank you, and I ran a yellow light to boot. Next thing I know, red lights were flashing behind me and a cop pulled me over. When he walked up to my window I told him I was taking an injured animal to the vet's, that as soon as I got care for the cat, I'd be happy to speak with him. I figured there was no time to lose and away I went. He just stood in the road looking after me. As the vet was placing the cat on the examining table, the cop flew in—super pissed—and wrote me up for everything but kidnapping the cat, probably only because he didn't think of it."

I was leaning back in my chair, laughing aloud by now. I wiped my eyes with my napkin. "So you had to go to court?"

"Oh, indeed. My father wanted to send a lawyer with me, but I figured the truth ought to do it. I admitted running the light and speeding and said I would pay any necessary fines. I insisted I was not driving recklessly and certainly did not endanger the officer's life—I never told him to stand in the middle of the road like a traffic cone. I definitely had not resisted arrest—I told him exactly where I was going and why. And I had not left the scene of an accident because it wasn't my accident in the first place. And the defense rested."

I shook my head in admiration. "You may be in the wrong business," I suggested. "You'd make a great lawyer."

"Could be," she agreed. "At any rate the judge dropped the charges since I was 'on an errand of mercy where timeliness was of great importance.' I was feeling pretty good, but then he lectured me in this superior, drippy voice. 'In the future, if something like this should happen, Ms. Hart, please try to exercise restraint. After all, in your zeal to assist an animal, you could have injured a person, and I'm sure you realize a person is more important than a cat, do you not?'"

"Condescending old fuddle, wasn't he?" I noted with a frown.

"You bet, and I wasn't about to stand still for it. I said, 'Your Honor, I can't answer such a hypothetical question. I would have to know both the person and the cat.' And the fusty old coot fined me fifty dollars for contempt of court."

I let out a laugh that had heads turning in the dining room. "You'll have to tell this all to Ellis. He'll love it. He has two Siamese of his own. I must say, between tying yourself to trees and rescuing animals, you've lived quite a life of crime."

I got a very knowing look in answer. "So you met Mimi Trinler. Isn't she a lovely woman?"

"Er, yes. Yes, lovely." I felt hot, and was sure my face went bright red.

Cindy flashed a wide-eyed look of innocence. "I think half the females in school were in love with her. Lord knows I was. I used to have really wild fantasies about her."

158

"Indeed?" I flashed a cool, Cary Grant smile. "Did anyone ever manage to make it with her?"

"Not that I know of. She lives with a sizable music professor, who would probably throw her piano at anyone who got within ten feet of her Mimi." She added casually, "Did you get to spend much time with her?"

I felt my face heat up again. "No, very little. I was on a tight schedule. On my way to Norwalk to check out another applicant," I said in what I hoped was a professional manner.

I guess Cindy decided she had tortured me long enough. I was certain she knew exactly what my reaction to Dean Trinler had been, right down to the blue quilt.

She asked, "So when do I find out about *your* secrets?"

"I don't think there are many, just ask anybody in town. I've been here forever."

"I may do just that. I've been thinking"—she changed the sub-ject—"Ellis didn't waste any time, did he? He called me yesterday afternoon to see if I could come up today. He offered me the job right away and wanted me here pronto. Any reason you know of?"

"Not especially. I know your new department is his pet project. He feels the bank waited too long to offer your type of expertise, and I guess he's making up for lost time."

"Makes sense. A private investigator," she said again. "And what sort of things do you investigate besides employee profiles?" She sipped her wine.

I was pleased at her reaction to my saying I was a PI. I don't usually tell that to people I don't know well. For some reason they invariably think it's either hilarious or sleazy—and either reaction annoys me. "I don't really have a specialty. I investigate a lot of per-sonal injury claims on-season, chase down people named in wills, handle some other insurance frauds, and—when I'm broke—divorce grounds."

"It sounds fascinating." I looked at her and realized she meant it. For some reason, I felt really good about that. She leaned forward now, relaxed, elbows on table. "Are you investigating anything exciting now—that you can talk about?"

"In a left-handed sort of way," I conceded. I told her a little of Schley's murder and its aftermath.

"Wow. I never realized—I guess I never thought—how investigations actually work. I do hope you can clear the two old dears. They sound innocent as lambs to me."

"I hope so, too. I'm getting quite fond of them, which may be a mistake. And don't make them pearly white. They *do* provide pretty, compliant houseboys for their inn guests."

She shrugged. "Better than their bringing in unknowns off the street, isn't it? Boys will be boys."

And then I did it. I reached for my wineglass and knocked it over, liquid spreading across the tablecloth at amazing speed. We both grabbed our napkins. The waiter came running. It only took seconds to get everything under control, but I was mortified. I had ruined everything. Cindy started to make a jocose comment, saw my face and backtracked. "Alex! Are you all right? Are you ill?"

"No." I sighed and explained my saga of the witch's curse and its following slips and falls, spills and breaks. "I'm at the point of looking over my shoulder to see if she's behind me," I finished.

She reached across and took my hand. "You poor dear. I know sort of how you feel. When I was a little kid, I decided our house was haunted and became terrified to go upstairs. One day I turned and ran back down the stairs so fast, I fell and got a really nasty bump on my forehead." I took a cautious sip of coffee as she continued.

"The next day the lady who helped Mom take care of the house came, and I told her of my accident. She said, 'Honey, now we know there's no such thing as ghosts. So they can't hurt you, but they can sure make you hurt yourself. So you got to not give 'em that power.'"

I looked at her quizzically, and she patted my hand and laughed. "I know—there's a dichotomy in there someplace, but it's also true. An old lady curses you, and afterwards a couple of odd things

160

happen. You start *looking* for odd things, and you get tense and apprehensive, so you *make* them happen. There . . . your curse is gone! And we'd better do the same, it's getting late."

"Thanks for being understanding," I said as we left the restaurant. "Between you and my mother, I really do feel better." I told her of mom's "exorcism" and she laughed.

"I think I'd like your mom."

"Me, too." As we drove back to Aunt Mae's for Cindy's car, I thought again of Cassie's lecture to me about being more assertive with women. That I should just go for it instead of waiting for the lady to make it crystal clear that she *wanted* me to go for it.

When we pulled in the drive, I cut the lights and put my arm across the back of her seat. "Look, Cindy, Providence is a long drive, and you've had a couple of glasses of wine. We could go back to my place and—"

She put two fingers across my mouth. "Shush. I am cold sober—with miles to go before I sleep. I'm fine. It was all lovely. We don't need to push it. Anyway"—she grinned—"I never date on the first kiss." She gave me a warm, soft kiss on the mouth—more than friendship, less than passion. She got out of the car. I sat there, feeling completely bewitched in the loveliest of ways.

Aunt Mae's porch light went on and Fargo came running across the yard. Cindy held the door open for him and he jumped into the front seat. She reached in and kissed his head. "Take care of her, Fargo. The world needs its wine experts."

I started the car, beeped a general goodnight and pulled out of the drive. "The hell with Cassie, Fargo, we're doing okay as we are. We got a goodnight kiss, didn't we?"

He gave me a toothy grin and slurped my hand on the wheel. Now I had two kisses. Hard to beat.

Chapter 17

For some reason I felt quite energized after our outing, and in entirely too good a mood to go home and attack the mail again, or to flop in front of the tube and hope the History Channel wasn't once more exploring the pyramids. I bribed Fargo with the promise of a hamburger for him and stopped in the Wharf Rat, which some snide acquaintances have dubbed my "other office." The Rat was busy this Friday evening, with the regulars, including Harmon of course, at their front table. He gave me a dirty look as I came in and I made a mental note to make my peace with him before the evening was out.

At that moment, I heard a "Yoohoo, Alex!" float musically across the room. It was Peter Mellon. He and Wolf were having dinner. I walked over and thanked them for the tape. They asked if anything was new, but I wasn't really in the mood right that minute to get involved with my nursery rhyme tale of dancing table legs that seemed to be multiplying like rabbits.

"I've managed to look at a few things. All rather in your favor, but I'm tired and you're in the middle of dinner. How about around ten tomorrow?"

"Fine," Peter said. "Come for breakfast." I agreed.

On the way back to the bar, I stopped by Harmon's table. "Harmon, I think you're a little peeved with me, and I don't much blame you. I shouldn't have teased you about anything so serious as murder. I'm sorry."

He gave me a skewed grin, and when he spoke the fumes were thick enough to make smoking dangerous. "Oh, thass okay, Alex. I know you was jus' fooling. I sure had Mitch goin' though. He couldn't seem to figure what I was talking about. Went round and round we did." He laughed in a happy alcoholic memory. "I ain't mad, Alex. You'n Sonny, you're okay. Shay, where is Shonny . . . Sonny? I ain't seen him."

"He's on vacation."

"No time fer that. We got bad things happening here. Bad things."

"He'll be home soon. I'll let you get back to your friends, Harmon."

At the bar, I almost ordered a beer, thought of a bourbon and finally asked for a stinger. I felt like something special. Joe presented me with one that was surprisingly smooth and oh, so innocent in its taste. I was just savoring it, when a voice behind me said, "Drinking a love potion? Waiting for a lovely lady? Or just being uptown?"

It was Cassie, smelling lightly of shrimp scampi. "Not waiting," I answered. "I already spent the afternoon with the lovely lady. And, no, you don't know her. And, no, I am not going to explain. It would be premature," I said regally. "Uptown? Why not? This place could use a little class. Between your breath and Harmon's I may need oxygen. How are you?"

"Fine. Gotta go pick up Lainey. She had to work late and her car's in the shop. Sorry to run."

"You're forgiven. By the way, let's have no more about my being more assertive with women. Those of us with a little *savoir faire* don't need to come on like Jackie Chan at a drug bust to impress a lady. A well-mannered, smooth approach does the trick with the more sophisticated type female." I went to take an elegant little finger-crooked sip of my drink and poured a bit down my sweater, but I think I still carried it off.

Cassie rolled her eyes and said, "Sure, Agent Oh-Oh-Seven, whatever gets you through the night. Bye."

I turned back to the bar, grinning, and lit a cigarette. Number six for the day, so I scolded myself roundly. It was the perfect partner to the stinger, especially as another glass took that moment to arrive in front of me. "Compliments of Peter and the Wolf," Joe said. I turned to thank them, but they were just going out the door. Facing that way, I noticed Jared Mather at the end of the bar in his regular place. As usual, he elected not to see me, and I felt no need to greet him. I turned back to my drink and began happily to relive the afternoon.

I heard a familiar loud, nasal voice call out, "Well, now, if it isn't Jared Mather!" It was my old nemesis, Ben Fratos, but at least I wasn't eating, and at least he was about to sit down beside Mather, not me. Still, my happy reverie dissipated.

Mather gave a curt nod and stared at Fratos with a look that would have frozen lava. Fratos muttered something about seeing him later and veered off to join Harmon and the others at Provincetown's answer to the Round Table, so I finished my drink in peace. I felt guilty ordering a third and figured I would shortly be right up there with Harmon. But I was enjoying myself. I had the feeling that Cindy might well turn out to be more than my aunt's tenant. I found myself hoping so, more than I would have thought.

Yet I was leery of any involvement anytime, and now was no different, in spite of Cindy's obvious appeal. My track record was hardly reassuring, and while I longed for togetherness, I lived in terror of suffocation. As my relationships went on, breathing room disappeared. I retreated into an emotional vacuum rather than ask for a window to be opened. And the chill eventually permeated the bed . . . and there you were. In avoiding what might have been a simple, reasonable conversation, I landed in the midst of a heart-rending or rip-roaring breakup every damn time.

I was not entirely sure why. A friend who was a therapist had once mentioned to me that many people who lose a parent at an early age fear abandonment later. Maybe I was afraid any confrontation would result in that. But, of course, avoiding the confrontation had the same result. Apparently when I got around to *cherchez la femme*, I turned into one of those dismal creatures who do the same thing over and over, blissfully hoping for a different result.

What to do now? Not having another stinger seemed a good idea. When I collected Fargo, I noticed that Mather and Fratos had left before me and were standing at the top of the alley near the street. I guessed Mather hadn't wanted his cocktail hour to be interrupted by Fratos, but then found himself cornered on the way out. I wondered what gossip the slimy Fratos could have that would interest the upright Mather. But mainly, I just wondered how soon I could get home. P.I. Peres was finally ready to pack it in.

Fargo and I completed our individual pre-bed routines quickly. He wolfed down his hamburger and we retired. I was so beat I didn't even turn on CNN for my nightly update. I was just reaching that marvelous space between sleeping and waking, when I realized with surprise—but maybe not all that much surprise—that Cindy had eased quietly into my bed.

I put my arm around her and realized she was in the nude, and I stroked her smooth, lithe body with drowsy sensuality increased by the sweet butterfly kisses she placed on my ear. My hand moved to her breast, rubbing the nipple, feeling it become rigid, feeling her turn, pressing harder against my hand. I moved my head so I could kiss her mouth and found her tongue already poised for the meeting. My drowsiness disappeared in a flood of hot excitement. My hand traveled downward, stopping here and there for an

exploratory caress, but inexorably bound for that soft, warm enclo-
sure I knew my fingers would find.

"Excuse me," the voice came from behind me, beside the bed.

I flipped onto my back, propping on an elbow. "Who the
hell . . . oh, I know you!"

It was that damned blonde from Kudlow's!

"I'm sorry to bother you, but I need to ask Cindy about the
Wexford account."

"How dare you sneak into my bedroom in the middle of the
night!" I roared. "Screw the Whoozits account! Get a life. Bugger
off, slug!"

"Right on!" Cindy barked.

Cindy barked?

I managed to get my eyes open and found I was sitting up looking at a very worried Fargo at the foot of the bed. I glanced to my
left—no chubby blonde stood there. I looked to my right—the
sheets were smooth, the pillow undented. I rubbed my eyes and
groaned. Fargo had apparently decided that either I had gone
crazy or we had been invaded by things he could not see. He
barked again.

"Oh, shut up. Everything is all right." He looked hurt and slithered off the bed, headed for the kitchen. I sat there for a minute—
confused, highly frustrated and actually embarrassed. I sighed, got
up and pulled a sweatshirt over my pajamas, slipped into a pair of
mocs and followed him.

I let him out and noticed the coffeemaker held some liquid—
probably brewed during the War of the Roses. I poured it into a
mug and shoved it in the micro. By the time he whimpered to
come in I'd had a sip of it and it wasn't too bad. At least it settled
me slightly. I gave him a hug and was forgiven. Why can't women
be like Fargo?

He put his head on my thigh. I stroked him gently and
explained, "It's like this, angel dog. In the past week I have met
three very attractive women. The first one I figured I had a very
good shot of separating from Lainey and Cassie's party and bring-

ing here for a lively romp. But that ended in the shoelace caper. The second was Dean . . . was Mimi Trinler. I was in the midst of a fabulous fantasy, which she interrupted by presenting me with a computer printout and, I think, reading my mind. The third, as you know, was a wonderfully realistic Cindy-dream turned into something by Monty Python. Put it this way—I can't get laid when I'm awake, I can't get laid in my imagination, I can't get laid in my dreams. I am doomed."

He gave my hand a cursory lick, lay down in his bed and was asleep in ten seconds. Neutering does have certain advantages.

Saturday morning, between the stingers, the esoteric dream and the midnight caffeine, I felt exactly like you'd figure I did. But Fargo cajoled me into a beach run out at Race Point, and we worked up a nice appetite for breakfast. It was definitely fall—the sun still held a tentative warmth, but a chill was sneaking in around the edges. The ocean was that almost royal blue and the sky a pale reflection . . . autumn. I began to recuperate. I made a mental note to watch the booze. I didn't want too much of my father's black humor, and I certainly didn't need his hangovers.

When we arrived later at Green Mansions, Peter met us at the door. Pewter took one look at Fargo, yawned and retired to the kitchen. Wolf called hello from there and said he'd be out in a minute. Peter and I sat and batted the weather around until Wolf stuck his head out. "You said the news was good. Orange juice or champagne cocktail?"

"I don't know if it's *that* good, and I would love champagne, but I think orange juice is a safer way to begin the day."

I told them of my last days' activities while we drank. Conversation took a hiatus when Wolf brought out scrambled eggs with bleu cheese, Smithfield ham and popovers with black cherry preserves. Sometimes I really wish I could cook.

Finally, over coffee, Wolf asked what my conclusions were. "Well," I summed up, "we have enough pine legs to put Robert

Louis Stevenson and Herman Melville out of business. I'll turn the list of names over to Mitch to finish checking out, but we have at least seven people in this area who had—or say they had—missing table legs. Any one of them could be lying. Of the ones I spoke with, a nasty character named Quinn and the Reverend Bartles seem only real bets. Quinn looks like he could go for rough trade, and Bartles lied to me . . . I just know it."

"So what should we do?" Peter asked.

"Nothing. We haven't proved a thing. We've just muddied the waters. But it does make it more plausible that you, too, had a missing leg—not that you used it for a weapon and then tossed it or burned it. And it makes it *possible* that one of those people got four perfectly good legs and used one to kill Lewis. And there is one other thing . . . identifying that SUV—or van—that Harmon saw."

"I hear he's been all over town saying he's now sure I'm the killer." Wolf sighed. "Because he's sure it was our SUV he saw late that night."

I reached and patted his knee. "Wolf, I'd hate like hell to be a lawyer knowing my case depended on Harmon's testimony about anything, especially something he saw at four in the morning. I'm surprised he didn't swear your vee-hicle was pink with big ears. Seriously, anybody might mistake a van for an SUV—or vice versa—in the middle of a rainy night, when it has just almost run you off the road at high speed. That doubles the possibilities right there." I sipped my coffee and returned the cup very carefully to the table.

"Now, just from memory. Choate Ellis has a white one and Jared Mather has a cream one. Diane Miller has a light green van that could be mistaken for tan in a bad light. Bartles himself has a light-colored van. Also, the famous Mary Sloan has a tan Santa Fe."

"Oh, delightful! Have her arrested on general principles." Wolf grinned.

"There you go. If need be, I'll ask Nacho to check registrations around the area. Five gets you ten she turns up at least a dozen.

And I'll bet not more than three of them could prove they weren't on Race Point Road. Mitch doesn't have a leg to stand on."

As I completed that reassuring statement, Mitch rang the doorbell, standing firmly on both legs. He was accompanied by Jeanine and Pete, both in full uniform with all the accoutrements. Somehow I knew they were not collecting for the Police Athletic League.

"May we come in, Mr. Wolfman? Mr. Mellon?"

I don't know who would have refused them. Wolf and Peter both nodded and retired to the couch. Mitch headed for the piano bench, I re-took my chair. Ominously Pete and Jeanine stopped behind the couch and stood there.

"Mr. Wolfman, Mr. Mellon, I need to ask some questions. Alex, this doesn't concern you, if you'd like to leave." Well, thank you, Mitch!

"We would like her to stay, detective. She is our advisor and friend. I think we need a friend here, don't you?" Peter still had claws and they were out. I looked at Mitch and grinned. He ignored me.

"Very well. Gentlemen, where were you last night, from eight p.m. till two a.m.?"

"Here we go again." Wolf sighed. "About seven-thirty we went to the Wharf Rat for dinner—in view of at least a dozen people we know. We left around nine and came home. We watched most of a movie on TCM. I can tell you all about it if you wish."

"Perhaps later, thank you," Mitch continued quietly. "Did you encounter Mr. Benjamin Fratos at the Rat?"

They both thought a moment and then looked at each other, as if deciding who would answer. Peter said, "Not *at* the Rat. Walking home, we passed him walking *toward* the Rat. His car was parked across the street from our place."

"Did you encounter Mr. Harmon Killingworth at the Rat?"

"Who? Oh, Harmon, yes, he was there, drunk as a lord."

"Was he still there when you left?"

Peter looked questioningly at Wolf before he answered. "I'm sorry, I don't recall. Wolf? Did you notice him?"

"Yes." Wolf gulped at his cocktail. "Yes, I remember, he was there."

"Did you steal Mr. Killingworth's truck?"

"Mitch!" I exploded. "Have you lost it completely? The other day you insinuated prostitution. You've practically accused them of murder and now you're trying *grand theft auto?* Nobody in the *world* is desperate enough to steal that old death trap. Don't say another word, guys, either he's crazy or it's a very un-funny joke."

"Shut up, Alex, or I'll book you for obstruction." What on earth had gotten into this nice young man? Focus was one thing—obsession was another.

"You can book me for grand treason," I snapped. "I still advise them not to say another word without a lawyer. The mood you're in, you'd call it a confession if they said the Lord's Prayer."

He looked hurt for a minute, before he put his tough face back on. It gave me hope he was still in there somewhere. "All right," he said. "If you don't want questions, I'll give you answers. Some I know, some I am pretty sure of." He yanked out his notebook and started making that noise with his tongue again. I didn't like it any better this time.

"I know that about eleven last night, Harmon rolled into the police station, wailing that somebody had stolen his truck from in front of the Rat. Sergeant Juvenal was in charge and, like all of Ptown, he knows Harmon always leaves the keys in. So, Juvenal figured one of two things happened. Either Harmon forgot where he parked the truck, or some kids swiped it and we'd find it in some silly spot come daylight. So he did exactly what I would have done—sent him home in a squad car and told him we'd find it."

Wolf and Peter were leaning forward, as if enrapt by an ancient storyteller. "Now, around three," Mitch continued, "Harmon got up to . . . er, relieve himself. At that time, Juvenal received a hysterical phone call from him. The truck was now in his yard. There was a bloody tire iron in the back that wasn't his and the truck bed was covered in blood. They got me up and I went over."

"What did you find, a gallon of ketchup?" I chortled.

170

"No. I found an old tarp in the back of the truck with considerable blood, and I found a tire iron with the business end caked in blood, hair and brain matter."

"Jesus," I breathed. "Was there a body? Who . . . ?"

"No body at Harmon's, but on a hunch I drove out to the amphitheater. There he was, laid out just like Schley . . . Ben Fratos."

I sagged in relief. "My God," I said. "Half the town would as soon see *him* dead. He spies on everybody. I swear he's a voyeur, he's got a brutal temper—he tried to break my jaw over nothing the other day. You'll be hard put to find six pallbearers for Ben Fratos." Wolf looked white and sick, but Peter was sitting straight and alert, not missing a word. I was beginning to change my mind about who had the real strength in that couple.

Mitch nodded. "I agree, Alex. You might like to know I recommended his private investigator's license be revoked last year. But he's an ex-cop and Anders wouldn't back me with the chief. Anyway, he has been brutally murdered and I have a job to do."

"Were there prints on the tire iron?" I asked. "Do you have any *real* evidence, Mitch?" I realized too late that my voice sounded condescending, not guaranteed to make Mitch more helpful.

"The evidence is a police matter, Alex, but here's what I think happened. Last night, Wolf, I think you and Peter ran into Fratos as you walked home—I'll even say he was waiting for you. He told you he knew something about the Schley murder that would incriminate you. He may have told you he was going to the police with it. More likely, I think he told you that for money, he *wouldn't* go to the police with it. Blackmail would not surprise me. I think you lured him to your garage, telling him your safe or your cash was hidden there. I think one of you picked up the tire iron and killed him."

It sounded too damned logical to reassure Wolf, Peter or me. We all looked at each other and then looked back to Mitch as he resumed his narrative.

"Then one of you remembered Harmon's nearby truck and

171

stole it and brought it to your house. You loaded Fratos in the rear, and late at night you drove him to the amphitheater, laid him out like Schley, took Harmon's truck home and left it. Complete with the tire iron from your garage."

I couldn't let him sound so sure. "Mitch, this is highly circum—"

"Oh, I forgot one thing," he interrupted. "I found this stuck in the brace of the tailgate. It was apparently used to wipe finger-prints from the murder weapon." Mitch took out a clear plastic bag with a man's handkerchief in it. It was stained with what looked like blood and perhaps oil and in the corner were the ini-tials *FW.* "Is this your handkerchief?" Mitch asked Wolf, holding out the bag.

Wolf took it gingerly and grimaced. Before I could say any-thing, he answered, "Well, I guess so. It looks like it. I've got about a dozen of them. They were a Christmas gift from Bobby Helms last year," he added, as if that explained everything.

"Have you any idea how it got into the truck?"

I had to intercede here. "Be quiet, Wolf. Mitch, I have no desire to impede your finding the killer. I hope you *do* find him—or her—Lord knows there are women in this town with plenty of reason to bash Fratos. But I do not think this interview should continue without a lawyer. I'll stop down later. I have some information you may find useful. Right now, I think you should go."

"You may be right." Mitch stood and for some reason we all stood with him. "Frank Wolfman, I arrest you for the murders, and Peter Mellon, I arrest you as an accessory to the murders, of Lewis Schley and Benjamin Fratos." He nodded to Jeanine and Pete. "Read them their rights and cuff them."

Wolf looked like he was going to collapse, but Peter was straight as a board. "Detective, please, handcuffs are not necessary. Neither of us would humiliate ourselves by trying to run. Alex, would you kindly call John Frost, I guess he's about the best crim-inal lawyer in town. And one big favor." He reached back to the couch and stroked the gray blob huddled there. "Would you please take Pewter to the vet and have him board her? Her carrier is in

172

the pantry. She'll be terribly upset." For the first time his voice broke. He turned and walked out the door, Jeanine lightly holding his arm.

They left, Mitch bringing up the rear like the sergeant of a sad platoon. I said *Shit!* loudly and Fargo looked at me in alarm. "Not you, sweetheart, just everybody else."

I called Frost. He was out, of course. I left a detailed message with his secretary, and she assured me he would contact Peter and Wolf as soon as he could. I found the pantry and took the cat carrier into the living room. I went back to the kitchen, stuffed our breakfast dishes into the dishwasher and hit "rinse and hold," wondering just how long "hold" might be. I turned the thermostat to fifty, put on a hall light and figured that was about all I could do.

Back in the living room I spotted Pewter, sitting in front of the door, staring fixedly at the doorknob, waiting for it to turn at Wolf's or Peter's hand. My eyes smarted badly and I yelled *Shit!* again. I took the carrier back to the pantry and stuffed it with cat food. Struggling, I picked up Pewter under the other arm—the damned tub must weigh thirty pounds! I managed to open the door, very nearly locked Fargo inside and finally made it to the car. Panting and swearing, I dumped Pewter and the carrier in back and let Fargo in front.

We made the surprisingly lengthy drive home with Pewter yowling piteously and Fargo barking threats at the windshield. Well, damn, what the hell else could I have done?

Chapter 18

Pewter had to explore the house inch by inch, with Fargo's nose about three inches behind her tail all the way. That chore finished, she went and sat by the back door and cried, and Fargo sat close beside her, whining in some apparent gesture of canine support. Figuring one or both might be feeling a call of nature, I went out with them. I was right on both counts. Technically, I knew Pewter could go over the fence; I just hoped she was too fat to try.

Then, kindly animal-person that I am, I opened food, freshened water and uncapped a Sprite for me. I reached the living room and just had the can tilted as great yowls and spits and growls and shrieks issued from the kitchen. Going on the happy assumption it was all talk, I sat down and took a mighty swig. They both immediately came into the living room and lay down amiably on the rug. It's hard to produce high drama when your audience is yawning. I know—I've tried it.

We had enough real drama. I felt tremendous sympathy for Wolf and Peter, even if they weren't guilty. Lord knows their lives would never be the same, no matter what the outcome. I went over the latest events in my mind.

That Ben Fratos was capable of blackmail was a given. If he knew, or thought he knew, anything damaging against Peter and the Wolf, he might well have tried it. But if Wolf and Peter were innocent of his accusations, I couldn't believe they were too dumb not to string him along until they could reach me and get some advice on what to do.

The tire iron was generic and might have belonged to anyone who'd ever had a car or truck. But the handkerchief was not. The initials were damning, and Wolf had virtually admitted it was his. It was easy to see why they might have killed Fratos. But Lewis was less clear.

Yes, he had disappointed them, inconvenienced them, hurt their feelings. But we've all had those things happen to us. If we all killed over it, you could shoot skeet in downtown Boston. Still, Lewis had damaged a much-loved heirloom and humiliated Peter in the so-called fight. Two dangerous things to do—no one likes others to be careless of their valuables, and no one—gay or straight—likes to be shamed in a fight. Despite the fact that Wolf was under arrest for the actual murder, I thought Peter the more likely candidate. I could see him getting even for many real and presumed wrongs with every blow he struck.

I knew Lewis was the key. Fratos was just an afterthought, whoever did it.

And I knew I had to do something or Pewter was mine for life. Maybe I'd try Bartles again. He was hiding something; the question was whether it mattered.

I mulled this over as I had another soda and a cheese sandwich, carefully watched by Fargo and Pewter. Apparently—obviously—she was used to tidbits. I shared. I freshened up and picked up the car keys. Not wanting to leave Pewter alone, I told Fargo he couldn't go. This resulted in a grand display of groveling and keening on his part and sympathetic mewing on Pewter's. I slammed the door on this opera and left, not in a charitable mood.

My first stop was the police station, to give Mitch my list of "legless" customers of Wood's Woods. He listened to my theory and agreed it had merit. He agreed to check out the people I had missed and look further into ex-cop Quinn. He also agreed to check on *vee*-hicles similar to Wolf's and Peter's. But I knew it would be perfunctory. In his mind he had the "doers" back in two cells of the jail. I asked to see them but was told they were currently "being processed." I was getting just a bit tired of Super Cop.

As I left, Jeanine pulled me aside. She was a buxom young woman in her thirties, married, with a couple of kids, and the epitome of kindness. She was also strong as an ox and had no compulsion about tossing an ornery drunk onto his backside and headfirst against a wall. She said softly that she had spoken with Wolf and Peter and agreed to bring them any personal items they needed. I explained about the cat, and she offered to tell them Pewter was with me. She was sure it would cheer them up.

She cheered *me* up, and I moved on to Bartles in a somewhat better frame of mind. The day was warm and sunny, and I guess that helped. Once again, the van was not in evidence, but I went around back and, once again, found the Rev. Bartles up to his elbows in dishwater.

"Well, hello," I said from the doorway. "Aren't you the diligent homemaker!" He nodded and turned back to his chore.

"Here, I'll dry." I picked up a towel and went to work, which earned me a small, grateful smile. We worked in companionable silence for a few minutes, before I asked the obvious question. "Well, Lawrence—if I may be informal—why did she leave you?"

He kept his head down so he didn't have to meet my eyes and turned on his plummy voice. "Bless her! She's just worn out with all our endeavors—plus the baby. I insisted she accept an invitation from an old college chum. Do her a world of good!"

"Can it, Lawrence! Where did she really go? Home to mother? Why? Did you abuse her? Abuse the baby? Cheat on her? Did she cheat on you?"

He carefully put a plate in the rack, took the dishtowel from me and wiped his hands. "Come and sit down, Ms . . . Alex. It's a crazy situation." He poured coffee into two mugs I had just dried and sat down. He took a deep breath, let it out in a puff. "Emmy is at her mother's. She really is tired. We have not broken up, and nothing is seriously wrong. Our marriage is fine."

"I'm glad to hear it. So what *isn't* fine?"

"We did have a row. Over money." He grinned sheepishly.

I laughed. It had cost him something to say that. I guess sometimes even preachers can need someone to talk to. "At least it's normal."

"Yes and no," he said. "Sunday when I went into the chapel to get ready for services, I noticed a thick envelope on the floor, pushed through the old mail slot in the door." He stood up and left the room for a moment, returning with a cheap white envelope, stuffed about to capacity. "Here."

It was full of money. Trying to touch both the envelope and its contents as little as possible, I eased the money and a sheet of writing paper out onto the table. "Did you count this?" I asked.

"Yes. There's three hundred seventy dollars there."

I gently pushed the money aside and unfolded the paper. The note was formed by letters cut from magazines and glued to the paper. The letters were in various sizes and colors, but the message was easy enough to read: THIS IS DIRTY MONEY CLEANSE IT IN THE SERVICE OF THE LORD AMEN. I looked questioningly at Bartles. He shook his head. "I have no more idea than you what it means or who sent . . . delivered it."

"And you and Emmy fought because . . ."

"We need so many things for the Mission. That kind of money looks like a million to us! I wanted to keep it and use it. She felt that someone had had a crisis of conscience over an illegal bet, or perhaps a drug sale. Or that someone had been robbed in some way, and the robber repented but was afraid to return the money. She hoped we could somehow return it to the rightful owner. We kept reading the paper for news of a robbery or mugging. The story about Lewis said nothing of robbery."

"I think the police were hoping if they didn't release that fact, someone might start flashing a lot of money he shouldn't have. Didn't either of you think of just giving it to the police?" I re-folded the note, trying to touch only the edges.

"Yes. But quite honestly, we thought it might just get shuffled around in the bureaucracy and finally get put into some general fund and disappear. We wanted either to return it to the owner or obey the letter and use it in God's work."

"Would it surprise you to know that Lewis Schley was believed to be carrying between three-fifty and four hundred dollars the night he was killed?"

"And you think he brought it here as some sort of atonement and then was killed? Poor Lewis. So he actually had gained something from his time here! He must have been so close—I think he really was beginning to work through his homosexual problem."

"What problem was that?" I asked smoothly. "The problem of being a liar? A thief? Of providing sex to anyone who made it worth his while? I was not aware those problems were limited to homosexuals."

Bartles set his mug sharply on the table. "Don't be condescending, Alex. You know perfectly well what I meant—the basic problem of *being* homosexual, a sin against God."

"Hold it, *Reverend.*" No way could I let that one go. "You *might* somehow, someday have made an honest man out of Lewis, but you could never have made a heterosexual out of him . . . any more than you made him gay. Neither of those things is done. There are two statements I have never, *ever* heard from a homosexual. I never heard, 'When *I decided* to become gay . . .' and I never heard, 'When he/she *made* me gay.' Many times I've heard, 'When I *dis-covered* I was gay . . .' or 'When I *finally realized* I was gay . . .' but not the others." I lit a cigarette and pulled over a saucer as ashtray. Like it or lump it, fella.

"I follow you, Alex." His voice was conciliatory. "You think being gay is genetic, and I'll admit to the possibility you are right. And remember, it's the sin we hate, not the sinner." Suddenly I had

178

a vision. I saw Bartles in a slick, shiny suit with a bright shirt and loud tie—standing in front of a sign reading *A-1 Used Cars and Redemption Center.*

He continued his smarmy pitch. "We have discovered that many gays can marry, have children, lead normal lives if they really want to. Faith in God, prayer, wise counsel and community support can truly work wonders. It's not the genes we have, it's what we do with them!"

It was fortunate there was not a loose table leg handy. I hate to think what I might have done with it. "Really, Lawrence? Funny, everything I've read on that subject says it rarely works for long and often has really bad emotional side effects on all the persons involved. Oh, and a question. All those *we's* in your little speech . . . were they the *royal we, the editorial we* or the *we* meaning *you*, too, have some naughty genes?"

He turned beet red and started to shake. For a moment I thought he was going to hit me. "I am not gay! I am perfectly happily married. I was trying to help Lewis because I sensed he was not happy in his life, and you are trying to distort it into something salacious!" He stood and turned away, staring out the window. "I think you had better leave."

I trotted out my sweetest smile. "I apologize for the crack about your genes. It was uncalled for. But, Lawrence, you're a bright fella. Now use your imagination. Pretend you are Gulliver. One night you are walking home, looking forward to being with your beloved wife. You step into a dark hole, and when you awake, you are in a society where the *norm* is for women to marry women and men to marry men." I reached for a cigarette but didn't light it. I didn't want to give him time to interrupt me.

"If you don't conform you are ostracized, punished socially, maybe legally and—in a few cases—killed. Finally, under terrible pressure you conform and marry a man. A nice guy, maybe a friend in another world. But to you it is abnormal. You dread his most casual touch for fear it may become amorous. You lie tight as a drum in bed, waiting for his breathing to change. But he's young and healthy, and he often wants you. The feel of him, his sweat, his body fluids . . . they disgust you. The smell of him, the taste of him makes you retch." I paused. "Do you think prayer and wise counsel would help you, Lawrence?"

He looked at me with pained eyes, pain from his imagined situation or a real one, I could not tell. "I do not know. That will take some thought. Not now."

"And we should get back to the immediate problem," I agreed. "Where did all that money come from? I don't think Lewis brought it here. I think his killer did."

"Why are you so sure?" He poured us more coffee and sat again.

"The word *cleanse* for one thing. Not Lewis's style, too literate, too biblical. And Lewis was drunk and high on mischief that night. He might have hit you up for dinner and made a big thing out of handing you ten dollars because he felt generous. But I don't think 'dirty money' was on his mind. Also," I quibbled, "I personally don't think he ever made it near here. I think he was killed early and taken to Race Point much later."

"I guess I'd better get this to the police." He tapped the fat envelope, rather sadly I thought.

"Sounds good to me. Sorry, it could have been your ticket to a dishwasher."

"Emmy says it keeps me humble. I'll have to call her. God, I miss her." He actually sounded human.

"By the way." I stood, prepared to leave. "While we're on this truth kick, was Emmy really here with you Saturday night?"

He sighed. "Yes and no. I wasn't entirely honest. In the early evening she and a girlfriend drove up to Hyannis to some mall to buy some baby things at a sale. They had pizza afterwards and Emmy got home something after ten-thirty." I nodded. Emmy's absence put Bartles alone during Mitch's favorite time frame of the murder.

Of course, it put her alone, too. Or had she walked in on something, grabbed a table leg and beat the hell out of the sinful little queer while her husband explained none of it was his fault?

I felt I had labored in the Lord's vineyards—or kitchen—long enough. Leaving Lawrence to explain to the police why he had sat on stolen money for a week, and—perhaps—why he lied about being alone Saturday night, I retired to "my other office" for sustenance. The subject of people hating themselves—or others—for whom they loved just made me sad.

It looked like half the town was in the Rat, all gathered around the front table with our star performer of the afternoon—Harmon. He had several free beers lined up in front of him and was telling his tale for the umpteenth time, each account more richly embellished than the last. I sat down at the empty bar and waited for Joe to find a minute for me. He finally came over. "Sorry, Alex, it's a little busy."

"You're getting rich. Give me a bourbon, Joe. It's already been a long day."

"I imagine so, Alex. They're your friends, I know. Do you think they're guilty?"

"No. But the police are pretty sure they are, or they wouldn't have arrested them. It's like I decided you belted Billie last night. Can you prove you never touched her?"

"Nope. I get your point. Well, I hear they got John Frost. He's good. Say, have you found my wicked witch yet? Cassie says you think she really put a spell on you."

"Cassie's mouth is sometimes in overdrive," I answered sourly. And wouldn't you know—I picked up my drink and slopped it. I sipped at the bourbon, but the noise and laughter in the Rat bothered me. I knew whom the laughter was about. Anyway, there was a call I should make. So I ordered two plain burgers for the kiddies, a fancier one for myself, along with some fries, and went home.

The house was intact. I—or at least the hamburger treat—was greeted joyously, and the kiddy dinner hour went without incident. I felt that bonds were being forged here, and it probably was just as well. Pewter might prove to be a permanent guest.

I called John Frost's office and managed to connect with him. He thanked me for recommending him, and I knew that in the future some of his P.I. needs would come my way, which was a happy thought, though the circumstances were dismal.

I told him about the table legs, assuming Mitch might not have. I was right. The little fink hadn't said a word to Frost about them. John was particularly interested in Quinn.

"Maybe there isn't an obvious connection between Lewis and Quinn in Ptown, but maybe there was one earlier in Worcester," John mused. "I know one of the prosecutors down there. I'll make a call."

And I told him about Bartles, who presumably would have been to the police with the letter and money by now. "You would have to decide, John, but that letter and money seem to put Peter and Wolf in a position at least to get bail. Right?"

"Oh, definitely. I can't get to a judge for a hearing before Monday, but I'll have them out of the Ptown Hilton as soon as I can." He laughed. "Of course, Mitch will probably try to say they did the letter themselves as a ruse to throw suspicion elsewhere."

"John, take my word for this. They might *possibly* have done the letter, but the thought of their giving nearly four hundred dollars to a born-again preacher man—even to stay out of jail—is ludicrous. They would sauté it and serve it with tartar sauce first!"

He laughed again and then said, "By the way, Alex, are you working for them?"

"It's a gray area. They sort of asked me to help them out and I sort of agreed. Nothing was signed or really discussed regarding fees. It doesn't matter. I haven't done all that much, and I hate to take my little tray of homemade cookies to the jail and then say, 'Oh, yes, here's my bill.'" I propped the phone on my shoulder and went through the contortions of lighting a cigarette.

"Oh, I'd say you've done quite a lot, and I'd appreciate it if you'd keep at it. What do you make of the two of them, anyway?"

I shrugged at the phone. "I've known them for years but never well until the last week or so. Could they have done it? Yes. Did they? I don't think so. Don't be confused by Wolf's willowy effete act. I think he's quite pragmatic. And Peter is far from the south-

182

ern belle with the vapors he wants you to think he is. He is a survivor and he's smart. And to me, they don't add up to two hysterical old queens who got all flustered and beat a guy to death, even over a valuable watch. I don't mean they weren't angry and humiliated by Lewis. I just hope they are too sensible to have murdered over it."

John was silent for a moment, then replied, "Okay, I can accept that. Not them, then. But somebody who had a better reason. Unfortunately, his—or her—reason may make sense only to him or her. You and I might have a hard time uncovering it—or recognizing it when we do."

"Yes. And to make it more difficult, I think you'll find he or she is otherwise quite moral, the old pillar-of-the-community routine."

"Why?" I heard a lighter click, followed by John's exhale.

"The money. He didn't know what to do with it. He didn't want to take it for himself. But like most of us, he couldn't bear to destroy it. So he gave it to a church."

"Interesting. And why that church? Not one of the more traditional ones. Although perhaps there are none needier than Bartles. But I seem to hear in your voice that you like Bartles for this. Right?"

I moved a few things aimlessly on the desk, trying to align my thoughts. "He's a definite maybe. What if he is gay, and all this 'help' is just cover? Say he and Lewis were lovers and had a fight. Maybe Lewis wanted money. Or he *wanted* Lewis as a lover and Lewis laughed or threatened to tell his wife. Or say Bartles is straight, Lewis made a grossed-out pass and Bartles freaked. Put it this way, I think Lewis's murder was very personal, mixed with a lot of anger. I don't think it was triggered by a broken watch and some unmade beds."

"Interesting," he said again. "Look, Alex, keep track of what your bill would be, and stay on this. We'll get these guys off yet. And when we do, the Town of Provincetown will happily pay your bill and mine and a few other things to avoid a suit for false arrest. Do anything you need to. I think you're closer than you know you are. It just hasn't clicked yet. Stay in touch." He hung up.

I was glad he hung up before I had to reply to his instructions to do whatever I needed. Frankly, I hadn't the faintest idea *what* I should do. Well, yes, I needed to eat.

So I heated up my burger and fries, popped a beer and clicked on the TV. Unfortunately, it was the pyramids again.

Chapter 19

Sunday was delightfully, wonderfully, *gloriously* normal. With an absolute minimum of guilt, Fargo and I left Pewter in the middle of my bed, looking like a furious Sitting Bull, and headed for the bayside beach. We walked along on the wet sand as the tide finished its ebb and were joined, as usual, by Toby the Terrible. He raced from his hiding spot under the deck of the Old Dockside Inn and attacked Fargo with gusto.

Toby needed all the gusto he could get to leap for Fargo's ears and tail. He rarely connected but got in an occasional nip, which would result in Fargo's bowling him over and literally rubbing his nose in the sand. This morning they contented themselves with chasing outgoing wavelets. Fargo would playfully prance out of the way of incoming waves while Toby ran in desperate arcs to keep from being inundated. Eventually he trotted home, swinging his little round bottom like a *fin de siecle* Parisian tart, headed—no doubt—for a well-deserved nap.

Fargo and I continued to the store, where we picked up the New York Times, some melt-in-your-mouth French crullers and Fargo's weekly rawhide, augmented today by kitty treats. On our return Pewter decided sweetness might be the best way to get some of the pastry and curled back and forth between my legs until I was ready to boot her through the goalposts. Finally, I got settled with food, my special Sunday Blue Mountain coffee and the crossword puzzle and was brilliant in the solving of it.

I did a couple of chores and then rewarded myself by settling on the sofa with cigarettes, a beer and the Titans-Steelers game. The Titans were somehow keeping the Steelers out of sync, and the score was a surprising and gratifying 21–3, Titans. I wondered briefly if Sonny and Paula might be in the stadium, and then decided Nashville was nowhere near Gatlinburg.

I hoped Sonny was having a good vacation. He rarely got much consecutive time off and I hoped he was having fun. I wasn't too sure, though. He'd sounded a little tense on the phone. And Mom said she'd gotten a postcard with the picture of some mountain called Clingman's Dome and the cryptic message: *You and Aunt Mae would love it here, Sonny.* He didn't sound especially thrilled. I yawned and felt my hand slide off the couch onto fur—I wasn't sure whose.

That's the last I remember until the phone rang. I picked it up and a man's pleasant voice said, "Hi. Alex? This is Larry Bartles." Gee whiz, we were getting chummy! "Something's come up. I've handled it, but I just thought you ought to know. Another letter and some money arrived. I've given it to Detective Mitchell."

I sat up, now wide awake. "How much? What did it say? How was it delivered?"

"It was there when I went into the chapel this morning, slipped through the slot like the other one. Looks like the same type of paper and says 'make this clean thru God.' It's made of pasted letters like the last one. And there was fifty-seven dollars in it."

"An odd amount of money." I deliberated. "But maybe not, Ben Fratos's wallet and watch were taken, of course, to raise—at least

186

theoretically—the question of robbery. And that amount would probably be about what the average person carries. You know, enough to cover most immediate needs, but not enough to ruin you if you lost it."

"Yes, that sounds right. Maybe his wife could tell you more."

"He was divorced, lived alone. Speaking of wives, what about yours?"

"Right here," he answered. I could hear a smile in his voice.

"Great! I'll say no more. Were the cops pleased with your good citizenship?"

"Not so you'd notice. The detective turned to a lady officer and said, 'Damn! They couldn't have done this one.' Whatever that means."

I laughed. "It means the two men they have under arrest just took a giant step toward freedom! Huzzah! They were the wrong ones anyway. Well, I won't keep you from your reunion. Stay in touch, ah, Larry."

We hung up. Larry Bartles grew on you, and I could see why my Aunt Mae liked him. I still didn't like his brand of religion, but maybe—just maybe—I had opened a tiny window in his mind yesterday. He seemed intelligent and there was always hope. Of course there was always the possibility he was a charming killer, too.

Which made me unhappy at the train of thought still chugging through my mind. Suppose Bartles was the world's most accomplished liar and all this religion was just a hoax. Say the kitchen table components had been spread out in the backyard for assembly. Suppose something triggered a fight between Bartles and Lewis. Bartles picked up a leg and hit Lewis. Maybe Lewis managed to get up and try to run, and Bartles downed him in the sawdust of the garden. Then he either lost it and kept beating him, or beat him on purpose to make it look like a crime of passion. I wished Mitch could have forensics examine Bartles's van and that sawdust mulching his garden.

Now, suppose Fratos saw something. He decides to approach

Bartles. If there is no money to be had for blackmail, he can still have Bartles under his thumb, which would be almost as rewarding to slime like him. Fratos has a few at the Rat to work up his courage. When he walks out, he sees Harmon's old truck with the keys in it and decides he can double his fun. He'll drive over and park it at the mission, where Harmon would never look for it in a million years, and have a nice threatening scene with Bartles. Only Bartles panics and kills him.

The only thing I couldn't account for was Wolf's handkerchief. Maybe Harmon had done some work for Wolf, needed a handkerchief and just picked it up, or Wolf gave it to him. Or maybe he simply found it somewhere. It could have been in the back of his truck forever with other junk and just used on the tire iron because it came to hand.

Bartles had all the time in the world to make up those letters, while his wife was gone, and then fake their delivery. Well, it was a reasonable theory. And with the case against Peter and the Wolf getting weaker, maybe Mitch would finally look into it. I almost hated to call him. Mitch and I really seemed to be at cross-purposes these days, and I hated finding us in an adversarial position. I'd considered us friends and wished we could get back on good terms.

I knew at least some of his problems. Sonny and the Chief were both away. Anders hadn't had an original thought since first grade. Mitch probably felt as if he were a lone sergeant who had suddenly been left in charge of D-Day. This was the first murder case under his responsibility. I remembered Sonny with his first homicide. He had a theory he was determined was correct, and he would have sworn the moon was blue cheese if it had reinforced that theory. Of course, he just happened to be right.

I'm sure Mitch felt I had been no help and was working against him. And now John Frost had been added to the equation. Well, perhaps if I was very tactful we could bring this mess to an accurate conclusion that would preserve Mitch's self-esteem. I would try. I called and asked him over for a drink, and he accepted, although I sensed reluctance in his voice.

When he arrived I mixed us a highball. I lifted mine, saying, "To friends."

He smiled and clicked his glass against mine. "Absolutely, Alex. To friends."

We kicked the case around, from first report to last, but made little progress. Neither of us could explain Harmon's ongoing peripheral involvement, nor could we believe he was seriously implicated. Peter and Wolf could not have sent the second letter to Bartles, since they were in jail.

"Of course, they could have gotten someone else to send it for them," Mitch said.

"Not unless they had considerable help from someone in your department," I retorted. "Nobody else would know what it looked like."

"Oh, I don't know," he said with a smile, "there's always Bartles . . . or you."

"Oh, go check the garbage for cut-up magazines—and while you're there, get your head stuck in the can!"

"Well, whoever it was, they meant it to be long-lasting. Forensics tried to get the letters loose, to see what magazine—or what kind of magazine—they came from. No go. The paper will have to grow old and rot around it before those letters fall off."

"Strange," I agreed. "Maybe it was all they had handy."

"Maybe. It's some kind of real strong stuff, I'm told. Something you might find at Wood's Woods, although I doubt Wood is involved." He looked at me impishly over the rim of his glass. "And you'll be happy to know, we found nothing like it at Peter and the Wolf's."

"You went back?"

"Yeah, I figured the warrant was still good. Look, Alex, I'm just trying to wrap this up, one way or another."

"Mitch, if you could just bear with me for a moment. If it is *not*

189

Peter and/or the Wolf, and if it is *not* a vagrant robber . . . who is it?"

"Could be the Governor, for all I know. I have no idea. Do you?"

"Not really. What about Bartles?" I recounted my scenario. "And he has no alibi for last Saturday night or for Fratos. He told me his wife was shopping with a girlfriend down at the mall Saturday night. Then they had a fight over the money in the envelope on Sunday, and she trotted home to Mum's."

Mitch covered a yawn. If I hadn't known his lost sleep was mainly due to pursuing Peter and the Wolf, I would have felt sorry for him. "I know," he said. "She didn't get home till this morning late. Bartles told me about the shopping and the fight. He was aware it put him alone at the time of both murders, but it didn't seem to bother him. His fingerprints are on letter number one and its envelope, along with smaller prints, probably his wife's. We're going to check that."

I got up and made him a refill as he continued. "The money has prints galore. His, the ones we think are the wife's, Wolf's, Peter's and enough unidentified ones to start a whole new file. And don't tell me—I know Peter and Wolf usually paid Lewis in cash."

"Well, at least that pretty well confirms it was Lewis's money. And I don't see Lewis dropping it off at the church on his way to Race Point to get himself killed. It's got to be from the murderer, Mitch. You know, Bartles could have done the letters and faked the delivery. That would give him a logical way to explain to his wife how he got the money."

Mitch looked stubborn, as if he didn't want to admit ministers had been known to kill. But I went on. "Look, he knew Lewis, and I still think it's a bit strange Lewis visited Bartles. There *could* have been something between them . . . sex, drugs. Bartles had what could be the weapon. And there's the sawdust. And his van. Come on, Mitch, it's more than you have against Peter and the Wolf."

"Maybe." He sounded part amused, part aggravated. "Well, I still say it's weak, but I'll see about a warrant to look at the sawdust and the van. Happy now?"

I grinned. "Yeh. And if it isn't Bartles, what about a hate crime? Lewis was openly gay, openly for rent and a wise-ass to boot."

He fought off another yawn. "Thought about that. But for one thing, a hate crime is usually committed by more than one person. Usually, one of the group gets drunk and has to brag, or somebody knows something and talks. And, more often than not, they take some sort of credit. Maybe a piece of paper pinned to the body. 'Queers Beware. The Committee for a Pure Town.' You know what I mean, the usual high-blown crap."

"Yes. You're right. No rumors? No tips?"

"Nada. Nil. Nothing, Alex. Nary a word. There's still Quinn. Thus far he's known at the Harbor Bar, but not where any of the gay guys hang out. On the other hand, his ex-sergeant tells me he was on report twice for roughing up suspects—both gay. They weren't sorry to get rid of him. We haven't written him off."

"Damn!" I was out of ideas. "Have you talked to Sonny, other than that once? Did he give you his number?"

"No. He didn't and I don't think it's necessary. I don't want to start W-W-Three, Alex, but nobody fits as well as Wolf and Peter."

"What about letter number two and the fifty-seven bucks?"

"A misguided friend."

Was he still thinking of me? It seemed so. Before I got good and mad, I shrugged and said, "Well, I suppose so. What about prints? I bet they belong to Ben Fratos."

"Bartles's are on the envelope. Not the letter. He says he remembered not to open it until he put on a pair of his wife's gloves, if you can imagine! Lots of unknown prints on the money—not Peter, or Wolf, or Bartles. I imagine you'll be right about Fratos."

"Fratos!" I slapped my forehead. "I forgot to tell you. The other evening he came into the Wharf Rat, started to sit with Chief Mather, but Mather gave him a dirty look and he moved on. Later, he cornered Mather up by the street. Fratos was talking and Mather looked disgusted . . . angry. Maybe Fratos was bragging about some dirt he'd uncovered somewhere. He'd love to know something foul about a man like Bartles. Maybe you should ask Mather. I'm sorry I didn't tell you sooner. I've been sort of . . ."

"Preoccupied lately?" Laughing, Mitch finished for me. "With the Curse of the Ptown Witch?"

"Shit. Is that going around now?"

Mitch drained his drink and smiled. "Oh, lots of people know. Joe has kept us all up to date. But I don't have to ask Mather. He mentioned it himself. It seems Fratos has been trying to get an increase in his pension but Chief Franks kiboshed it. Fratos was trying to exert some pressure through Anders and the selectmen and anybody else who might lean on Franks. He begged Mather to put *his* oar in the water. Mather was disgusted, said there was nothing wrong with his leg in the first place."

I looked at him quizzically. "You going steady with Mather these days?"

He had the grace to blush. "Ah . . . well . . . he's been kind of nice to me. He said he knew with Sonny and Chief Franks away, I might feel a little uneasy and he'd be glad to help any way he could—even if I just wanted someone to talk to. He's really a stand-up guy, Alex, though I can understand why you don't care for him."

"He's okay in his own way." I set my glass down. "Has he been helpful?"

"Some. You'll be glad to know he's not at all sure about Peter and the Wolf. He thinks maybe Lewis came on to some skinhead-type tourist who got mad and killed him, maybe having seen he had a lot of money on him. Then the killer posed him at the amphitheater just for kicks."

"What does he think was the weapon?"

"He didn't have anything specific. He thought there might have been more than one—and maybe more than one person. Like maybe somebody hit him with a block of wood or a hockey stick, and the other wounds came from the handle of a jack, or even somebody wearing a large ring and hitting him with his fist."

Mitch stood. "Well, we haven't come up with anything really

new. I will check into Bartles, and we haven't crossed off Quinn or the skinhead theory. I am really sorry, Alex, but I still think it's going to end up Peter and the Wolf."

I wanted to stamp my foot and scream, "Is not, not, not!" But that would not convince Mitch of anything but my lunacy. We said a muted but cordial farewell.

I let Fargo and Pewter out and stood in the doorway as they went on final patrol. Something was nibbling around the edge of my thoughts but wouldn't take hold. Maybe tomorrow.

Chapter 20

I had let the animals out for their Monday morning patrol—I was getting entirely too used to saying *animals* in the plural—while I showered and donned my usual sweatshirt, jeans, crew socks and sneakers. I let them in, gave them dry food and fresh water. Then I sat down with my first cup of coffee and cigarette. If there is any better combination than those two things I haven't found it yet. And I don't need a lecture. This was number one and today I was counting. I would not exceed five, in all probability.

I finished the news portion of the paper and turned to the week-ahead horoscope for my morning's intellectual touch. I looked at *Leo* and learned I would benefit from the generosity of friends but might have an unpleasant experience dining out. I looked at *Sagittarius* and was told that Fargo should be careful playing games and not to be judgmental in making new friends. "Okay, Fargo, we hope for a check, eat at home, stay away from Frisbees and be nice to Pewter."

At that, Pewter began to run frantically between the back door and the front, yowling shrilly. Fargo looked at me in confusion: what was this? I didn't know either. For an absurd second I wondered if Pewter was upset because I hadn't read her horoscope. A car door slammed, and Fargo joined the racket, lustily, if late.

I looked out the door and did not recognize the car but shortly recognized its occupants. Wolf and Peter came in, laden with two bottles of Moët champagne, Russian caviar, a dozen long-stem yellow roses and a dozen red, plus an enormous rawhide and a catnip toy. The reunion was unanimously joyous. Eventually I got the flowers into vases, while Peter made toast points and boiled a couple of eggs for the caviar and Wolf wrestled the shrink-wrap off the presents for the kiddies.

Finally, we got ourselves settled at the dining table. The champagne was cold and beautifully dry, the caviar the best I had ever tasted. Did drinking in the morning count if you had caviar with it? It didn't seem as if it should. Peter and the Wolf were exultant at being out of jail and reunited with Pewter, who pretended she didn't care.

"John Frost must have gotten the judge out of bed at six a.m.," Peter told me. "We were in court at nine sharp and out in twenty minutes. But would you believe Mitch got the D.A. to make John promise to collect our passports and turn them over to the court. Does he think we have a Swiss bank account and a *pied a terre* on the Riviera?"

I thought it mere petulance on Mitch's part, but I just smiled. "Well, at least you're back in your own home, and things look better all around."

"Don't count on that," Wolf said. "Guess who was waiting when we got home?"

"Not Mitch!" I couldn't believe it. Hadn't our conversation last night gotten through to him at all?

"Give the lady a silver dollar. I guess you noticed we're driving a rental." I shook my head; I hadn't thought about it. "Well, we are. Mitch took our Explorer last week and now our old Nissan.

He said Ben Fratos's killer had got blood on the clutch of Harmon's truck, and he—Mitch—wanted to make sure there was none transferred from the truck to our car. He won't find any. I just hope he doesn't put some there."

"He won't do that." I put more caviar on my plate and reached for the little bowl of chopped eggs, trying to look casual, not greedy.

"I'm not sure of anything anymore, Alex. He really wants us for this."

"It's not really that he wants you two so much as he wants *somebody*. And he can't come up with anyone else who really makes sense. Except Bartles, and Mitch has a mental block there. I'm sure you didn't do it," I added hastily. "But I can't prove it yet. And Mitch is getting pressure from Anders, who's getting it from the selectmen, who're getting it all over town."

"What about Righteous Brother Bartles?" Peter asked.

"It's a gray area." I wasn't about to go into details. "And Lewis never mentioned anything going on with Bartles to any of his buddies. The cops asked around."

"Well, *somebody* did it and I'm getting damn sick of it looking like us." Peter tossed off his remaining champagne and reached for the bottle in the ice bucket. He didn't seem to care if he looked greedy.

"Yeah, I'm sure," I sighed. "I don't suppose any of your guests had reason to want Lewis dead." I made it a question.

They looked at each other and shook their heads. "I can't think so." Peter shrugged. "There were a couple of incidents. It must be three weeks ago now. Walter Harris was a guest and came to us saying he was missing a ring. He was sure it was taken off the bureau. We were asking what it looked like and when he'd last seen it, when Lewis came downstairs with the ring. Said he found it behind a bureau leg while cleaning. I just assumed Walter had missed it when he first looked. Now I think maybe Lewis conveniently found it when he heard us talking. But I doubt Walter killed him."

"No. You said a couple of things . . . ?"

"Oh, back the end of September, a guest thought he was missing fifty dollars. We were very upset. Wolf offered to make it good. Then the guest got all flustered and said he wasn't really sure, he'd been drunk the night before and may have given it to Lewis as a tip." Wolf stretched. "Excuse me . . . my back. I don't recommend the beds in that hotel."

"Are you saying Lewis figured he deserved a tip and helped himself?" I asked.

"Possibly. Or the guest was drunk and gave it to him, or spent it somewhere or lost it. Again, I doubt it would have ended in murder. Anyway, he hasn't stayed at the inn since, if he's been in town."

"Maybe he came back to town, stayed somewhere else, got in a dust-up with Lewis and killed him," I suggested.

"Where would he have gotten a table leg, assuming that was the weapon?" Peter inquired.

"Oh, just about anywhere." I gestured around me grandly. "They seem to be popping up all over town. Even my Aunt Mae now has a spare."

Wolf laughed and topped off my glass. "Have a little champagne, Alex. The caviar is getting to you."

Peter and I giggled and we gave up any hope of serious talk. Eventually, they left with many thanks to Fargo and me for our hospitality toward Pewter. Wolf took Pewter in his arms and they walked toward the door. Fargo gave Pewter a farewell sniff, and she bopped him on the nose with her claws out. Fargo sat down looking dismayed, and I led him away by the collar before he could jump into my arms. It was Panalog time—and good stuff it was. My leg was healing nicely.

First aid complete, I realized I was getting a whopping headache. Champagne and caviar for breakfast might be terribly sophisticated, but obviously I wasn't meant for it. Cool fresh air seemed a good idea but I didn't think driving was, so we walked down the bay side. Of course, here came Toby, abbreviated legs churning through the sand, bright beady eyes alert with mischief. He had picked the wrong day.

Having lost his playmate and been given a bloody nose by her as a final humiliation, Fargo was in no mood for small-dog antics. Poor Toby spent their entire meaningful moments with his head pushed into the sand and Fargo's broad, heavy paw in the middle of his back. Finally Toby managed to free himself and stomp—if dachshunds can be said to stomp—off the field, whiskers puckered into a moue of disgust.

As my head cleared, I realized that while caviar made a delicious and unusual breakfast, it did not make a filling one. One of Joe's pastrami sandwiches and some fries took care of the emptiness. Iced tea helped the sudden thirst. As Joe cleared my plates he asked, "Any news on the murder . . . murders?"

"Not really. Peter and the Wolf are out on bail, which is overdue, as far as I'm concerned."

"Yeah, most people I talk to can't picture those two great ladies killing anybody. You don't figure this for a hate crime, do you, Alex?" His forehead creased in a frown.

I took a good-sized gulp of tea. "It's hard to believe in Provincetown. Of course, anything is possible. But if that was true, why kill Ben Fratos? He wasn't gay. Though he was sure easy to hate. Have you heard something?"

"Oh, nothing about a hate crime. The majority say Ben saw something and tried to blackmail the killer, who then killed him, too. A few folks vote for Ben having killed the Schley fellow for his money, and one of Schley's pals killed *him* in revenge. But that's pretty far out. Of course, Harmon is still saying it's something about drugs and cigarette boats and a Hollywood connection. But his story is now so confused, *he* can't even remember how it goes."

"God, poor Ben was sure popular, wasn't he? Thief, blackmailer, murderer. Makes you scared to get killed around here for fear of what people will say!" I laughed.

"Yeah. Say, how's the wicked witch? Did you find her yet? I hear you've been patrolling the streets."

"She was last seen circling over your house, coming in to land."

"What the hell, I'm already married. What's one more?" Joe ended the conversation and went to wait on another customer. I felt better after eating and figured Fargo might, too. I took him out some sliced chicken and water, and then we walked home via the street. I didn't think either of us was up to Toby.

The phone was ringing as I walked in the door. I almost let the machine pick up. I was working toward a nap and didn't need irritation. But I picked it up and was glad I did. It was the bank's decorator, calling from Boston.

She would be over on Friday, she said, for a 10 a.m. appointment with a Mr. Jared Mather to look at some carvings. Could she come to my house around 11:30, or would that be too close to lunch? I said it was fine and suggested I take her to lunch afterwards. I thought that was what she was angling for, and sure enough, she became considerably more gracious. But I didn't care. I wanted that photo of Fargo and the gull and/or the one of him with the squirrel used at the bank. Maybe buying lunch would make that happen.

Nap forgotten, I went into my office/studio and started looking at photos. I grouped them, shifted them, discarded some, but somehow my heart wasn't in it. As I looked at photos of Fargo laughing, a cat smiling, a starling glowering, I thought of Jared Mather and didn't know why—perhaps wondering how a man so blatantly miserable could carve birds in such obviously joyful flight.

I moved to the kitchen and a beer, sat down at the table and just let my thoughts drift. They moved, like a compass needle returning north, to Jared Mather. I saw him in his uniform, straight and military. I saw him relaxed and pleasant with Sonny and my mother. I saw him in jeans and T-shirt on his back porch that fateful Saturday I'd walked up his driveway. Always when I thought of Jared, it was in connection with his years as a policeman. I rarely thought of him in connection with his woodworking and carving skills.

I set the beer down carefully, back in its same little circle of wetness on the coaster. But Mather was a man who worked with wood. And wood meant splinters, chips, sawdust.

I remembered Mather talking to both Lewis and Fratos before each was killed. Maybe a few hours before their respective deaths, possibly only a few minutes.

It seemed strange that Mather would have been talking to either of them *at all*. Mather was obvious in his disapproval of Lewis. That had been easy to see all along, and his "Well done, soldier," speech to me had underscored it. Yet just a few minutes after that speech, I had seen them talking together at the head of the alley. Certainly, their voices had not been raised in any confrontation, nor were they whispering, they were just . . . normal.

And Fratos. I could visualize Fratos walking into the Rat and heading for the stool next to Mather. Mather gave him a ferocious glare, and he veered off. Then I saw them on the street. Tension. How did I know? Heads forward, voices low, urgent, not wanting to be heard. Fratos was leaning toward Mather, pressing a point. Mather looked tight, nodded, said a word or two.

The unthinkable thought floated up unasked—could Mather be the killer?

He had the possible weapon and the opportunity. But was he a killer? He disliked gays but had never used his official position to mistreat them. Fratos had been a fellow officer, but Mather didn't like him, and didn't support his try for more money. Mather seemed a man of high morals and the guts to live up to them.

But what if he'd had sex with Lewis and Lewis threatened to go public? And what if Fratos knew it and tried some form of blackmail?

I couldn't believe Jared would let two innocent men be convicted. By serving as advisor to Mitch, he would be kept abreast of the workings of the case and could promote his skinhead theory. Anders would support that—it was close enough to his own solution, and the investigation would simply wither into "unsolved."

Assuming they were innocent, neither Peter and Wolf nor—to a lesser degree—Rev. Bartles would consider it a happy ending.

200

They would never be free of suspicion, even though they were never tried. But it would probably be about the best Mather could arrange. It would be like it had been in the old eighteenth-century Scottish courts: a verdict of innocent, guilty or "not proven."

I knew I could never, ever convince Mitch of my new theory. I needed to get a good look at that table leg in Aunt Mae's kitchen, and I needed to do it without her knowledge. She would be terrified and horrified if I simply walked in, explained my thoughts and crawled under the table with a flashlight. I'd have to think of a way.

I drained the beer and stared out the window for a while. Then I went into the office and dug around until I found the card with the phone number of the Mekong Mariott or wherever Sonny was staying these days, and sat down to make the call. "Fargo, the time has come to call the Mounties. I am not easy about all this. I think it's time we update Sonny."

Hearing Sonny's name, Fargo looked hopefully at the door. "Not yet, angel dog, but probably soon."

After various recorded messages, menus and instructions I reached their room and Paula picked up. "Helloo-o-o."

"Hi, Paula, it's Alex. I hope I didn't catch you at a bad time."

There was a momentary pause, just long enough to tell me she had to stop and think who I was. Gee, I loved this girl. Then she began to gush.

"Not a bad time at all! I've just been to the spa and had a massage. Don't you just *love* them! So-o-o relaxing; stress just *melts* away. I may take a swim before dinner, just to stay loose. Although I need my hair done. And I've got to have my nails done, but they'll take me anytime. And I want to check this little boutique that the masseuse recommended. But I'll fit it in somehow!" She sighed with the enormity of it all, and I spoke quickly before she pressed the "play" button again.

"Is Sonny by chance around?"

"Oh, dear, no. He's out with Dave, golfing or riding . . . canoeing. Shall I have him call you?"

Dave? Who the hell was Dave? "Yes, would you, please?"

201

"Absolutely. And you have a good afternoon, now, honey." She giggled. "I'm just getting *too* Southron!"

I said "Um" and we both hung up.

Sonny didn't call until after six and sounded as if he might have had a drink or two. My opening words were, "Who's Dave? I thought you were down there with Paula."

"Just a guy I met. We've been having some fun together."

"Working my side of the street?" I laughed. "Paula's apparently about to make you turn gay. She'd have me in a nunnery in a snap. But at least the hotel seems to meet with her approval . . . sounds like the Boston Sheraton to me."

"It is. That's the whole idea—you travel a thousand miles and you stay in a hotel just like the one two blocks from your office." I heard ice cubes rattle.

"I hope, for the sake of your evening together, she's not hearing this. Anyway, things are perking right along here in the old village. We've had another murder."

"*Another* one! No kidding?"

"Sonny," I answered sharply. "Ben Fratos was killed. I didn't like him either, but you sound like a kid who's just been given a three-pound Milky Way."

"Sorry. It's just that a second murder gives me a perfect . . . Well, never mind. Fill me in a little here."

I did so, and at the end of it Sonny definitely thought it time to come home. Much as it pained him, duty called.

"I'll get there as soon as I can. That may not be easy. Knoxville is not the airline capital of the world. But I'll get there."

I'm not sure who was happier—Sonny saying the words, or me hearing them. Then he had to go and spoil it all.

"Oh, and Alex, you've done a great job for your clients. You have also helped the police with their inquiries. Now get the hell out of it. It could be turning dangerous now. You hear me? Leave it alone."

Chapter 21

April may be the cruelest month, but November is high in unpredictability. Wednesday morning felt like a warm spring day, thereby giving me immediate spring fever. There was nothing I had to do. I had to admit I was tired of chasing table legs. And I had been warned off the case by none other than Detective Lieutenant Edward J. Peres. That was my cachet for a do-nothing day. Yay!

I started with a leisurely shower, followed by a pot of my treasured Blue Mountain coffee and cigarette number one. Resolutely, I did not think of dead villains or living suspects. I thought of my now-cozy relationship with the bank and the possibility of adding a "master suite" to the house—how cosmopolitan it sounded. *Oh, I was somewhat fatigued and spent the evening relaxing in the master suite.* Maybe I'd include one of those showers that came at you from every angle and possibly a delightful female who did the same.

My main decision come spring would be whether to have the contractor go up or out. Up would be cheaper to build and to heat. Both my mother and my aunt voted for, "Up if you're going to sell it soon, out if you plan to grow old in it. When you get to be our age, whatever you want will be upstairs if you're down, and downstairs if you're up. Avoid stairs." My contractor agreed.

He had done a back-of-the-envelope sketch that showed not only how easy it would be, but how I would lose little of my yard and gain both a breezeway to the garage and a sheltered patio that would be very usable on a day like this. I sighed my indecision and Fargo took that to mean I needed his advice. He went to the back door and stared at me with deep meaning. Obviously *out* was his choice, so I filled a covered mug with coffee and we made our way to Herring Cove.

The day was such that tourists had reemerged in our midst. They never entirely went away anymore. Fargo immediately found a playmate, a large golden retriever who raced him pace for pace along the shallows. Then, at some unheard signal, they made a turn into the sea and began to swim, breasting the waves easily, burnished heads smoothly parting the water at amazing speed. I'd begun to wonder if their next planned stop was the Azores when they turned again as one, again for no visible reason, and streaked for shore.

After a great shaking off of water and rolling in dry sand and shaking some more—earning black looks from nearby strollers— they seemed ready for rest. Fargo and I started for the car and a drink of water and coffee. I asked the goldie's owner if he'd like a drink for his dog—I didn't offer to share the coffee—but he said thanks, he had a stash in his own car. Manners minded, Fargo and I went our way.

As I approached the turnoff to Aunt Mae's house, I had to stop to allow a huge moving van to swing wide and make the turn into her street. The lettering on the van said: *Hart Brothers Moving and Storage, Providence, R.I.* Being a trained detective, I swiftly deduced this would be the van carrying Cindy's household effects to my aunt's cottage.

Cleverly, I decided to follow it, inferring that if the van was here, Cindy would not be far ahead or behind it. I stopped again and held my breath as the van negotiated its way into Aunt Mae's narrow driveway. And sure enough, there stood Cindy and Aunt Mae, signaling it toward the cottage.

I parked out of the way and strolled toward them. The van looked even bigger up close. "Boy, when you say you're going to get a moving van, you really mean it," I commented. "That looks like you could furnish the White House out of it."

"Don't be fooled." Cindy smiled. "My stuff is taking up about a tenth of the space. The rest belongs to some people moving to Freeport, Maine. This is just a little side trip and a brief stop."

"Ah." I nodded. Cindy was holding a rather skinny half-grown cat in her arms, black with three white socks and a chin that looked as if she'd dipped it in the milk. Her face looked sweet and very feminine. "Who's your friend?" I asked.

"Wells."

"Wells?" I stared at the cat and then at the dog. "Fargo?"

"Very good! Her Wells, him Fargo."

I must have looked as stupid as I felt, for Cindy couldn't keep a straight face.

"You should see your expression," she chortled. "It's priceless! Actually, I doubt if the poor thing even has a name, and she just now became mine, I guess. The people who lived here deserted her. Your aunt has been feeding her and looking for a home. She can't have her inside the house—she's allergic, as you doubtless know. So—o, it seems she's mine. I haven't given a thought about a name—I just wanted to tease you."

"Wells sounds fine to me. She's a pretty little thing."

"Yes. Does Fargo like cats?" He was sitting at Cindy's feet, looking up at the cat with a phony ingratiating grin. He wouldn't hurt her, but he'd love to put her up a tree. It took a Sumo wrestler like Pewter to bring him into line.

"Oh, he's harmless," I temporized. Cindy gently put the kitten on the ground. Fargo put his *derriere* up and his front paws out in

205

front, the universal play signal, and pounced toward the cat. She bristled, hissed, bopped his nose and then jumped back into Cindy's arms. Fargo sat, stunned, with hurt feelings. Clouted *again?*

I saw him stiffen, about to jump into *my* arms, which would have resulted in my landing ignominiously on my back. Quickly, I grabbed his collar. "I'll take him up to the house and put some cream on his nose," I said. "Tell Aunt Mae where I've gone. Be right back."

At that point, Aunt Mae joined us. "I'm glad you came by, dear. Would you run up to the house and turn the soup to simmer. I forgot. And give it a stir. I'll just stay here and make sure these young men don't drive across the herb beds on their way out."

God help 'em, I thought, if they nick a dill sprig. She'd be less upset if they took the porch off the house.

"By the way," she continued, "I'm making the soup for dinner tonight. I've asked Cindy, she certainly won't be prepared to make her dinner. Your mother's coming, and Sonny will try. You must come, too, if you can."

"Sure, love to. You said Sonny? He's back?"

"Yes. Jeanne said he got in early this morning, looking exhausted. But he's gone to work anyway."

So, he did make it home. I was glad he was back. I left Aunt Mae and Cindy directing men carrying things into the cottage and walked toward the house. I heard a car toot its horn and looked up. It was Jared Mather in his SUV, driving toward his home, lumber sticking out the back. I assumed the horn was a greeting to Aunt Mae and didn't bother to raise my hand.

Walking across the back porch, I noticed the spare table leg still propped against the wall. Apparently Aunt Mae had been in no hurry to return it to Wood's Woods. In the house, I rummaged through Aunt Mae's medicine chest and found some Neosporin and rubbed a bit gently onto Fargo's battered nose.

Back in the kitchen I turned the heat down under the soup. A large spoon was propped nearby, and I removed the lid from the pot and gave the soup a stir. She was making Portuguese soup—my personal favorite—thick with pieces of sausage, fresh kale, navy beans, tomatoes and onions. I knew she'd serve it with hot home-made bread. She had one of those machines where you dump all the ingredients in one end, and about eight hours later a loaf of bread comes out the other. I've never understood how it works, but I understand hot fresh bread and sweet butter all too well.

Sonny's orders aside, here was my chance to get a look at the table leg without upsetting my aunt. I put the spoon down and crawled under the table. Even in the poor light I could see the top of the leg was slightly battered and had a sizeable splinter or two missing. There was a widespread discoloration on the top and part-way down one side of the leg. It could have been oil or stain . . . or blood, but it was definitely more than just "a flaw in the wood." Obviously, whatever it was, there had been some effort to wipe it off. I was glad Sonny was around. For my money, this leg was now a police matter. I sat there, under the table for a moment, wondering how on earth to explain this to Aunt Mae without absolutely horrifying her.

Footsteps clattered across the porch and I peeked out. But instead of Aunt Mae's sensible low heels, I saw highly shined military oxfords topped by sharply creased khakis.

"Mae, are you home?" Mather called pleasantly. He stepped inside the screen door and called again. "Mae, it's Jared." I was not pleased to see he was holding a fresh-wood-smelling table leg in his hand.

I had the childlike impulse to shrink small against the wall and hope he wouldn't see me. Unfortunately, I wasn't sufficiently childlike in size to have that work. Mather bent over with an amused look. "Well, Alexandra! Are we playing hide and seek? I'm seeking your aunt."

"Aunt Mae's not here, Chief. No hide and seek today." I managed a small laugh and held up my hand. "I dropped my ring and it rolled under the table. I'll tell Aunt Mae you stopped by."

"Fine." He waggled the leg. "Mae's been using a faulty leg on her table. I made her a good one. I'll just put it on for her while I'm here." Obviously he was going to brazen this out.

207

Certainly I couldn't let him leave with the stained leg. It would be gone forever. "Well, gee, Chief, I wouldn't feel quite right changing her things around when she's not here, you know?"

"Alexandra, I am simply replacing a bad leg with a good one, not redecorating the house. Now stand aside, please." He gave a small smile. If it was meant to be reassuring, it failed.

I crawled out from under the table and stood up. I didn't feel quite so helpless on my feet. I took a deep breath. "Sorry, Chief. The answer is no." I was not happy to see him scowl and begin to swing the leg in little circles.

His voice was sharp. "You think you have things all figured out, don't you? You think you know something about these murders, don't you? Well, you don't. You're dead wrong. You've let your imagination run away with you. You always were flighty. Let this end here and now and we'll both just forget it. Stand aside."

"No, Chief. I can't do that. The leg is evidence. You cannot take it away." There, it was said. Fargo nuzzled my hand nervously—he probably heard fear in my voice. I hoped Mather didn't.

He answered gently. "Now just what makes you think it's evidence? What dastardly thing do you think you have *detected?* What are you confused about? What could be so bad?"

I made my first mistake. "It's nothing so bad at all, Chief. I've known it for years. And I never thought badly of you. I've felt sorry for you, that you made yourself carry such a burden. But I'm not the least confused. I do know."

He seemed stunned. "You know what?" Then the penny dropped. "That day . . . Mae's broken window . . . you came to my house. That must be it." The circles became faster, his voice higher. "You peered through my bedroom window, you prying bitch. Listened outside my house! You wanted something on me. So you could tell your family, poison me with Sonny. Ruin me in the town! Who have you told, bitch?" He swung the leg wider. Fargo and I back-pedaled, stopped by the chair behind us.

"No, Chief, I never told a soul! And I didn't look in your window. I wouldn't do that. I just accidentally heard you and . . ."

He was white as a snowball, and his whole body began to shake. "Never told a soul. Hah! You think your ill-gotten knowledge gives you power over me, well it doesn't. Power! *I am the one with power!* I am the one who keeps down Satan's serpent!"

He swung the leg dangerously close. "You have no idea what it is like. My father caught me with another boy when I was young. We weren't actually doing anything, but my father knew where it was leading. He beat me nearly unconscious so I would know the depth of my sin."

His eyes widened so the whites showed large, and his voice dropped almost to a whisper. "Then the preacher came and I was on my knees throughout the night. Praying for forgiveness. My mother sobbing and praying for my soul. My father and the preacher reminding me of the hell that would await me. But I beat Satan's serpent! I beat it down and I keep it down every day of my life! Sometimes it tries to rise, rise! But I beat it back. I am pure. I have the power! I have the pain." He touched his chest. "But I have the power."

He took a shuddering deep breath and spoke calmly. "Look, Alexandra, it was quite simple. You saw—outside the Rat. I'd heard Lewis say he was going to Bartles's place. I offered him a ride if he'd help me load some benches I'd made for Bartles's church into my SUV. And it was about to rain, no reason for him to get wet. Simple."

I wondered if I could edge around him to the door, but he side-stepped with me. "But he had to make it dirty! He laughed and said, 'I've never done it on a church bench, might be fun. Sure, Pops, I'll *help* you.' Help me! Help me! We got to my shop and he came up behind me, rubbing against me. His hands went around the front and I . . . you know . . . got hard."

I swallowed a bolus of pity and disgust and tried to calm things down. "Listen, Chief, if there was some accident with Lewis—or provocation—and if Fratos was blackmailing you, you know Sonny, and the prosecutor, would both help you all they could."

His laugh was awful to hear. "So you could take the stand and tell the world I'm queer? You want still *more* power over me? Never. You will never have it. I have power, you are a sniveling les-bi-an sinner! No, Alexandra, I got enough *help* from Lewis. I shoved him away, harder than I meant, but I was angry—at him, myself, God. I pushed. He fell against the lathe. A terrible, terrible head injury. I should have called the police. It was an *accident!* A simple, tragic accident. But you know what I did? I picked up that leg." He gestured toward the table. "And I beat him until you couldn't tell what had caused the wound. And he was very, very dead. So lovely—and so dead. Satan's serpent was dead." His eyes teared up.

Now I made my second mistake. I'd had enough of his cant and my own temper flared. "Cut the shit, Mather. I used to see you drive round and round 'patrolling' Gay Beach, to make sure there was no 'raunchy behavior.' Yeh. Getting an eyeful of all those cute buns and the bikinis showing off the size of the equipment. Probably masturbating as you drove."

I read his eyes and grabbed for the wooden kitchen chair behind me, holding it up in front of me, rather like a lion tamer. He spat at me. "You have no idea of the torture it is. You Whore of Babylon! You bed with any pretty woman as casually as you drink a cup of coffee." I thought that was a bit overstated, but it didn't seem the time to be picky. "You have not felt the pain of looking, longing, even loving in vain, knowing it can never be. Rarely have I given in, the agony is not worth the moment's pleasure. The Serpent will die!"

He swung again and the score immediately went to Lions 3, Tamers 0. I was left holding the top of the chair with a few dangling slats. The rest of it splintered and fell to the floor.

Aunt Mae picked that moment to walk quietly in the back door, eyes wide, mouth slightly agape. I didn't want Mather to become aware of her—she might still be able to get out. So I tried to keep his attention.

"What happened, Jared baby? You sobbed over his body while

210

you jerked off? And Fratos saw it and blackmailed you, so you killed him, too?"

"Filthy-minded fornicator!"

Several things happened at more or less the same time. Jared swung, the rest of the chair disintegrated and my right arm went numb. Fargo made his terrified "leap to safety," pushing me into Mather's embrace, as it were. And Aunt Mae poured the soup over Jared's head.

He screamed in surprise and pain and I didn't blame him. I could feel stinging little needles of spatters hitting my neck and forearms. My feet began to slide on the wet, food-strewn kitchen floor. My right arm now felt on fire to the elbow. I clutched desperately at Mather with my other arm, and we began a kind of clumsy, slow-motion skaters' waltz in the soup. We went down together and he lost hold of the leg. I fell on top of him, trying to keep him from reaching it again, but he was strong. My right arm was useless and my left arm wasn't going to stop him for long—it had barely recovered from its Halloween sprain.

At this point Fargo landed on top of both of us. I think he had it figured for a new and wonderful game. He barked excitedly into Mather's face and my ear, pausing from time to time to lick a morsel of food from Mather's neck and shirt. Mather looked distraught, but wasn't distracted enough to quit inching his hand for the leg, and I was losing my grip on his arm.

Aunt Mae stood over us, looking fearful and distressed, still clutching the soup pot. "Hit him on the head!" I yelled. She looked at me blankly. "Hit him!"

Finally she tapped him on the head with the empty pot. He bellowed with anger but was very much still with us. "Hit him *hard!*" I screamed desperately.

"I don't want to *kill* him," she wailed.

"Why not? It's what he's going to do to *us!*"

That got through to her. She brought the pot down on his head like a woodsman felling a tree. Mather's eyes rolled back and I felt him go limp beneath me. I dumped Fargo off my back, rolled off of Mather and sat up.

Cindy ran through the back door, did a surprisingly graceful *glissade* across the kitchen, crashed into the sink, grabbed it and turned around—a little pale and out of breath. "I—I called—cops. Cell—phone. They're on—the way."

"Splendid! How did you ever know to do that?"

"The noise."

She looked as if I should have known that, and probably I should. I was a little scattered right then. "You done good. Could you give me a hand up?"

"Oh, sure." She walked carefully to me and extended her hand.

"Other hand, please."

She then looked at my visibly swelling right hand and arm, and put out her other hand. "You're right," she said gently, "definitely not that hand." With great care she got me to my feet and over to a chair.

"Now," I said, "Please kick that table leg aside. Don't touch it. If Mather moves, break his ankle with the pot."

I turned and rested my arm on the table, which helped. Police sirens sounded comfortingly near. Cindy picked up the pot and stood alertly near Mather. Aunt Mae and I sat quietly.

And thus were we posed when Mitch ran through the back door, .38 in hand, slipped, fell flat on his back and fired his pistol through the kitchen ceiling.

Chapter 22

I sort of lost the picture for the moment. At the report of the pistol, Fargo leaped for my lap and I yelped in pain as he jarred my arm. Aunt Mae screamed. Cindy looked as if she thought she should hit *somebody* and waved the soup pot threateningly. A large chunk of the on-duty Provincetown Police Force tumbled through the back door and went through various contortions to maintain their balance, and everybody began to talk at once.

Finally, Sonny yelled, "Everybody shut up!" and everybody did.

By the time I had given a fairly coherent description of the recent events, Mather groaned and stirred. Pete Santos and Jeanine got him into the only remaining chair and stood beside him watchfully. All four cops looked at my tumescent arm and then at Mather, and I got the feeling his prior rank would earn him no favors at the Ptown jail.

Mather blinked and then looked at me, completely calm. "I've hurt your arm, Alexandra, and I am truly sorry. Could I have some

213

water? So much has gone wrong . . ." He looked around until his eyes met Sonny's. "Oh, Sonny, so much."

Sonny hoisted himself onto a counter. "You want to tell me what happened, Jared? Shall we do the Miranda thing?"

"Don't be silly, I know the Miranda warning perfectly well. Oh, yes, I'll tell you what happened . . . what little Alexandra hasn't already spread around town!" He was revving up again. "Mae, she used our friendship to try to gain power over me! I never knew it at the time. She sneaked up to my house and peeked through windows and listened from outside." He sipped the water Aunt Mae handed him. Sonny and Ptown's Finest were staring open-mouthed as he rambled on. "I assure you, it was one of the few times I gave in! *I* have sought the Lord's forgiveness, but Alexandra, here, thinks—"

Sonny leaned forward. "Jared, I'm not quite sure where you're going with this."

"Oh, of course . . . the murders. Ah, Lewis, that beautiful, beautiful boy, headed for hell. Yes, I killed him. He called me 'old man.' I hated that."

Mather reached in his shirt pocket. We all tensed. He pulled out a cigarette pack and lit one. His eyes were slightly unfocused, as if he were watching a distant scene unfold. "Frankly, I think the wound was fatal, but I should have tried."

He closed both fists and beat them gently on the table, cursing himself, I thought. He went on softly. "But I was—still very excited—and mad. I was afraid people would guess what had happened, and what a joke that would be! The anti-gay cop—of course I had been anti-gay. I hated the sin within me and within them all. Now the anti-gay cop would be the laughingstock of the town." He stopped, as if he were finished.

Sonny finally spoke. "Jared, I'm not quite clear . . ."

"Alexandra will tell you later. I'm tired."

I asked, "Why did you take him to the amphitheater?"

He shrugged. "It was off the beaten track. It could have been days before he was found. Who knew that damned meddling

Harmon would be on one of his drug-busting crusades? And, it seemed appropriate. Lewis . . . so handsome lying on stage, like a young Greek god fallen in battle. He deserved that. His life had been so sordid. In death he was glorious."

My arm was throbbing with a drumbeat far from glorious. I mouthed the word "ice" to Cindy. She quietly picked up a tea towel, put some cubes in it and placed it softly on my arm. It helped some, and I didn't want to miss this. Jared Mather had tried to be a good man—by his lights—and he had tried to be a good cop. It seemed tragic his efforts to attain those ambitions had led him to madness.

Sonny noticed the ice pack and asked, "Are you all right? We can finish this later, and I'll take you to the clinic. That looks broken to me."

"It feels broken to me, but I want to hear this. Maybe some Tylenol."

He nodded and slithered off to the bathroom, returning with four capsules. I can count on Sonny's knowing when to be generous. Now Mitch was asking, "Mr. Mather." It was strange how nobody was calling him *chief* anymore. "Mr. Mather, did you empty his pockets?" Poor Mitch had to be furious and humiliated, knowing now that Mather had used him as a handy tool for getting information and planting false ideas.

"Sure. I wanted to suggest simple robbery. I found a handker-chief that probably belonged to Frank Wolfman. I put that in my pocket, mostly to get it out of my way. I emptied his wallet, you know what I did with the money. It never occurred to me Alexandra would wrangle it out of Larry Bartles that he had received it. I thought he would have spent it on the mission in an hour. The wallet itself and Lewis's watch I tossed in one of the ponds."

He was beginning to sound spent. "At home I shoveled the bloody sawdust around the garden. I rinsed the table leg in solvent and tossed it on the scrap heap. Another mistake, I should have burned it. But then, Sergeant, you had Mellon and Wolfman burning things, didn't you?" He gave a sour grin. "They certainly did all they could to look guilty until Alexandra started butting in and until Mae showed up without her glasses and said the leg looked fine."

Sonny put him back on track. "Why did you kill Fratos? Blackmail?"

"Yes. Slimy bastard. He cornered me outside the Rat. Told me he'd been at Race Point the night Lewis was killed. He saw me driving back, thought nothing then, but put it together later."

"Why had Fratos been at Race Point in the middle of the night?" Mitch queried. "Did he tell you?"

"No. But it was his favorite pastime. He loved to sneak up on couples parked out there, shine a light into the car and scare them half to death. Thought it was funny. Sometimes he would show his old police badge, and offer not to arrest them for 'public indecency' if they gave him money. But nobody was ever willing to go into court against him, and we could never prove it. He was a rotten cop!"

Mitch was writing quickly in his notebook, with no clicking noises, thank God. He looked up as Mather spoke. "Anyway, Fratos demanded money. I told him I'd have it at my house at ten o'clock. Then I noticed Harmon's old truck . . . with the keys in it. I saw a way to take care of Fratos and get a little revenge on Harmon. I took the truck and hid it behind my shop."

In the midst of this Aunt Mae had somehow made a pot of tea. She placed a steaming mug in front of me, laced with rum and heavily sugared. Nothing had ever tasted better. I smiled my gratitude silently. Jared still had the floor. Like Bartles, when he decided to talk—he talked.

"I was ready for Fratos, with a spare tire iron, when he got out of his car. I put him and the iron in Harmon's truck and went to wash up. I noticed Wolfman's handkerchief on the window ledge, where I'd tossed it, and put it in the truck. I drove to the amphitheater and arranged the body . . . no reason, just mischief. The same with his money, more confusion. I drove Harmon's truck to his house, Fratos's car to his apartment—and went home."

He smirked slightly. "Incidentally, Mitchell, I knew you would never get any real evidence on Mellon and Wolfman. Much as I detest them, I wouldn't have let them go to trial. I figured it would just fade away into one of those unsolved murders, assumed to be a transient hate crime or robbery."

Sonny slid off the counter and stretched. "Well, I guess that covers it, Jared. We'd better get moving. I want to get Alex down to the clinic."

"Yes. Yes, of course. Again, I'm sorry, Alexandra, but you shouldn't be so nosy. It's unbecoming." I was feeling worse by the minute. I nodded silently. I guess there was nothing to say.

"One thing, Sonny," Mather added. "I want you to know I greatly regret Lewis's death. I would do anything to reverse it. As to Fratos, I could as easily have killed a fly."

Mather stood up but grabbed the table, grimacing. "Sorry, I'm still a little dizzy, and I seem to have done something to my knee. Jeanine, Pete, can you help me here, please?" Automatically both officers walked over to him.

Sonny turned to Mitch with some litany of instructions. I cradled my aching arm and started for the back door. Mather had an arm over the shoulders of Pete and Jeanine, limping heavily and groaning with each step. I followed them out, telling Cindy and Aunt Mae I'd catch up with them later. Cindy looked like she wanted to cry.

Mather seemed to stumble on the top step, but his grip on the two cops looked, if anything, tighter than ever. They all tumbled down the steps into a heap.

I heard Pete yell, "Shit!"

Jeanine wailed, "Oh, goddammit! Noo-oo!"

Mather was already on his feet, backing away with no sign of a limp, and with Pete's .38 revolver in his hand. "Stay back!" he called. "I don't want to hurt anybody. Don't come this way." He reached the driveway as Sonny reached the top of the steps.

Jeanine had her pistol out and pointing at Mather. Pete stood clasping and unclasping his fists helplessly. Mitch had gone out the front and come around the side of the house. Mather saw him and swung the .38 toward him. "Stop, Mitchell, I'll shoot if you come closer."

Sonny spoke calmly from the porch, his gun still holstered. "Jared, you know you can't escape. Please don't make this worse. Toss that piece onto the grass and stand still."

"I'm not going to hurt anybody, Sonny. Try to remember I was an honest cop. Mae, I'm sorry to do this here."

He put the barrel of the pistol to his temple and pulled the trigger.

Chapter 23

In the open air the crack of the pistol sounded more like a medium-sized firecracker than a lethal weapon, but there was no doubting the reality of the blood, bone and brains that spewed across the driveway. For two or three eternal seconds nobody moved, and nobody spoke, as Jared Mather still stood there, a slightly bemused look on his face. Then he began slowly to crumple and the police converged.

Pete got there first and knelt beside him, looking sick, as he felt for a pulse. "He's gone. He shot straight."

"He would," Sonny said with infinite sadness. "He was a cop."

I looked at Sonny and said softly, "That's why you didn't remind them to cuff him when they took him out? You figured he would do this."

Sonny shrugged. "I don't know. Maybe. I know there was no way would he go to prison. No way."

He turned and said to Mitch, "Wrap it up. I'm getting Alex patched up now."

"Yes. Good luck, Alex, hope it's minor. Sonny, should I put Pete and Jeanine on report?"

Sonny looked startled. "Whatever for?"

"For neglecting to cuff Mather, plus Pete let him take his gun."

"Sure. And add your name to the list. You're their superior officer."

Mitch blanched. "Yes, sir."

"And add mine, too. I'm senior officer present. And Alex's, she noticed the omission but said nothing. And Aunt Mae's. She bopped Jared in the head, although she did manage to subdue him without shooting up the ceiling. Mitch, there are times I despair. Come on, Alex." He actually held the car door for me.

He stayed with me as we sat in the waiting room, and sat in the examining room, and sat in the X-ray room and sat in the examining room again. Sometimes my brother could be quite sensitive. As time passed, I began to get shaky. I wanted something to take my mind off the events of the day and the throb of the arm. "I'm tired of murders and suicide. I want something more pleasant. Tell me about your vacation."

"The most amazing thing about my vacation is that it didn't end in murder and/or suicide."

"That good?"

"It started as we drove down the main drag of Gatlinburg. Paula thought it looked hokey. Well, it does, but it never claimed to be the Vatican. We got to the hotel I showed you in the brochure. It was too rustic. We never even got to the room. She didn't like the *lobby*! So, we went to this big hotel downtown . . . just like any fairly good hotel in any town you've ever been in. I swear even the pictures in the rooms are the same." He walked to the window, spread the blinds with two fingers and stared out.

"What's the town like? And the people?" I asked.

"Very friendly. And what scenery! You've got to see those mountains someday! Anyway, we went horseback riding, and the horses were nags. We went on a helicopter sightseeing ride in one of the little bubble-canopy jobs and she got vertigo. We took a hike and she was afraid of bears. We went fishing and the rocks were slippery. The town was too touristy and the people too hill-billy."

I was dying for a drink and a cigarette but didn't know where to find the one and figured two oxygen tanks in the corner precluded the other. "What did you do, hang her in the closet?"

"Fortunately, we met this couple, Dave and Ann. Ann was Paula's soul mate and Dave and I got along. The women spent all day in the beauty salon or spa or the boutiques. Dave and I took some horseback rides, tried some golf, hiked, had a little fun. We got to some of the real craft shops, and they were interesting. I had never seen a dulcimer before, much less watched one being made. They come in different ranges, like a sax." Count on Sonny to find the unusual.

He gave a half-hearted chuckle. "The most fun was the trip home. We get to the Knoxville airport and Paula announces she's not riding to New York, Cattle Car Class. She asks the agent about upgrading to First Class, and he says three-fifty plus the ticket she holds. She says fine and whips out the old plastic. I say I'm not spending that kind of money for a two-and-a-half-hour flight. She shrugs and says she'll see me at LaGuardia. So we fly to New York—separate tables, if you will."

"I don't believe this." I did believe it. It sounded like Paula.

"The best is yet to come. In New York I say we have to hurry to get a late Boston shuttle. She says she's going to spend the night in the suite her father's business keeps at the Helmsley, and asks if I wish to accompany her there. I thought for a minute and then had to say I really couldn't think of *any* place I would wish to accompany her. And that was that. She caught a taxi, I caught the shuttle, missed the last Ptown flight and spent the rest of the night on a bench."

"You should have called Cassie." I sounded grumpy. Actually, I wanted to cry. He looked like a hurt little boy.

"I was so mad I unfortunately didn't think of it."

The doctor finally showed up again, waving a soft cast. "Had a heck of a time finding this in the right size," he said. "Sorry for the delay. Now let's see." He put the cast on my arm and snugged it down, and I felt immediately better. "Okay!" His round cheerful face moved on into a smile. "We'll leave that for a couple of days. Come back when the swelling subsides and we'll see if you need a hard cast. Maybe not—it is a simple fracture a couple of inches above the wrist. By the way, how did you do this? You work in a restaurant and slipped in some grease or something?" He sniffed. It was a logical assumption. I was generously perfumed in Aunt Mae's soup.

Before I could answer, Sonny spoke sharply. "I don't think we need to get into a lot of detailed history, doctor. If you're finished, we'll be leaving."

The doctor stared up at Sonny, totally unintimidated. "Please return to the waiting room, sir, I wish to speak with this young lady alone."

"Look, doctor, I'm Lieutenant Peres and—"

"I don't care if you're Captain Marvel. Wait outside." Sonny rolled his eyes and left. I stuck my tongue out at him and he sort of growled. The doctor looked at my chart and said, "Now, Ms. Peres . . . Peres? The same name? What's going on? How *did* that arm get broken?"

"Doctor, the lieutenant is my brother. He's a cop. He's very tired and has lost an old—acquaintance today. Please forgive his rudeness. It's been a tough time. I guess he just doesn't want to release details yet. I don't really know why. Right about now, the guy who did this"—I lifted my arm—"is being carried through your backdoor in a body bag. Believe it or not, Sonny is one of the good guys."

"I'll take your word for it," he said, running his fingers through crinkly red hair. "A body bag—livens up a dull day. I guess I'll get some details sometime. Well, here." He handed me a small envelope and a pill and a small cup of water. "Take this now and one every four hours for pain, as needed. Watch the alcohol and don't drive as long as you're taking them. I'll see you in three days—sooner if the pain and swelling don't improve."

"Thank you. And thanks for making sure everything was all right."

"I like to check. You'd be surprised how often the injury was inflicted by the doting companion."

"Doctor, while I'm here . . . this may not be your bailiwick but . . . well, oh, hell." I took a fast pace around the room, his eyes following me patiently. "Over Halloween, this witch—this old lady dressed like a witch put a curse on me. Ever since, I've been tripping and walking into doors and dropping things. I know curses aren't *real*, but could it be? Is it coincidence? Or am I making myself do these things, or what?" I ran down.

He walked over to the cabinet and murmured something. "I'm sorry," I said. "I didn't hear you."

"I said that you seem to have a hearing problem in your right ear. That's the third time you've asked me to repeat when I've been on your right."

"Oh, God," I said. "You mean I'm going deaf? That is all I need!"

"No, I said you weren't hearing well in your right ear. Let me have a look." He got out that little gizmo with the flashlight on the end and stuck it in my ear. "Yep. Eardrum is inflamed, and I imagine there's a low-grade infection of the inner ear. It has thrown your balance off a bit and made you clumsy. Nothing to worry about."

He walked over to the desk. "I'll give you a prescription for antibiotics that should do it. If they don't, call Dr. Ewing . . . he's our ENT man. There you go."

"You mean that's it? That's my curse? An infected ear?"

"It's nice when a curse will respond to an antibiotic, isn't it? Ding, dong, the witch is dead."

I thanked him profusely as I left.

Lighter than air, lighter than air! Bright as a feather and lighter than air! Huzzah! I felt a hundred pounds lighter. What was a mere broken arm, a little infection? *Ding, dong, the witch is dead. Mean old witch! Wicked old witch!*

"Well?" Sonny asked.

"I told him you're having a bad hair day but are essentially harmless. Ding, dong, let's go!"

At home, I managed a fairly successful, if somewhat painful, shower by the simple expedient of removing the cast and holding my arm over my head so I couldn't bump anything. I dressed slowly but without incident and was replacing the cast when I heard Sonny come in from the drugstore. The phone rang and Sonny picked it up in the kitchen, and a moment later he came into the bedroom.

"Mom is at Aunt Mae's. They've ordered antipasto and pizza for all of us, but Mom says if you'd like just to go to bed, she'll come over and make something here."

"No, no! Tell her I'm fine, never better. Don't let her come over here, Sonny, for God's sake. She'll make poached eggs. She thinks poached eggs on dry toast cure everything from a hangnail to a fractured skull. I *hate* poached eggs."

"I know," he laughed, "she's my mother, too. Okay. I'll ward her off."

We arrived at Aunt Mae's to find all back in perfect order. The floor was mopped and the kitchen table was replaced for now by a card table. Fargo had been bathed. My mother held me very tight for a moment and tried to control the tears. I hugged her back, suddenly terribly glad she was there . . . poached eggs or no.

Cindy told me, in an aside, that Jeanine and Pete had cleaned and hosed the driveway. When they came in to take the table and extra leg to forensics, Aunt Mae had given strict instructions that they were never, ever to be returned. The dining room table was set, and as soon as the food was delivered, we went in to eat. I, for one, was starved.

We were a rather silent group, all doubtless thinking of the day's events. I looked around the table and realized that had things gone as Mather planned, I wouldn't be here. I'd be down at the morgue. So, quite probably, would Aunt Mae and—less likely but possibly—so would Cindy. It was disquieting and I was glad when Sonny opened the wine and poured. It was a Portuguese red that would have been perfect with the soup but went quite nicely with the antipasto and pizza. I figured a half-glass wouldn't be more than the doctor would approve.

I lifted my glass, took a sip, smooshed it around in my mouth and swallowed loudly. "A-ah-ah, a rough and ready little wine, yet—"

Cindy interrupted me. "Yes, the definite sturdy character of the Tagus hill country with just a touch of the warm, open plains."

My family looked at her askance. Finally, Mom said, "So, Cindy, may we assume you are a wine expert?"

"Well, I suppose you might," she answered smoothly. "Alex taught me everything she knows."

There was silence, then a roar of laughter, and the tenor of the evening improved greatly, although every few minutes my mother would reach out and touch my arm, as if to make sure I was still there.

Sonny recounted some amusing events of his vacation. He had been introduced to grits and red-eye gravy and found he liked them both. He recounted how he'd enjoyed—from a safe distance—a mother bear with her cub, flicking fish from a quiet pool in a mountain stream. He told of the grizzled guide who had led them on a horseback ride. As they had passed under a giant stone overhang, one member of the party had questioned its stability. The guide had answered, "Them geologist fellers say she's been right thar a million or so years. Still, if I'se you, I wouldn't jump up and down on her."

"Sounds like Harmon," I noted.

"Don't talk to me about Harmon," Sonny grumbled. "I hope this at least teaches him to be careful who he ID's and to take the keys out of that damn truck. Not that it really would have changed anything."

Sonny turned to me and raised his glass. "Well, you're the heroine of the day. You and Aunt Mae. What the hell was Jared rambling on about you and his big secret and power?"

I told them what I had known about him and why I vowed to keep quiet about it.

225

"Very noble," my mother said dryly. "So noble it almost got you killed! And I've known it all my life."

"Jeanne!" Aunt Mae looked stunned. "I had no idea."

"His younger sister Betsy was a friend of mine in high school. She told me her father caught him with another boy and just lost it. I guess he beat him half to death when he found out—raving about sins against God. Calling in some preacher, I don't know what all." She took a sip of her wine. "The father was sort of nuts, he was just as bad with Betsy going out with boys. You know, no makeup, no dances, no dates except on her own front porch. Poor Betsy nearly wore out her bedroom window climbing out it almost every night. She was a wild one."

"She left home shortly after graduation, didn't she?" Aunt Mae asked.

"*Very* shortly. After graduation we all went back to the gym to turn in our rented caps and gowns. She picked up her suitcase and went from gym to bus."

"Well, we'll be looking for her," Sonny announced through a bite of pizza. "I guess she's next of kin. Any idea where she is?"

"Portsmouth, ages ago. We wrote for a while. She got a job, did pretty well. Then we both got married and, you know . . ." Mom made a little waving motion with her hand. "Christmas cards and then nothing. I've got her address somewhere."

Between the pain pill and few sips of wine, I was feeling rather dreamy. "Strange how things go. Nobody has a single good thing to say about Ben Fratos, and not much good about Lewis. Nobody had too much bad to say about Mather, but he killed them both and now he's gone. Would have liked to take me with him."

"Not really, Alex." Sonny came to his defense. "He just finally snapped. First he feared Lewis would smear him all over town, then Fratos blackmailed him. He was carrying those two murders on his conscience. Plus the stress of years of secrecy and dread of exposure. Then you got him right between the eyes."

"You mean he finally had to face who he was?"

"Okay, okay. You're right." Sonny pushed his plate away. "But the way he told it, the way Mom recalls it, you can't blame Jared entirely. Blame the father, it was his fault."

"That would have been a great comfort to me if my daughter and sister were lying dead tonight," my mother snapped.

"Yeah!" I chimed in belligerently and reached for my wine-glass, only to find that Cindy had quietly moved it away. I looked at her owlishly and then grinned. "Good idea. I'm a little squiffed. But the three of them . . . all very different, but all just as dead." I giggled. "God works in mysterious ways."

"Or as we say in the police department, sometimes you wonder whom to arrest, the victim or the perp." Sonny sounded a little squiffed also.

Aunt Mae sat Victoria-like, unamused. "Three men are dead and others have been hurt and endangered because Jared's emotional pain and guilt overcame his good sense," she said testily. "We may never understand it all, but I think we can surely hope that all three have found peace . . . something they never apparently enjoyed in life."

Mom nodded in agreement. Cindy gave Aunt Mae a slight smile. And Sonny and I, I suppose, looked suitably chastened.

The party broke up shortly after that. Sonny offered to drive me home, but I thought the walk would be a good idea, especially after Mom announced she would be over in the morning to help me with a shower and make me a nice breakfast. The doctor had been right—the pills and wine were not the best mix. Sonny and Fargo and I walked Cindy down to the cottage.

Sonny walked on ahead with the dog, and I took Cindy's hand with my good one, recalling Cassie's advice once more. "Cindy, if you're afraid to stay alone after all that's gone on today, I could sleep on your couch and—"

She gently put two fingers across my lips and said, "Sssshh. That's the wine and pills talking. I'm not at all frightened. I am worn out. You are hurt and strung out. Go home, rest. Come over tomorrow and help me unpack. We have time, my dear, and all is well." She pulled my head down to hers and gave me another one of those kisses. And everything did seem fine.

Sonny and I strolled home in the chilly darkness, with Fargo trotting ahead and making occasional little side trips to explore some intriguing smell. It was home. It was my town. It was peaceful. Indeed, I thought, never to feel peace must be a terrible thing.

Suddenly an old woman came out of a darkened yard, walking swiftly, almost running toward us. She seemed to be wearing nothing but a nightgown and one slipper. "My God, Sonny, it's my witch!"

"What witch? Are you crazy?"

I had no time to explain. I grabbed her arm as she would have passed us. "Excuse me, ma'am, but aren't you the witch who cursed me in front of the Wharf Rat a couple of weeks ago?"

"Now why would I curse a pretty girl like you? Unless, of course, you are a prostitute." She shook her finger at me. "If you sell yourself upon the street, you will cringe when Saint Peter you meet."

Poor thing was mad as a hatter. I had let *this* send me into a spiral for three weeks? I must be as nutty as she!

Sonny was looking pole-axed as a heavy, middle-aged woman panted up to us, carrying a slipper. "Oh, thank you for stopping her! Mama, how did you get out *this* time? We try to keep up, but she's too slick for us. Here, put on your slipper. Over Halloween my daughter left her witch's costume on the hall chair. Mama found it and wandered off. It was hours before we found her, 'way downtown, half frozen and yelling curses. She used to work for a greeting card company and all she does now is talk in verses. Oh, Lord! Now I'm doing it! She's going to a lovely h-o-m-e next month if we all live that long. I tell you . . ."

I've no idea what further news might have been imparted to us, but my brother could stand no more. "Excuse us, ma'am, if you're both all right, we have to get going." Not waiting for an answer to his implied question, he strode off, pulling me with him.

"Have a lovely wedding day, enjoy your happiness in every way!" my witch sang after us. We looked at each other and started to giggle . . .

"You *are* going to explain all this aren't you?" Sonny asked.

"Yes, not now."

"Okay, later. I wonder if that lady could figure out how to rhyme the curse Harmon already put on us a while back. Remember?"

"Kind of. What exactly was it?" I asked. I was fading fast.

He altered his voice to imitate Harmon's high-pitched rasp. "Them two Peres kids, they never did have no luck with women. Hell, even th' dog's fixed, so he can't have no luck neither."

We both laughed, and Fargo barked to join the chorus. I took Sonny's arm. I smiled to myself and felt a warmth in the chill night. Harmon wasn't always right.

About the Author

Jessica Thomas is a native of Chattanooga, Tennessee, where she attended Girls' Preparatory School. She later graduated cum laude from Bard College, Annandale-on-Hudson, New York, with a bachelor's degree in literature.

After an early retirement, Miss Thomas spent a bit of time doing some rather dull freelance assignments and ghostwriting two totally depressing self-help books, always swearing someday that she would write something that was just plain fun. When her friend Marian Pressler "gave" her Alex and Fargo, Jessica took them immediately to heart and ran right to her keyboard.

Miss Thomas makes her home in Connecticut with her almost-cocker spaniel, Woofer. Her hobbies include gardening, reading and animal protection activities.

FALL GUY by Claire McNab. 200 pp. 16th Detective Inspector Carol Ashton Mystery.
ISBN 1-59493-000-7 $12.95

ONE SUMMER NIGHT by Gerri Hill. 232 pp. Johanna swore to never fall in love again—but then she met the charming Kelly . . .   ISBN 1-59493-007-4 $12.95

TALK OF THE TOWN TOO by Saxon Bennett. 181 pp. Second in the series about wild and fun loving friends.   ISBN 1-931513-77-5 $12.95

LOVE SPEAKS HER NAME by Laura DeHart Young. 170 pp. Love and friendship, desire and intrigue, spark this exciting sequel to *Forever and the Night*.
ISBN 1-59493-002-3 $12.95

TO HAVE AND TO HOLD by Peggy J. Herring. 184 pp. By finally letting down her defenses, will Dorian be opening herself to a devastating betrayal?
ISBN 1-59493-005-8 $12.95

WILD THINGS by Karin Kallmaker. 228 pp. Dutiful daughter Faith has met the perfect man. There's just one problem: she's in love with his sister.   ISBN 1-931513-64-3 $12.95

SHARED WINDS by Kenna White. 216 pp. Can Emma rebuild more than just Lanny's marina?   ISBN 1-59493-006-6 $12.95

THE UNKNOWN MILE by Jaime Clevenger. 253 pp. Kelly's world is getting more and more complicated every moment.   ISBN 1-931513-57-0 $12.95

TREASURED PAST by Linda Hill. 189 pp. A shared passion for antiques leads to love.
ISBN 1-59493-003-1 $12.95

SIERRA CITY by Gerri Hill. 284 pp. Chris and Jesse cannot deny their growing attraction . . .   ISBN 1-931513-98-8 $12.95

ALL THE WRONG PLACES by Karin Kallmaker. 174 pp. Sex and the single girl—Brandy is looking for love and usually she finds it. Karin Kallmaker's first *After Dark* erotic novel.
ISBN 1-931513-76-7 $12.95

WHEN THE CORPSE LIES A Motor City Thriller by Therese Szymanski. 328 pp. Butch bad-girl Brett Higgins is used to waking up next to beautiful women she hardly knows. Problem is, this one's dead.   ISBN 1-931513-74-0 $12.95

GUARDED HEARTS by Hannah Rickard. 240 pp. Someone's reminding Alyssa about her secret past, and then she becomes the suspect in a series of burglaries.
ISBN 1-931513-99-6 $12.95

ONCE MORE WITH FEELING by Peggy J. Herring. 184 pp. Lighthearted, loving, romantic adventure.   ISBN 1-931513-60-0 $12.95

TANGLED AND DARK A Brenda Strange Mystery by Patty G. Henderson. 240 pp. When investigating a local death, Brenda finds two possible killers—one diagnosed with Multiple Personality Disorder.   ISBN 1-931513-75-9 $12.95

WHITE LACE AND PROMISES by Peggy J. Herring. 240 pp. Maxine and Betina realize sex may not be the most important thing in their lives.   ISBN 1-931513-73-2 $12.95

UNFORGETTABLE by Karin Kallmaker. 288 pp. Can Rett find love with the cheerleader who broke her heart so many years ago?   ISBN 1-931513-63-5 $12.95

HIGHER GROUND by Saxon Bennett. 280 pp. A delightfully complex reflection of the successful, high society lives of a small group of women.   ISBN 1-931513-69-4 $12.95

LAST CALL A Detective Franco Mystery by Baxter Clare. 240 pp. Frank overlooks all else to try to solve a cold case of two murdered children . . .   ISBN 1-931513-70-8 $12.95

ONCE UPON A DYKE: NEW EXPLOITS OF FAIRY-TALE LESBIANS by Karin Kallmaker, Julia Watts, Barbara Johnson & Therese Szymanski. 320 pp. You've never read fairy tales like these before! From Bella After Dark.   ISBN 1-931513-71-6 $14.95

FINEST KIND OF LOVE by Diana Tremain Braund. 224 pp. Can Molly and Carolyn stop clashing long enough to see beyond their differences?   ISBN 1-931513-68-6 $12.95

DREAM LOVER by Lyn Denison. 188 pp. A soft, sensuous, romantic fantasy.
ISBN 1-931513-96-1 $12.95

NEVER SAY NEVER by Linda Hill. 224 pp. A classic love story . . . where rules aren't the only things broken.   ISBN 1-931513-67-8 $12.95

PAINTED MOON by Karin Kallmaker. 214 pp. Stranded together in a snowbound cabin, Jackie and Leah's lives will never be the same.   ISBN 1-931513-53-8 $12.95

WIZARD OF ISIS by Jean Stewart. 240 pp. Fifth in the exciting Isis series.
ISBN 1-931513-71-4 $12.95

WOMAN IN THE MIRROR by Jackie Calhoun. 216 pp. Josey learns to love again, while her niece is learning to love women for the first time.   ISBN 1-931513-78-3 $12.95

SUBSTITUTE FOR LOVE by Karin Kallmaker. 200 pp. When Holly and Reyna meet the combination adds up to pure passion. But what about tomorrow?   ISBN 1-931513-62-7 $12.95

GULF BREEZE by Gerri Hill. 288 pp. Could Carly really be the woman Pat has always been searching for?   ISBN 1-931513-97-X $12.95

THE TOMSTOWN INCIDENT by Penny Hayes. 184 pp. Caught between two worlds, Eloise must make a decision that will change her life forever.   ISBN 1-931513-56-2 $12.95

MAKING UP FOR LOST TIME by Karin Kallmaker. 240 pp. Discover delicious recipes for romance by the undisputed mistress.   ISBN 1-931513-61-9 $12.95

THE WAY LIFE SHOULD BE by Diana Tremain Braund. 173 pp. With which woman will Jennifer find the true meaning of love?   ISBN 1-931513-66-X $12.95

BACK TO BASICS: A BUTCH/FEMME ANTHOLOGY edited by Therese Szymanski— from Bella After Dark. 324 pp.   ISBN 1-931513-35-X $14.95

SURVIVAL OF LOVE by Frankie J. Jones. 236 pp. What will Jody do when she falls in love with her best friend's daughter?   ISBN 1-931513-55-4 $12.95

LESSONS IN MURDER by Claire McNab. 184 pp. 1st Detective Inspector Carol Ashton Mystery.   ISBN 1-931513-65-1 $12.95

DEATH BY DEATH by Claire McNab. 167 pp. 5th Denise Cleever Thriller.
ISBN 1-931513-34-1 $12.95

CAUGHT IN THE NET by Jessica Thomas. 188 pp. A wickedly observant story of mystery, danger, and love in Provincetown.   ISBN 1-931513-54-6 $12.95

DREAMS FOUND by Lyn Denison. Australian Riley embarks on a journey to meet her birth mother . . . and gains not just a family, but the love of her life.   ISBN 1-931513-58-9 $12.95

A MOMENT'S INDISCRETION by Peggy J. Herring. 154 pp. Jackie is torn between her better judgment and the overwhelming attraction she feels for Valerie.
ISBN 1-931513-59-7 $12.95

IN EVERY PORT by Karin Kallmaker. 224 pp. Jessica has a woman in every port. Will meeting Cat change all that?   ISBN 1-931513-36-8 $12.95

TOUCHWOOD by Karin Kallmaker. 240 pp. Rayann loves Louisa. Louisa loves Rayann. Can the decades between their ages keep them apart? ISBN 1-931513-37-6 $12.95

WATERMARK by Karin Kallmaker. 248 pp. Teresa wants a future with a woman whose heart has been frozen by loss. Sequel to *Touchwood*. ISBN 1-931513-38-4 $12.95

EMBRACE IN MOTION by Karin Kallmaker. 240 pp. Has Sarah found lust or love? ISBN 1-931513-39-2 $12.95

ONE DEGREE OF SEPARATION by Karin Kallmaker. 232 pp. Sizzling small town romance between Marian, the town librarian, and the new girl from the big city. ISBN 1-931513-30-9 $12.95

CRY HAVOC A Detective Franco Mystery by Baxter Clare. 240 pp. A dead hustler with a headless rooster in his lap sends Lt. L.A. Franco headfirst against Mother Love. ISBN 1-931513931-7 $12.95

DISTANT THUNDER by Peggy J. Herring. 294 pp. Bankrobbing drifter Cordy awakens strange new feelings in Leo in this romantic tale set in the Old West. ISBN 1-931513-28-7 $12.95

COP OUT by Claire McNab. 216 pp. 4th Detective Inspector Carol Ashton Mystery. ISBN 1-931513-29-5 $12.95

BLOOD LINK by Claire McNab. 159 pp. 15th Detective Inspector Carol Ashton Mystery. Is Carol unwittingly playing into a deadly plan? ISBN 1-931513-27-9 $12.95

TALK OF THE TOWN by Saxon Bennett. 239 pp. With enough beer, barbecue and B.S., anything is possible! ISBN 1-931513-18-X $12.95

MAYBE NEXT TIME by Karin Kallmaker. 256 pp. Sabrina has everything she ever wanted—except Jorie. ISBN 1-931513-26-0 $12.95

WHEN GOOD GIRLS GO BAD: A Motor City Thriller by Therese Szymanski. 230 pp. Brett, Randi, and Allie join forces to stop a serial killer. ISBN 1-931513-11-2 $12.95

A DAY TOO LONG: A Helen Black Mystery by Pat Welch. 328 pp. This time Helen's fate is in her own hands. ISBN 1-931513-22-8 $12.95

THE RED LINE OF YARMALD by Diana Rivers. 256 pp. The Hadra's only hope lies in a magical red line . . . climactic sequel to *Clouds of War*. ISBN 1-931513-23-6 $12.95

OUTSIDE THE FLOCK by Jackie Calhoun. 224 pp. Jo embraces her new love and life. ISBN 1-931513-13-9 $12.95

LEGACY OF LOVE by Marianne K. Martin. 224 pp. Read the whole Sage Bristo story. ISBN 1-931513-15-5 $12.95

STREET RULES: A Detective Franco Mystery by Baxter Clare. 304 pp. Gritty, fast-paced mystery with compelling Detective L.A. Franco. ISBN 1-931513-14-7 $12.95

RECOGNITION FACTOR: 4th Denise Cleever Thriller by Claire McNab. 176 pp. Denise Cleever tracks a notorious terrorist to America. ISBN 1-931513-24-4 $12.95

NORA AND LIZ by Nancy Garden. 296 pp. Lesbian romance by the author of *Annie on My Mind*. ISBN 1931513-20-1 $12.95

MIDAS TOUCH by Frankie J. Jones. 208 pp. Sandra had everything but love. ISBN 1-931513-21-X $12.95

BEYOND ALL REASON by Peggy J. Herring. 240 pp. A romance hotter than Texas. ISBN 1-9513-25-2 $12.95